THE SUBURBS HAVE SECRETS

A SADIE MCINTYRE MYSTERY

BARBARA WALLACE

BARBARA WALLACE

ISBN: 978-069293279-7

ASIN: B075KNQ833

Cover Design: Ecila-Media www.ecila-media.com

❀ Created with Vellum

1

EVERYONE HAS SECRETS.

Take, for example, the good folk of Woodbridge, Massachusetts, population 7,256.

Like many of the leafy suburbs outside of Boston, Woodbridge has beautiful, tree-lined streets and acres of manicured community athletic fields. It's the kind of town that routinely places high on those *Best Places to Live* lists.

And it's just bursting with secrets.

Trust me, I know. Having sold real estate in Woodbridge for the past nine years, I can safely say I've seen more dirty laundry than most. Just this past week, for example, my client opened what she thought was a utility closet in the basement and found the seller's dominatrix supplies. Needless to say, the riding crop collection discouraged them from making an offer.

That's the thing about secrets. Eventually, they get out. And when they do...

The fallout can be murder.

2

IT WAS HALF PAST SEVEN, Sunday night. I was on my way home from a wildly unsuccessful open house and debating whether or not I wanted to drown my sorrows in a bottle of Riesling when *wham!* Out of nowhere, a dark figure stepped in front of my car.

I slammed on the brakes. Thankfully, I wasn't driving fast, so I screeched to a halt inches shy of a collision. The person—whoever it was—didn't notice. Head down, the figure crossed the street...

And promptly crumpled to the ground.

I got out of my car and hurried around the hood, stopping short when I reached the left headlight. The person sat cross-legged in the middle of the road, face obscured by a dark navy hood. "Are you all right?"

The person muttered a reply. From where I stood, it sounded like "stupid street."

I stepped closer. Probably not the best idea, seeing as how I was alone and dealing with a potentially crazy person. Then again, curiosity has always been my downfall.

"Hello?" I said, reaching for their shoulder. "Do you need some help?"

"Don't touch me!" the person screeched, and jerked away from my touch. In the process, they fell backward, knocking the hood away.

"Marylou?"

"Stupid street. Freaking tilted off balance."

It was Marylou Paretsky.

At least she had Marylou's voice and pudgy face. The Marylou I knew wore pastel twin sets and chirped her words like an excited chipmunk. The woman in front of me looked like a street person. Her navy-blue sweatshirt was two sizes too small. I could see her stomach protruding out from beneath the hem. And her hair, normally neat as a pin, hung in a half-done ponytail, the sandy brown curls flopping in her face. When she turned, I caught raccoon circles of mascara lining her eyes.

I watched as she struggled to stand up, only to get her feet halfway under her body before sitting again. "Stupid street. Stop moving," she muttered.

She was drunk as a skunk. "Here, let me help you up."

"Leave me alone. I'm fine." The protest might have had more oomph if she hadn't tipped over trying to slap my hand away. Not even trying to save herself, she fell and lay with her cheek smushed into the blacktop. "Perfectly fine."

We weren't going to get anywhere this way. Grabbing her upper arm—this time she was too busy lying down to wave me off—I tugged her into a sitting position.

"Stop it! Gotta stay here. Gonna listen to me."

Listen? If she kept hollering in the middle of the street, the whole neighborhood was going to hear her. I looked around at the houses with their curtains drawn. Thankfully, we were on the north side of town where the houses were set farther back from the sidewalks. Plus, everyone would be settling in to watch the eight o'clock game.

"You can't stay here," I told her. "We're in the middle of the street." Dear Lord, but she reeked. Alcohol. Mothballs. There was a third smell in there too I couldn't identify. It might have been sweat. "Tell you what. Let's get you home, and you can sit there."

"No! Gotta stay. It's impo-portant."

Impotent or important? I didn't get to ask because she managed to yank free of my grip and crawled on all fours toward the curb. Dignity was clearly off the table at this point.

At least we were out of the street though. We were making progress.

That's when she threw up.

We're talking super ugly, power retching. The kind that poured out of you and turned the air sour. I jumped onto the grass, praying the splatter didn't hit my pants. How much had Marylou had to drink anyway? Considering the volume coming out of her, it was obviously a lot. Afraid to look down in case there was a stream of vomit in the gutter, I stared at my car that was still running in the middle of the street.

Marylou continued retching long after she'd emptied her stomach. Harsh, gasping heaves that made her body shake. I stood behind her and rubbed circles between her shoulder blades, the way I used to when my son, Tim, had the stomach flu. Someone was going to find a very unpleasant surprise when they stepped outside tomorrow morning, that was for sure. I wondered if I should ring the doorbell and let them know. Then again, did I really want to be publically associated with this debacle?

"...loser."

I looked down. Marylou had managed to push herself upright. Sitting on her haunches, she rocked back and forth, her arms clutching her stomach. "Lousy, stupid loser."

"You're not a loser," I told her. "You just had too much to drink. Happens to everyone. I'll bring you—"

"Not me. Her. Them."

She spoke so harshly, I jumped. This was not the chipmunkian woman I thought I knew. "Who are they?"

"Thinking I can be ignored. Well, I can't. 'M not some stupid kid anymore." She swiped her hand hard across her mouth. "I'm a winner now. She'll see. A. Win. Ner." She punctuated each pause with a jab of her finger against the Native American logo silkscreened just above her heart. "She'll be sorry. Gonna stomp her on her head."

"You don't mean that." At least I hoped not. Hearing her talk about violence freaked me out. As the past five minutes had shown, I didn't know Marylou as well as I'd thought. For all I knew, those twin sets she normally wore concealed the heart of a serial killer. Wouldn't be the first time I misjudged a person's character, although I thought I'd gotten better over the years.

"Yes, I do," Marylou snapped. "I hope they all die in a hole. Every single one of them."

"Who?" I asked again. With all the various pronouns being bandied about, I was getting confused. "What did they do?"

But Marylou was too deep into her angry pity party to hear my question. Instead, she rambled on about winning and making "them" see. "Lying bitch. But I know. Got proof."

"Okay," I said, "let's get you home." My car was still in the street. It'd be just my luck to run out of gas listening to her blather. Taking her elbow, I finally succeeded in pulling her to her feet. Because no good deed goes unpunished, the moment she stood, she leaned into my side, along with her rancid breath. "I'm not stupid, you know."

"I know."

"He thinks I am, but I knew he didn't buy that aftershave for the smell. He bought it for her."

"Who?"

"Her!" She spit the word like it was leftover vomit on her tongue. "Ungrateful bastard. Screwing around with his assistant. After everything I'm doing for him."

"Paul's having an affair? Are you sure?"

"Course I'm sure. No one works that many late hours. No one. Why does everyone think I'm stupid?" Her head separated from my shoulder. "You think I'm stupid too, don't you?"

"No," I replied, feeling her glazed glare. "It's just... he doesn't seem the type." I'd only met Paul Paretsky once, at a volunteer's mixer for our town's local cancer fundraiser. He was a quiet, awkward man with palms so sweaty, I'd had to wipe my hand on a napkin after he shook it. If I remembered correctly, he spent most of the mixer avoiding any actual mixing. Hard to imagine him having the nerve to cheat on Marylou. "I meant how do you know?"

"Cause I know, that's why. Dinner and the game. I know better. I know lots of things. Important things."

As her index finger assaulted the emblem on her chest a second time, I realized how stupid I was in trying to have this conversation. "Why don't we go sit in my car?"

"I'm serious. You have no idea how many things I know. You should respite...respect me."

"I do respect you."

Her head lolled toward mine again, bringing a new waft of rancid breath. "You promise?"

"I promise."

Only a few more feet to the passenger door. Never had such a short walk felt so long. With every step, Marylou's voice grew more slurred, and her steps more sluggish. It was like dragging a giant sack of flour. If she passed out before I got her into the passenger seat, I was screwed, because there was no way I would be able to lift her into my SUV by myself, and I didn't relish knocking on some stranger's door to ask for assistance.

Finally, after what seemed like forever, she was in the front seat. "Can you buckle your seatbelt?" I asked.

"I threw up on my sweatshirt."

Make that a no.

"I can't believe I got vomit on it. Now it's all ruined."

How could she tell? I hadn't noticed when we were outside, but under the dome light I could see the thing was covered with stains, including a crusty one on the front pocket.

The spot offending Marylou was near the emblem. She rubbed furiously at the peeling image, trying to clean it. The poor silhouette was getting its share of abuse tonight. Reaching into the glove compartment, I handed her a clump of napkins and a small bottle of hand sanitizer. "Here," I said, "these might work better." Not to mention she could clean her hands. "When you get home, you can throw the shirt in the wash, and it'll be like new."

"Can't. Got to keep it or won't work. I don't feel well."

Oh no, not in my car. "Hold on," I said, buckling her in. "Let me get you something for the ride. If you get sick before I get back—" I pushed the passenger door as wide as it would go. "—lean out."

Keeping one eye out for her head, I ran around to the rear of my car to look for something I could use as a bucket. Underneath the open house signage was my obligatory stash of canvas grocery bags. The ones I was supposed to use but always forgot about until I was halfway through the groceries. Too bad I didn't have a plastic bag to use for a liner, but my collection of plastic grocery bags was hanging by the back door of my house for me to remember to take them for recycling.

Hopefully, the fate of the environment didn't rest on my memory.

"You're so nice," Marylou slurred when I returned. She'd stopped wiping and was picking at the white shirt bulging from beneath the sweatshirt hem. "They would leave me in the gutter. Wait!"

Her head, which had started to drop against her chest, smacked against the headrest. "I gotta show her. So she knows."

"How about you wait until tomorrow," I said, stuffing the bag between her feet. "When you're not so...sick and can talk better."

She nodded. "In the morning. I'll show her. They'll have to listen to me."

"Let's get you home. You can get some sleep and tomorrow be at your best when you talk to them. Her."

Honest to God, she was killing me with all the pronoun switches.

Sticky fingers clamped themselves around my wrist. "You're the best, Sadie."

"Yeah, that's me. Sadie McIntyre, living saint." I tried to pull my hand away so I could shut the door, but Marylou's grip tightened. Where was this strength when we were walking?

"Seriously," Marylou said. "You're real nice, not fake, two-face nice. You've been nice to me since the day I got here. Not like those other lying witches."

"I appreciate that."

"I appreciate you. That's why I didn't..." Whatever she was about to say, she stopped, increasing her grip on my wrist instead. Her eyes grew serious and strangely sober. "I will never betray our friendship, Sadie. You have my word."

The October wind picked up, causing the skin on my neck to prickle. She was drunk. Drunks tended to get dramatic. "Your word, huh?"

"Till the day I die."

She flashed me a sloppy smile. It was the start of a head-to-toe relaxation. Gaze growing unfocused, she leaned against the headrest and let her fingers grow slack. "Swear to God."

She set a low bar. Marylou and I weren't exactly what you'd call friends. Beyond seeing her at Cuppa Joe's Café every morning, and serving on the Night Walk Charity Planning Committee, we had very little interaction. In all honesty, I'd always thought her a kind of an odd duck.

"Let's get you home," I said, finally breaking my wrist free.

It didn't dawn on me until I had buckled my own seatbelt that I didn't know where Marylou's home was.

"Hemlock Street," she said when I asked. Seriously? We were currently in Upper Woodbridge. The good side of the tracks, if you will, where the people with large incomes lived. Not *very* large—that was yet another section of town. Both areas were several miles from Hemlock Street, however.

A horrible thought hit me. "You didn't drive, did you?"

"Walked," she said, shaking her head. "Would never drink and drive."

Thank God for that small favor. "Pretty long hike."

"I didn't mind. I had... Did you see my bottle? I had a bottle. I'm thirsty. What did I do with it?"

Dropped it, empty, on somebody's lawn was my guess. "We'll get you some water when you get home," I told her.

"Oh-kay." The words came out a disappointed sigh. Her head rolled to the side, and she looked out the window. "Rather have a drink."

Her and me both.

———

MARYLOU LIVED in a modest Cape Cod with neatly trimmed landscaping. Like a lot of her neighbors, she'd decorated the yard for the season. There was an artful arrangement of hay bales and potted cabbages that I recognized from a Pinterest photo by her garage door, and another arrangement of mums by the lamppost.

From what I could tell, the only light inside was in the rear of the house. A soft glow could be seen through one of the front windows. No one was home, just like Marylou said.

I pulled into the driveway. "We're here," I said, in case she'd fallen asleep.

"Told you he was with her."

"You don't know for sure. Maybe he's out with friends getting ready to watch the game." Football was akin to religion in New England. In God and Bill Belichick we trust.

"Paul hates sports."

"Oh."

"S'not right. He owes me. I didn't have to, you know. I could have let him be a loser, but I didn't. Because I don't do losing anymore."

"You're a winner," I filled in before she could.

"Damn right. He's gonna do what I want him to do. Everyone is gonna. They'll see. I'm the boss."

"I'm sure they will."

"Oh, they will, all right. *They will.*"

God help Paul Paretsky when he got home. Marylou was going to have his head on a platter.

Then again, who could blame her? I know that if my late husband, Jack, had ever cheated on me, I would have gone ballistic.

Now that I thought about it, Paul Paretsky owed me a big, fat thank you. Marylou had clearly been on her way to confront him and his mistress. By bringing her home, I'd managed to derail what might have been a very messy, *very public* confrontation.

Messes were always better off private, in my opinion.

"Come on," I said, unbuckling my seatbelt. "I'll help you inside."

I got out and walked around to the passenger side, where she had —finally—opened her door. I watched as she slowly slid like sloppy Jell-O out of her seat, her feet landing with a wobbly plunk.

"Don't," she said, when I reached to prop her up. "I can walk."

She *did* seem a little more sober. Still, I walked along beside her in case she stumbled. I couldn't tell in the dark, but her driveway felt uneven, like it needed to be redone.

"You got a key?"

"Yeah. In my pocket. Hold on. The garage door light is broken." The sigh she gave was one of the longest I'd ever heard. Seconds later, I heard the jingle of keys followed by the screen door and then the front door, opening wide.

"I can take it from here," she told me.

"You sure? Because if you need me to stay..."

"Do you ever wish things could be different? That you could go back in time and change how life worked out?"

It was a strangely serious question for someone so drunk. I was about to brush it off with a joke when she turned her face and I saw her eyes. Hopeless and regretful, they were the same eyes I'd caught out of my own mirror some mornings.

She was tired. The kind of tired that came from carrying a load by yourself for too long. Made me wonder how long she'd known about Paul's affair.

When you had no one to lean on, secrets could get heavy.

"Only all the time." So many days I wondered how my life might have turned out if I'd opened a different door, made different decisions. "I'm good at playing 'what if.'"

"Me too."

Our eyes met and a bond made from past regrets formed between us. I made a note to reach out to her more often.

"If only life came with do-overs," I said.

"Doesn't work anyway. You can try, but in the end nothing changes. People still suck."

I didn't argue. I'd be jaded too if I were in her shoes.

"Are you sure you're going to be okay?" I asked instead.

"I will be."

Something about the way she spoke made the skin on my neck itch. She might have sobered, but underneath the fatigue, her anger still simmered. "What are you going to do?"

"You'll see."

That wasn't exactly the most reassuring of answers. She flicked on her foyer light, and I saw a face set in stone. Also not reassuring. "Will you at least promise not to do anything until you've slept?"

She smiled. "Don't you worry about a thing. I know exactly what I have to do."

Okay, rule of life here. Nothing makes a person worry more than telling them not to worry. Especially when you've already found them wandering the streets spoiling for a drunken confrontation.

I put my hand on the door. "Marylou, don't"

"Thanks for the ride, Sadie. I'll see you tomorrow."

I barely had time to pull my fingers away before she shut the door, leaving me staring at her corn-husk wreath.

"Do anything stupid," I finished under my breath.

Talk about famous last words.

3

"Give over. Nervous little Marylou pissed off her rocker?" Rob Carmichael sat in his chair, his gray eyes wide with astonishment. "There's something you don't see every day. She doesn't even drink caffeinated coffee."

"Tell me about it," I said. "It was surreal."

It was the following morning, and the two of us were having our regular morning coffee at Cuppa Joe's Café.

If there is one thing people in Woodbridge take seriously, it's their coffee. Well, that and their children's intramural sporting careers. (Although as any parent who has ever attended an early Saturday morning practice will tell you, the two go hand in hand.) At last count, there were at least seven coffee chains, convenience stores, and cafés in town where you could grab a cup of coffee. Meanwhile, we didn't get our first grocery store until five years ago.

Cuppa's was by far the town favorite. A no-frills kind of place, with large tables and lower prices, it was the town's daytime social hub. The go-to escape for stay-at-home moms and the self-employed.

Unless I had an early showing or Renee needed me in the office, I set up shop there for a few hours every morning. One never knew when they might overhear talk of a transfer out of town or of a family looking to upsize. At least that's the justification I gave myself. Honestly, I just liked hanging out with Rob.

Usually, he and Marylou had their laptops fired up and were deep into their work by the time I arrived. Marylou did something with computers. I was never quite sure what; technical speak tended to make me zone out.

Meanwhile Rob... Who knew what Rob did with his day? Technically, he taught British history at the local community college, but he only taught one class a semester. The rest of the time he spent managing his fantasy sports empire. It was also apparent he didn't have to work at all, although he remained tightlipped as to where he made his money. I knew, but only by accident. He much preferred cultivating his reputation as the town's mysteriously wealthy and handsome Brit.

First thing I noticed on Monday was that Marylou's table by the window was occupied by someone else. I don't know why her absence surprised me—she had to be nursing one heck of a headache—but it jarred me nonetheless.

"Do you think I should have gone inside with her?" I asked.

Rob shook his head. "You gave her a ride home, which was the important thing. If she was as bad as you said, I bet she passed out for the night. Probably still out. Know I would be. What I wonder is, what had her out wandering the streets in the first place? She didn't say?"

"Nothing that made sense." Nothing, that is, except the part about Paul's affair, but that wasn't my secret to tell. Not even to Rob. Airing people's dirty laundry only led to your own laundry getting aired.

"How was your weekend?" I asked, reaching for my mug. "Do anything interesting?"

"Nothing as interesting as picking up a drunk Marylou."

"A sign we both live extremely boring lives."

"I prefer the term sedate," he replied.

"Tomato, To-mah-to, it's still sad."

He grinned. "Least we've got each other, luv."

And thank goodness, too. Dull as my life might be, I could only imagine what it would be like without him in it. Rob was the one who brought me back to the living after Jack's heart attack. Dragged me out into the world and forced me to interact with it. Without him, I'd have become a shut-in widow suffocating my only child with my anxiety and loneliness.

People in town loved to speculate why a guy like him—rich, handsome, and charming as hell—would want to hang out with a middle-aged broad like me. I would have loved to give them some kind of scandalous answer, but the truth was we simply clicked.

Rob reached for his coffee. "Come to think of it, I did learn something interesting this weekend. Did you know you can make coffee by roasting dandelion roots?"

"Sounds like someone's been talking to Tim." My police officer/survival expert son. Ever since he joined the National Guard, he'd been feeding us a steady diet of do-it-yourself tips in case of a natural disaster.

"I got that same tip earlier in the week. I told him that if there was a natural disaster, making coffee wouldn't be my first concern."

"Would be mine. I'd rather hack my arm off than go without caffeine."

"Says the man whose idea of roughing it is using non-dairy creamer."

"*Anyway...*" Lines formed between his eyes as he shot me a dirty look from across his cup. "One of his guard mates had an extra ticket to the game, so I tagged along."

"So, while I was sitting in an empty open house and shuttling drunks across town, you were hanging about, drinking beer and swapping survivalist tips with a bunch of twenty-something soldiers? I take it back," I said. "I'm the only one living a boring life."

Rob grinned. "If it makes you feel better, I had to hitch a ride home with one of Tim's mates. Your son had to cut out early."

No, that didn't make me feel better. "Tim left the game?"

"In the third quarter. Fourth and one and they bloody punted, can you believe it? No wonder we needed overtime to win."

I was far more interested in what dragged Tim away from the stadium. "Tim didn't say anything about why he was leaving?"

"Work emergency, he said." From behind Rob's cup I could see his mouth twitching into a smile. "Something about a pair of drunks puking on people's front lawns."

"Very funny. It was one drunk."

"Who was drunk?" a female voice asked.

I swallowed a groan. Just once I'd like to finish a conversation without part or all of the yoga posse interrupting. Erin Koufax and Jennifer Falcone were two members of the quartet that sat at the table next to us every morning. They claimed to be coming from hot yoga, but their hair and skin always looked perfect. I know that if I spent sixty minutes twisting myself into a pretzel while standing in a sauna, I wouldn't look nearly as put together. But then, Erin and Jenn were part of the cool crowd. By definition they didn't sweat.

The propensity toward attractiveness was one of the downsides that came with living in Woodbridge. When I first arrived in town, I seriously feared I'd landed in *Stepford Wives* territory. Almost everyone was either genetically blessed with good looks or compensated by having an innate knack for style.

Maybe that's why Marylou came across as such an odd duck. She tried hard, but missed the mark in both categories. I'm pretty sure I missed the mark in both too, but I preferred not to try at all. I'd rather be bland and unmemorable.

Jenn and Erin—along with the rest of their posse for that matter—were deeply blessed in both categories. They had toned bodies, skin that never broke out, blond hair that always looked perfect, and clothes that looked magazine ready without having tried hard. Plus, they lived in *Home Beautiful* level houses. Not far from the street where I found Marylou, in fact. Despite having known them for several years, I still hadn't made up my mind as to whether or not I actually liked them. I didn't dislike them, per se; they were certainly nice enough—to my face, anyway—but I could only take them in small doses. Maybe it was because they were so freaking perfect, or because they roamed in a pack, but they reminded me of the popular girls from my teenage years. The kind of people who would as easily cut you as friend you.

The pair of them plopped themselves at the table next to us. Jennifer's attention, as usual, focused on Rob.

"Don't tell me you went out partying," she said, brushing her long blonde bangs away from her eyes. I'd decided a long time ago she wore fake eyelashes because no one beside Rob could have eyelashes that thick and luscious naturally. "You told me you wanted to watch the game."

"I did. In Foxborough," Rob replied. "Jenn wanted me to come to a beer and pizza thing yesterday," he explained to me.

"Aren't you Mr. Popularity," I replied.

"It was mostly a neighborhood thing. I would have asked you too, Sadie, but I knew you had that work thing."

"An open house," I said, forcing myself to sound unaffected. Rejection didn't feel any better in my forties then it did as a teenager. "And no worries. I'll catch you next time."

"Definitely," Jenn said. "That goes for you too, neighbor. You know how everyone *craves* your presence."

"Yeah Rob, we *crave* it," I said.

"People always do," he replied. From behind his cup, his grin widened. "Just ask my ride home."

I choked on my coffee. "Ewww, seriously? One of Tim's friends?" That was not an image I needed in my head. "They're babies."

"I didn't say it was reciprocal. Only that there was craving."

"And naturally you did nothing to encourage said craving," I said, taking the napkin he offered.

"Can I help it if I'm incredibly charming?"

"No," said Jenn.

"Yes," I said. The man was incorrigible.

Jenn flipped her ponytail. Posse code for dismissing my comment. "So who was drunk? If it wasn't you."

"Marylou," Rob said, before I could cut him off.

"You're kidding," Erin said.

"Nope." Come to think of think of it, Jenn's house was only a couple blocks from where Marylou and I ran into each other. Maybe that was where she'd drowned her sorrows over Paul? "Must have been some party. I'm assuming she was invited."

"Me-ow," Rob said under his breath.

The comment was a bit more passive aggressive than I intended. But, I thought Marylou, Jenn and Erin had gotten friendly over the past few months. In fact, the other night I drove past the three of them going into dinner at Gilroy's Tavern.

I wasn't invited to that, either.

The two blondes shared a look. "Marylou wasn't there," Jenn said.

"She wasn't?"

"I told you, it was a neighborhood thing. I only asked Erin and Lindsay because I mentioned it at travel soccer."

Lindsay Herrara was the posse leader. No surprise Jenn would invite her. A bigger surprise was not asking Lindsay to help plan the event. The posse didn't do anything without Lindsay's blessing.

Speaking of... "Where is Lindsay, anyway?" She and their fourth member, Andrea Baronelli, had yet to arrive. I actually had a slight soft spot for Andrea since she was the only non-blonde in the group.

"Lindsay had a nail emergency," Jenn replied. "She and Carlos are having dinner with one of his start-ups tonight and she needed the polish to match her dress."

But of course she did. Things like this were why I'd never be one of the cool kids, because I failed to see the point.

"And Andrea's sick," Erin added. "A cold or something. She sounded horrible on the phone when I called her Saturday to tell her about the..." She shoved her coffee cup to her mouth.

In my mind, I shook my head and wondered if the two of them were always this bad at lying or if I'd caught them on a bad day.

"The schools are full of germs. Brandon's had two colds since the year started." Jennifer took another sip of her drink. "Of course, Nick's all pissy about it because B's been sick on his weekends. Like I'm purposely giving my son colds to spite him. Trust me, if I were going to infect Nick, it wouldn't be with a cold."

"Well then," Rob said, "looks like it's the four of us today. Unless Marylou decides to drag herself in after all."

Just then, the bell over the front door—Cuppa's one annoying feature—signaled the arrival of another customer. Turning around, I saw a block of blue crossing the threshold. It was my baby boy, all six feet two inches of him.

A quick swell of pride washed over me. He looked very handsome in his uniform. I say that with the most unbiased of opinions, of course. The way he stood, square-shouldered and tall... That was his father's posture. He had his father's sense of honor and his decency, too.

I, on the other hand, contributed the ash brown hair and, sadly, the stubbornness.

I waved to him, getting a lackluster smile in return. His pretending-I'm-not-crabby smile; after twenty-two years of childhood dramas, I recognized the look immediately. Mother's radar on full alert, I got up and met him by the retail coffee display. "Hey, you." Much as I wanted to, I refrained from giving him a hug and kiss on the cheek. The man was in uniform after all. "You're not just getting off work, are you? Rob said you got called in last night."

"Actually, I'm still working. Bartlett ordered me to get coffee for everyone. Even gave me an itemized list, the jerk."

Dan Bartlett was Woodbridge's new chief of detectives. I didn't know much about him, but according to Tim he was bossy, arrogant, and had no sense of humor. "Finally something good happens and I get stuck with the crap jobs."

An uneasy shiver ran along my spine. During Tim's short police career, I'd learned that what cops called "good" was something the rest of us would consider bad. I was torn between wanting to ask what happened and trying not to be a nosy mother. This was his job, after all.

Plus, what he really wanted was a sympathetic shoulder from the one person he knew would let him whine.

"Sorry, sweetie, but that's what happens when you're the new guy."

"It sucks. I mean, I didn't mind standing outside the crime scene all morning, because that, at least, that had a point. But getting coffee? That's just Bartlett's way of letting everyone know he's in charge."

I refrained from pointing out that Bartlett *was* in charge. "You sure it's not simply because you're the new kid?"

"Yeah, well it still sucks. Bad enough I have to put up with it from the other guys in my unit. "

My poor baby. All grown up and learning adulthood was still one big high school. "Cheer up," I told him. "Soon as you get some experience, they'll stop hazing you."

"And if they don't," I added, brushing imaginary lint off his uniform, "I'll go talk to them like I did when you were in third grade and Tommy Robinson threw rocks at you during recess."

He gave me a stony look.

"I'm kidding," I said. Detective Bartlett wasn't the only one who didn't have a sense of humor. Come to think of it, my kid could be a wee bit arrogant too. No wonder he and his new superior clashed. "I'll send your Uncle Rob. He loves men in uniform."

"Very funny, Mom. I already had to deal with him being all flirty last night. I'm pretty sure Wilcox's got the hots for him."

I was about to suggest he might want to warn his buddy about getting too enamored when the two-way radio on his hip crackled and a muffled voice barked out a series of numbers which, based on his eye roll, was directed at Tim. "For crying out loud, I've only been gone five minutes," he muttered.

Sighing, he grabbed the radio and barked his own coded sentence back. "Ten-nineteen 30 Hemlock. ETA seven minutes."

My breath hitched. 30 Hemlock Street was Marylou's house.

Oh no, Marylou. What did you do?

4

Drunk as she'd been, I could easily see Marylou smashing things in anger. And by *things,* I meant Paul's head. I could see her now, being carted off in handcuffs in that ratty sweatshirt of hers, ranting about getting even.

Question was, how even?

I decided to follow Tim to the crime scene and find out. In a way, I felt responsible, having been the one to leave her alone last night.

It was complete chaos when I pulled onto Hemlock Street. Twenty-something years in town, and I couldn't remember ever seeing so many police cruisers in one place. Every officer on the force had to be there. Two of them stood at Marylou's front door, their somber appearance jarring with the cheery fall decorations. Two more officers were walking slow lines up and down the front yard, their attention glued to their feet.

I got a sick feeling in my stomach. That was an awful lot of blue for a simple domestic dispute.

Tim was crossing the street with his trays of coffee. He spotted my car, scowled, and pointed to the police tape blocking the driveway.

Small clusters of people dotted the lawns along the street. Flashing blue lights in the neighborhood always brought out spectators. I spotted two women drinking coffee in front of the Cape Cod across from Marylou's. Seeing how I wasn't going to get any information from Tim, they were my best bet at finding out what happened.

There are two great myths about small town life. One is that everybody in town knows everybody else. Not true. Not in Woodbridge, anyway. It's impossible to know seven thousand people.

The other myth is the idea strangers stick out like sore thumbs, and are therefore universally mistrusted. Exactly the opposite. Until they prove otherwise, a person is always thought to have a local connection. Took me over a year after I moved to town to get used to strangers waving hello when they drove past me on the street. To tell the truth, I'm still not 100% comfortable with the practice.

Needless to say, neither woman blinked an eye when I joined them with a coffee of my own.

"Such a shame," said the tall one of the pair, a silver-haired woman wearing a blue chenille robe. "All that time Marylou spent planting those mums and they've gone and trampled them."

"What are the police doing here anyway?" I asked. "What happened?"

"One of the officers said she fell down the stairs," said the other woman. She wore a barn coat over her flannel nightgown.

She? My stomach dropped to the ground. "Do you mean Marylou?"

"Poor thing. She was so young, too." A cold hand brushed my wrist. "Are you all right?"

No, I wasn't. "Marylou's dead?" It couldn't be. "When? Ho" I started to ask how, only to remember they said she fell.

"The police showed up around ten o'clock, I think. Wasn't that the time Phyllis?"

"Closer to ten thirty," Phyllis replied. "Her husband found her apparently."

"Can you imagine? Coming home and finding your wife lying there for who knows how long?"

No longer than three hours, I thought. She went inside at seven-thirty. Three hours was long enough.

I should have gone inside with her. Shouldn't have assumed she'd be okay.

"My guess? She was drunk."

"Phyllis!"

"What?" The woman in chenille frowned and raised her coffee. "It's hardly a secret. The whole street knew. For crying out loud, Gail, you could see the bottles in the recycling every week."

"Still, it's not nice to speak ill of the dead." Leaning toward me, Gail added softly, "She occasionally liked to have a cocktail or two in the evenings."

"More like a cocktail or six," Phyllis muttered.

So, last night wasn't an anomaly. The knowledge didn't make me feel any less guilty. I imagined Marylou stumbling around her house railing at the world. Had she kept drinking after I left her?

I should have gone inside.

"Her poor husband." It was Gail again. "He must be so upset. Such a nice man too. Mowed my lawn last summer after my lawn man got sick and wouldn't take a dime."

Where was Paul? I searched the crowd until I saw him. He was sitting on the curb behind one of the police cruisers staring at his hands. Every now and then an officer would walk by and he would look up. For the most part, however, he just sat and stared. He looked shaken and in shock - exactly what you'd expect a man whose wife had died to look.

"Will you excuse me?" I asked Gail and Phyllis. "I should see how he's holding up."

"Of course, dear," Gail said. "Tell him we'll be by later with some sandwiches."

I nodded. People always brought food in times of trouble. They'd brought baskets full when my Jack had his heart attack. I remember not having the heart to tell them food had lost its flavor.

By most standards, Paul Paretsky wasn't a good-looking man. He was pudgy and balding, with a pronounced overbite that made him look like a woodchuck. His elbows were propped on his knees, and despite the cool October temperatures, sweat dampened the armpits of his gray zippered sweatshirt. I tried to imagine him having an affair, but frankly, I couldn't imagine him having the nerve.

He looked up at the sound of my loafers scraping the gravel, the expression in his eyes one I knew well, the same reflection having stared at me for days after Jack's death. He was waiting for someone to tell him there'd been a mistake.

I gave a small wave. "Hey, Paul."

"They told me I couldn't go into my house," he said, his voice flat and lifeless. "I have to wait out here until they're finished."

"Don't tell me you've been sitting here all night?"

"I wanted to. Didn't feel right leaving." He rubbed his arms absently. "They, um, took my shirt. It had blood on it."

Marylou's blood. The thought made me queasy. "I'm so sorry," I said.

"I can't believe she's gone. Only yesterday, she was in the kitchen talking about how she'd found a way to..." Features crumpling, he buried his face in his hands.

For the second time in two days, I found myself sitting on a curb comforting a crying Paretsky. Reaching over, I rubbed circles between his shoulder blades, not much differently from what I did for Marylou. The thought made my own eyes tear up.

After a few minutes, he stopped shaking. "I'm sorry," he said, swiping his eyes. "I can't seem to..."

"You don't have to apologize." All things considered, the guy was holding things together pretty well. "I know it's hard."

Trite, but it was true. Grieving *was* hard. The world demanded you maintain this outward appearance of stoicism to make others feel at ease, while inside you feel like broken glass.

He offered a weak smile. "Thanks. You're Sadie, right? From the coffee shop?"

I nodded.

"I thought I recognized you. Marylou talked about you and your British friend a lot. Said you and he made her laugh."

"Mostly Rob," I said. "I'm more his straight man."

"Either way, she loved her mornings at the coffee shop. She used to say she needed to be there. That's how important they were to her."

I thought of how she'd become a fixture at her table over the past several months. The fact she had a designated table said as much. Rob used to tease her about needing the outlet to run her laptop. *"Not everyone needs shiny and new,"* she'd tell him. *"Like cars and music. Some of us prefer the classics."*

"Except not every song or car is a classic," he'd toss back. *"Like that computer."*

"We might not have known her long," I said to Paul, "but she will be missed."

"Thank you for saying that. It's good to know she managed to make some friends while we were here."

His sweaty palm closed over my left hand and squeezed tightly. The grip lasted a little too long and was a little too tight, sending an uneasy tingle up my arm. Only my guilty conscience kept me from pulling my hand away. Clearly the man was grasping for a connection to his late wife. Adulterer or not, Paul Paretsky was obviously mourning his wife. Letting him hold on for a moment was the least I could do.

We sat there in silence, Paul gripping my hand, me staring at the cement beneath my feet until a shadow fell over us. Looking up, I saw a muscular mountain of a man standing in front of him. Taller than Tim by at least a couple inches, he had shoulders I swore were as wide as he was tall. They were the only things that were wide on him, it should be noted. The rest of his body was shaped like a great big capital V. I could tell from the hands resting on his narrow hips.

He had one of those faces that looked permanently scowled, lined, and rugged from the sun, and the sharpest blue eyes I had ever seen. He looked like a man who didn't mess around.

"They told me you were still here, Mr. Paretsky," he said in a gravel-laced voice. For the first time in nearly a decade, awareness slid along my spine. "Didn't the officer who took your statement tell you it was all right to go somewhere and get some sleep?"

"He did, but I wouldn't have been able to sleep. Not until things were settled."

"I'm afraid gathering the necessary information is taking longer than anticipated. Hopefully, you weren't too uncomfortable." As he was saying the last part, he arched a brow in my direction.

"This is Sadie McIntyre," Paul said.

The man looked me up and down like I was a piece of evidence. That his eyes were a preternatural shade of blue intensified the scrutiny. "Dan Bartlett," he said, after a moment.

Bartlett? As in Tim's nemesis? I sucked in my breath, earning another arched brow.

"Sorry, I didn't realize who you were." That earned me another eyebrow. "I'm Sadie McIntyre. You work with my son, Tim. McIntyre," I added, since his expression didn't change. "The patrolman who brought you coffee."

"I know who Tim is."

"Sadie came by to offer her condolences," Paul told him. "She was friends with Marylou."

"Is that so?"

"We have coffee together every morning."

"Here?" Detective Bartlett asked.

"No, at Cuppa Joe's Café. A group of us have coffee there every morning. When she didn't show up this morning, I assumed she was sick."

"You didn't call her to find out?"

"It's not that kind of group."

He could have been made of stone the way his face didn't change expression. "I see. Then, how did you know to come to her house? Never mind," he said, holding up a hand. "I can guess."

I was sure he could. The dots being pretty easy to connect. Glancing behind me, I saw Tim watching our exchange from his guard post by Marylou's front door. If looks could kill...

"It was nice of you to rush over here to comfort Mr. Paretsky when you heard the news," Detective Bartlett said.

The implication in his words made me bristle.

Turning around, I realized Bartlett's attention was focused on my knee where Paul's hand still held mine. Unfortunately, the guy had my fingers in a death grip. Nothing short of yanking would get him to let go, and since that would mean making a scene, I let my hand stay put. "I didn't know about Marylou until I arrived. I thought..."

"Thought what?"

"Actually, I don't know what I thought," I replied. No need for Paul to know I'd been worried Marylou had nailed him with a fry pan. "I only knew something had happened so I came to find out. Then, when I heard Marylou was..."

I couldn't get the word out. Disbelief kept it stuck in my throat. "Well, I figured I should see if Paul needed anything. I know what it's like to lose someone unexpectedly. My husband, Jack, died of a heart attack while on his shift."

"So I've been told. I'm sorry," Bartlett replied. There was a flicker of compassion in his voice, although it had faded when he turned his attention to Paul. "We'll be wrapping up shortly and then you'll be able to go inside. We appreciate your patience."

Funny. He didn't sound all that appreciative.

Paul didn't notice. He looked over his shoulder and stared blankly at the police walking his front lawn. One of them kicked over a mum and bent to set the pot to rights.

"I don't know what I'm supposed to do next," Paul said. "Marylou did everything. Do...do I call a funeral home? I don't... I'll have to ask my assistant..."

"McKinnon's Funeral Home," I blurted out. Marylou deserved better than having Paul's sidepiece make the arrangements. "On Main Street. Bruce McKinnon will know what to do."

"Thank you."

I felt Detective Bartlett's stare making note of the way Paul squeezed my fingers even tighter. I was right; his eyes didn't miss a thing. Wasn't hard to imagine him intimidating a confession out of someone. All he needed to do was zero in with those eyes and wait for the person to start squirming. Here I was, innocent, and I felt like an ant trapped beneath a magnifying glass. A guilty person would probably burst into flames.

Hoping I looked casual—although I probably didn't in Detective Bartlett's eyes—I stood, letting the momentum force Paul into releasing me. "If there's anything else I can do," I said as I wiped my hand on my slacks, "please let me know."

"I..." He paused. "You'll let the others know about what happened? Rob. Lindsay. The other ladies?"

"Of course. I'll call them this afternoon." Definitely not calls I looked forward to making. "They're the other people in our coffee group," I told Detective Bartlett, largely because I could feel him listening. "A couple of them were more friendly with Marylou than I was."

"I thought you said it wasn't that kind of group?"

"It wasn't. But that doesn't mean individual people weren't friendly with one another." What did it matter anyway?

Maybe it was being at the crime scene that made the man's question sound ominous, but I was beginning to understand why Tim thought the way he did. Bartlett's gravelly voice could make a simple comment like "Are we out of coffee?" sound like an accusation.

I turned to Paul. "I'm so sorry. I just saw her last night." I refrained from mentioning her condition. "I'm really sorry."

"Thank you." He stood, and I saw his arm start to swing forward. Thanking God for jacket pockets, I stuffed my hands in mine before he could grab hold. His hand hovered awkwardly, before he rescued himself by finding pockets of his own.

"I'll walk you to your car," he said.

"If you don't mind, Mr. Paretsky," Detective Bartlett's voice stopped us before we could make a first step. "I have a few additional questions about last night."

"I've already told the officer everything I know," Paul said.

"There are a couple of details I want to double check for my report. With these kinds of cases, we like to be as accurate as possible. I promise it won't take long."

The detective pulled out a pencil and pocket-sized notebook. Classic old-school. Marylou would have appreciated it.

"You told the responding officer you arrived home around ten-thirty?"

Paul nodded. "Around then."

"Where were you before then?"

"At a bar watching the game."

"By yourself?"

"Marylou hates—hated—football, so I go out to enjoy it."

"I thought..." Both men turned in my direction. I shook my head. "Nothing."

Only I could have sworn Marylou said it was Paul who hated football.

"The game was still going on when you got home, though," Detective Bartlett said. He was right; Rob said Tim had to leave Foxboro early.

"Today was a workday. I didn't want to stay out late."

"Did you talk to anyone while you were there?"

"Not really."

Because he was lying! Poor Marylou had been right last night. Bastard *was* with his girlfriend.

What did it matter at this point, though, right? Admitting his infidelity wouldn't bring Marylou back.

Detective Bartlett, meanwhile, said nothing while he scribbled the information in his notebook. "You told the responding officer that you got home at ten-thirty, and that's when you found Mrs. Paretsky."

"Yes." The word came out a cross between a whelp and a sob. "She was at the bottom of the stairs. I tried to wake her up by shaking her, but... There was all this blood. On her. On the wall. I warned her those stairs were slippery and she should use the handrail..."

My heart cracked a little when he sobbed a second time. No one should have to find their spouse under those circumstances.

"Anyway," Paul said, wiping his nose on his forearm. "That's when I called 9-1-1."

"You didn't try to move her or touch anything while you were waiting?"

"I...I touched her hair. Told her the ambulance was coming. I wanted her to know I was there in case she woke up.

"She didn't," he added in a whisper.

His face not showing so much as a crack of emotion, Detective Bartlett closed his notebook. "Thank you, Mr. Paretsky. If we need anything else, I'll let you know."

"Can...can I go inside now? My phone, it's in there and I need to call that, um..."

"McKinnon's," I supplied.

"Right. McKinnon's."

Bartlett nodded. "The officer at the door will let you in."

"Thank you." With a parting sniffle, he started shuffling toward his front door, his earlier offer to walk me to the car clearly forgotten. Which was just as well, since I hadn't wanted the escort anyway. His head and shoulders were slumped as though bearing the weight of the world. Guilt will do that to you. My own shoulders felt heavier themselves.

Poor Marylou. I pictured her lying there alone as the life seeped out of her. A horrible, terrible, unnecessary end to a humiliating night. If only...

The world was peppered with *If only's*. Hadn't Marylou and I decided that very point? *You can't change the past,* we'd agreed. All the wishes in the world wouldn't bring Marylou to life. Best I could do was figure out a way to deal with my guilty conscience.

Good thing I was good at letting go.

There was one thing though. I sure would have liked to know why Marylou was wandering that side of town. Had she heard about Jenn's party and decided to crash it? Or was there another reason? Guess I'd never know.

I headed for my car.

"Hold on there, Ms. McIntyre," Detective Bartlett said. "I'm not quite finished with you."

5

What did I do?

Slowly, I turned around, feeling very much like a child called to the carpet, a feeling I resented, by the way. "Is there a problem, Detective?"

He tucked his hands in his pockets, calling attention to how well his khakis fit. I had to fight not to look him up and down. In retrospect, I should have, because no gawking meant looking him in the eye.

Back under the magnifying glass.

"The guys at the station speak highly about your late husband," he said. "They're happy his son decided to follow in his footsteps."

"Jack would have been proud, too." My husband loved being a cop. I used to joke he was born wearing a badge. "He taught Tim a lot while he was growing up."

"I can tell. The kid's got potential."

"Good to know."

"The thing is..." He shuffled his feet. "I'd hate to see that potential snuffed out because his mother couldn't cut the apron strings."

"The apron...?" Because I followed him to Marylou's house, he was accusing me of being some kind of clingy mother? "There are no apron strings. The only reason I'm here is because I heard Marylou's address on the radio and got concerned."

"If you say so. I wouldn't want people to get the wrong impression, is all."

He smirked. I smirked back. The two of us smirked at one another for several seconds. Now I understood why Tim disliked him. Condescending jerk.

"Thanks for the concern," I replied, making a point to drawl my words as strongly he'd drawled his. "But, if Tim has a problem with my being here, he'll let me know." In no uncertain terms, too. I was expecting an agitated phone call as soon as his shift ended.

"Now if you'll excuse me..."

I squared my shoulders, and tossed my head. When push came to shove, I could do haughty as well as anyone in Woodbridge. Especially to broad shouldered police detectives who should be minding their own business. "I have to go let people know our friend passed away."

———

IN THE END, the only person I told was Rob. My other four calls went straight to voice mail. I left messages for each of them to call me, but none did.

No matter. By the next morning, the whole town knew about Marylou's death. As the six of us gathered around our usual tables, Marylou's table remained conspicuously empty. Whether by coincidence or some silent mutual agreement, none of the other customers moved to sit there.

"I feel horrible," Andrea said, sniffing loudly.

I believed it. Unkempt wasn't something posse members did, and she looked a mess. Her eyes were watery, and the skin under her nose was red and raw. Generally speaking, I thought her the most approachable of the posse, a fact I attributed to her being quiet and not being blonde. Brunette solidarity, and all that. Although her hair was far more shiny and bouncy than mine. That is, normally it was. Today it hung in a limp ponytail.

"Why'd you drag your germs here in the first place?" Erin asked. She slid a napkin across the table, which Andrea grabbed to wipe her nose. "You look like death warmed over."

Talk about a bad choice of words. I waited to see if she would realize what she said, but she kept sipping her pumpkin spice latte without batting an eye. The woman was as mellow as I had ever seen her.

"I know I do, but I wanted to know more about Marylou," Andrea said. "Does anyone know what happened? How she fell?"

Erin shrugged. "Probably tripped over her cat. She seems the type."

"To trip or to own a cat?" I asked.

"Both. She wasn't exactly the picture of grace."

Remembering her four-legged crawl across the street Sunday night, I had to agree.

"And doesn't she seem like a 'cat person' to you?"

She'd directed her question to the other members of the posse, but it was Rob who answered. After sitting a little stiffer in his chair. "Exactly what kind of person is a cat person?" he asked.

"You know. Lonely. Odd."

"Don't worry," I leaned over and whispered before Rob could retort. Now wasn't the time or place to argue cat owner demographics. "You wouldn't count anyway. We both know Eliot is a human in a tiny fur suit."

"Damn right, he is," Rob whispered. "Trip a person on purpose, he would. It's why I always use the hallway light."

"My neighbor lets her cat sleep on the top step of her stairway," Jennifer said, flicking her ponytail, which, in contrast to Andrea's, looked freshly washed and curled. "Whenever Brandon goes over for playgroup, I'm terrified he'll trip over it. You'd think the other mother would pay closer attention to hazards."

"Oh for goodness sakes. It's only a cat. Just tell Brandon to step over the darn thing."

And there it was, the proclamation to end the discussion. Uttered by none other than Lindsay, she of yesterday's nail emergency. If the yoga posse reminded me of the high school popular girls, then Lindsay was the queen bee. The prom queen, head cheerleader, class president, most-likely-to-succeed queen bee. The kind of woman people claimed to dislike when really, they secretly longed to be her best friend. She and her dot com CEO husband moved to Woodbridge three years ago and immediately established themselves as town royalty—as only rich, pretty people can do. As a result, Lindsay was the major player on most parent committees, chair of the Night Walk Committee, and of course, de facto leader of the yoga posse.

Using her re-useable water bottle—Lindsay didn't drink caffeine—she pointed to Jenn's cell phone. "Are you going to get that? It's been buzzing all morning."

Jenn glanced at the call screen, before flipping the phone face over. "It's Nick," she said, rolling her eyes. "Undoubtedly calling to complain because I sicced my lawyer on him again. According to him, it's my fault he won't make his payments."

"How late is he this time?" Erin asked.

"A month. I got two checks before he started crying poor again. News flash." She grabbed her coffee. "Try spending less on the skanky girlfriends."

"Too bad he didn't fall down a flight of stairs like Marylou."

Wow, Erin was on target with the tasteless comments today, wasn't she?

"Never happen," Jenn said. "He doesn't own a cat."

"Why is everyone blaming the blooming cat?"

I patted Rob's hand and tried to pull the conversation back on track. Call it my guilty conscience, but I was feeling Marylou's absence. "I know she was only around since this winter, but it's going to feel weird not having Marylou joining us. I'm going to miss her."

I expected more of an acknowledgement. Okay, acknowledgement period. Instead, only Rob nodded in agreement while the other four reached for their coffees.

"Does anyone know when the wake is going to be?" Rob asked. "We should pay our respects."

"End of the week," I guessed. "Unless she's got family traveling from out of town."

"Where was her home town anyway?" He looked over at the other table where all four shook their heads before looking at me. "Do you know?"

I copied the posse. "No clue. Subject never came up."

"Hopefully the wake won't be this week. Carlos has us going to so many dinners. Everyone and their brother in the Greater Boston area want him to invest in their company. My calendar's a nightmare."

Lindsay pressed her fingers to her temple as though to ward off a stress headache. "How am I supposed to fit another event in my schedule?"

"I'm sure Carlos would understand you needing to beg off a dinner for a wake." My tone might have been more irritable than necessary. Honestly though, she was acting as though Marylou toppled down the stairs to purposely jam her schedule.

"Don't forget we also have the Night Walk meeting next Sunday," Jenn so helpfully noted.

"That's right. And there's no way we can reschedule either. Not with the event right around the corner." Again, her fingers went to her temple. This time it was both hands. "What a nightmare."

"What's the big deal? We'll skip on the wake if there's a conflict. It's not like any of us want to go in the first place."

"Erin!" My eyes nearly bugged out of my head. The woman had been insensitive all morning, but this comment took the cake.

"Well, I don't," she replied, meeting my stare.

"What Erin means, Sadie..." Jenn gave me a condescending smile, although not before she shot Erin a glare with eyes so narrow, her lashes looked like tiny black daggers. "...is that no one likes going to wakes. I think we all wish we had an excuse to get us out. Isn't that right, Erin?"

"Exactly."

But was that really what she meant? She and Jenn were having an entire conversation with their eyes.

Once again, it amazed me how little the four women had been affected by Marylou's death, especially Jenn and Erin who'd had dinner with the woman just the other night. I'd always assumed the posse had more depth than their shallow behavior implied. Apparently I'd given them too much credit.

Meanwhile, I felt kicked in the stomach every time I looked at her empty chair.

If only I'd stuck around on Sunday night.

The bell over Cuppa's front door jingled. "Hel–loo," I heard Rob say under his breath.

A strange tickling sensation tiptoed along my spine. Hello indeed. Swiveling in my chair, I looked to the front door to see what had caused the disturbance in the atmosphere.

Oh.

Detective Dan Bartlett stood in the doorway. Rob's whispered remark made sense now. After a night of careful contemplation, I'd nearly convinced myself yesterday's arresting appearance was my imagination. He wore the same leather jacket and similar dark slacks. Both fit as well as I remembered. What I hadn't noticed was exactly how hard and chiseled his features were, giving him a very been-there-done-that appearance. No wonder the guys on the force didn't give him the same new guy treatment they gave Tim. This guy had top dog written all over him.

What on earth was a man like him doing in a town like Woodbridge? He belonged in a city kicking in doors and flashing his gun.

The whole café registered his arrival. I thought the barista's knees would buckle when he stepped up to place his order—and this was a woman who had waited on Rob a half hour earlier. Jose, the other barista, stood on tip toes so he could stare at him from behind the espresso machine handles. Even the posse ceased their conversation in favor of coyly finger-combing their ponytails.

Order in hand, he turned and scanned the tables until his eyes landed on our group.

"Looks like he spotted something he liked," Rob murmured. "He's coming straight for us."

"Down boy," I whispered back. "He's Tim's nemesis."

"That's the soul-sucking Detective Bartlett? Your son did not do the man justice."

No, he did not.

Bartlett stopped at our table and smiled. "Good morning, Ms. McIntyre. I see your coffee group is meeting as usual."

"Minus one." I reminded him. "So, it's not really usual at all. In fact, we were just talking about how strange it was to be here without Marylou."

"Were you now?" His blue eyes moved around the two tables, where Rob and the posse were all nodding in agreement.

"Gonna miss giving her a hard time about that old computer of hers," Rob said. "Never did talk her into better technology."

"We'll miss her," Lindsay said. "She was starting to blend in with the town."

"Mmmm," the others echoed.

"Always hard saying good-bye to a friend. I'm sorry for your loss." He turned to me. "I was wondering if I might buy you a cup of coffee."

Any other time, a handsome man asking me to coffee instead of one of my other companions would have me silently gloating, but the gleam in his eyes looked a little too...intense for me to revel in the attention. He wanted something.

"If you've stopped by to continue your lecture from yesterday, you needn't have bothered," I said, once we'd moved to a new set of chairs. Behind me, I could feel five pairs of eyes watching our every move. "Tim talked to me last night."

Treated me to a lecture about respecting his boundaries was more like it. "Hard enough to follow in Dad's footsteps," he'd said. I hate it when kids have a point.

"Unless of course, you wanted to apologize," I added.

Bartlett nodded. "It had been a long night. My social skills might not have been at their best."

Not quite an apology, but close enough. His voice was less husky this morning. There was a satin finish to the gravel that took the gruff edge off. "Are you saying your social skills are better now?"

He gave a soft snort. "Somewhat."

I watched while he removed the plastic lid from his cup. Green tea. Interesting. I'd have pegged him for the black coffee type.

The bag floated on top of his hot water. Using his index finger, he poked it into the water. "I have to admit, you're not what I imagined after hearing the guys talk at the station," he said.

We were even then. "What exactly were you expecting? Never mind, I can guess what Tim said." After all, we were talking about a kid who once argued the words *maid* and *mother* should be inter-changeable.

"Someone less..." Bartlett paused to poke the bag again. "Memorable."

My fingers gripped my cup. "I see." I wasn't sure whether to take the word as a compliment or not.

"It's a compliment," he said, reading my mind.

"Thank you, then."

Still, I didn't feel like I should be completely flattered. Especially when he looked up from his drink, and I saw that the predatory gleam had returned to his eyes.

Another shiver ran down my spine. And it wasn't the good kind.

His next comment proved me right. "Paul Paretsky certainly seems fond of you. Are you two close?"

"Hardly. I've only met the man a couple of times through Marylou."

"With whom you also weren't close, even though you have coffee with her every morning."

"I told you, it's not that type of group. I have coffee with those four ladies there, too." I gestured at the yoga posse with a nod of my head. "I'm not best buddies with any of them, either."

"Interesting you didn't mention the guy sitting with them."

"Because he and I... Why are you asking?" This conversation had taken a strange turn. I doubted his interest in my social circle was idle curiousity.

Leaning forward, I raised my coffee to my lips, doing my best to mimic his penetrating stare. "What is it you want to know, Detective?" I asked.

"Oh, there's lots I'd like to know." He leaned forward too. To anyone watching, we looked about to share a secret. "How about we start with, are you having an affair with Paul Paretsky?"

6

I SPIT OUT MY COFFEE.

Not figuratively, the way people say when talking about being caught off guard. I literally sprayed liquid all over the table.

Bartlett wiped the front of his jacket with a napkin. "Should I take that as a 'No'?"

"Hell yeah, it's a no."

From over my shoulder, a handful of fresh napkins appeared, courtesy of Rob.

"Let me know if you need any more, luv," he said.

As it turned out, most of the coffee had landed on Detective Bartlett's side of the table, so I handed him half the stack. "I can't believe you'd even ask."

"Well, according to the neighbors, Mr. Paretsky had been spending a lot of time away from home. Add in the fact he joined a local gym, started touching up his hair..."

I stopped dabbing at coffee drops. "Paul dyes his hair?"

"His neighbors seem to think so. You didn't notice?"

"I wasn't exactly checking out his hair yesterday. And if I were, I wouldn't be impressed. Next, you'll be telling me he was getting manicures."

"You have a problem with manicures?"

"Not if they're on women." Men's hands, in my opinion, should look like they weren't afraid to do work. The kind of hands like my Jack had. Or Bartlett. Those chapped knuckles of his weren't from being inside all day.

I looked to where our hands were cleaning up coffee side by side. He had strong, meaty hands. Large enough that I swore you could fit two of mine on the back of one of his. I certainly wouldn't want to be a criminal being held by those hands.

Bartlett crumpled his napkin in a ball and moved it to the side. "In my experience, a guy starts paying extra-special attention to his appearance all of a sudden, he's trying to impress someone who's not his wife," he said, "and the two of you certainly looked friendly yesterday."

"The man had just lost his wife and was looking for a way to steady himself. Since I could relate, I let him hold on to my hand."

"Nothing more?"

"Definitely not. As far as Paul's girlfriend is concerned, you're barking up the wrong tree."

"Is that so?" he said. "What tree should I be barking up, Ms. McIntyre?"

"I..." My senses went on alert. These were awfully personal questions for an accidental death investigation. "Why are you so interested in knowing whether or not Paul was cheating on Marylou?"

Rather than answer, Bartlett flipped to another page of his notebook. "Did you ever socialize with Mrs. Paretsky? Beside morning coffee, that is?"

"We both serve on the Night Walk Committee."

"I saw a flyer about that at the station," he said. "It's a cancer fundraiser, right?"

"We create a luminaria course and hold a candlelight 5K. The police and fire departments have a running competition to see who can do the most fundraising. So far the fire department's ahead. Again, though, why are you asking?"

"And these committee meetings, they were the only other time you saw Mrs. Paretsky?"

"Yes. I told you, we didn't socialize."

He jotted something. I tried to see what, but the angle made it impossible to tell without being obvious, so I risked a sip of coffee instead. At least the liquid had cooled. If I spit out the contents again, I wouldn't burn anyone.

"Was there a committee meeting yesterday?" he asked.

"No. We don't meet on weekends because there are too many kid conflicts."

Suddenly, it dawned on me where he was taking this conversation, and I sat up in my seat. "Wouldn't it be easier to ask if I saw Marylou last night?"

He chuckled. "Okay. Did you?"

"Yeah. I ran into her on Daffodil Lane when I was driving home from an open house. She was in a bad way, so I offered her a ride to her house."

"By bad way, do you mean drunk? The neighbors mentioned she liked to 'unwind,'" he added.

"She was definitely unwound. I thought..."

The guilt I'd been trying to ignore pushed itself to the forefront, and I had to clear the lump from my throat. "I thought she'd be okay on her own. If I'd known she was so unsteady on her feet..."

But I had known. I'd watched her stumble and fall in the street. I looked to the tabletop and the silhouette of my head reflecting in the polyurethane. The thick glossy coating distorted my head into a shapeless blur.

"You would have what?" Detective Bartlett asked.

Was it my imagination or had his voice grown gentler? Added another layer of satin.

I shrugged. "Taken her upstairs and tucked her into bed? I don't know. *Something.* If I had, maybe she'd still be..."

My eyes started to tear up. I looked around for a clean napkin to dab them dry.

"Here." A white paper square slid into view. Pushed by a strong, red-knuckled hand.

"Thank you." Sniffing back the dampness, I gave as much of a smile as I could muster. "I'm not usually the emotional type."

"Death tends to make people emotional."

"I know." Some people anyway. Others were barely affected. I glanced over my shoulder at the others, who, by this time, had given up any pretense of ignoring the conversation. Of the five, only Rob and Andrea bothered to look somber, and I half-suspected Andrea's mood had more to do with her cold than grief.

"Takes a while for reality to sink in," I said. "I mean, I still haven't readjusted the seat from when she sat in my car."

"What street did you say you found her on?" he asked.

"Daffodil Lane."

"And that's where?"

"Sorry." I forgot he was still relatively new in town. "The other side of the Common. It's part of the subdivision off Hunter Street. I sometimes use it as a short cut rather than go up and around the fire station."

"Huh. I'll have to remember that. Pretty far from where she lives though, isn't it? " His brow furrowed. Visualizing the area no doubt. "Did she say why she was there?"

"Not really. She wasn't exactly dressed for socializing." I told him about her ratty, ill-fitting sweatshirt. "The Marylou I knew never dressed like a slob in public.

"Actually," I added, thinking things over, "she wasn't herself at all."

Bartlett looked up. "Because she was drunk?"

"No, because she was angry. I mean like really angry."

"And that was unusual?"

"For her? So far as I know." I paused, remembering her bizarre ranting. Her threats about making "them" see. Across the table, Bartlett's tea bag was still floating in his drink, the color of which was now a sickly green.

"The Marylou who joined us for coffee barely raised her voice," I told him. "When I found her Sunday night, she was ready to kill someone. Paul," I corrected. "She was ready to kill Paul. She knew about his affair."

"Really?" That got his attention, and he sat up a little straighter—if it was possible for his shoulders to get straighter. "Did she give you a name?"

I shook my head. "All she said was that he was seeing his assistant..." For Marylou's sake, I cleaned up the language. "And that she was going to show them."

"Interesting choice of words," Bartlett said, pen pausing. "I'm going to go out on a limb and guess she didn't elaborate."

"Elaborating would require coherency," I replied. "I assumed that the assistant lived nearby and she was planning to confront them somehow."

You know what happens when you assume, a voice whispered in my brain. I chalked it up as a side-effect to being interrogated by the police. Despite having lived nearly two decades with one cop and giving birth to another, face-to-face questioning still made me uneasy. Especially since Bartlett's gaze hadn't once lessened in intensity.

Not even when lost in thought, like he was now. He tapped his pen against the top of the table, each tap counting a half a second. "So far as you know, she didn't. Confront anybody, that is."

I shook my head. "I suggested she wait until she sobered up. Figured it was safer for Paul if she had a clear head."

Meanwhile, I should have been her safety. My conscience reared up again, bringing another batch of guilty tears.

"I should have insisted on staying after she told me she was fine," I said. "If I had, she'd never have fallen down the stairs."

"If she fell down the stairs," Bartlett said.

I stopped dabbing my eyes long enough to stare at him. "What do you mean, *if she fell*? Isn't that what happened?"

"So the initial evidence suggests."

"But..."

"You were a cop's wife. Surely, you know it's important we do a thorough investigation."

There was thorough, and then there was *thorough*.

Seriously, though, how could Marylou's fall be anything other than a tragic accident unless...

Someone had pushed her.

7

THE DOOR HAD BARELY CLOSED behind Detective Bartlett before the posse pounced.

"What was that all about?" Lindsay asked.

Her question was immediately backed up by Jennifer. "Was Marylou's husband really having an affair?"

Followed by Erin's "Why on earth would he think it was with you?"

"Give over. Sadie's an attractive woman. I bet there are tons of men who'd cheat on their wives with her."

"Give over yourself, Rob. I meant because she's such a straight arrow. She won't even jaywalk."

"Erin's got a point," Rob said to me. "You're hardly the running-around type. Although you completely could if you wanted to."

"Thanks." I shot him a smile. Only a good friend would turn the accusation into a compliment. "As for why. He saw Paul holding my hand yesterday and misinter"

Andrea coughed into the crook of her arm. "Paul was holding your hand?"

Again with the incredulity. "I was consoling him, and... Whatever. It was no big deal, and that's what I told Detective Bartlett."

"But he *was* having an affair with someone," Jenn said. "Wonder who? Do you think Marylou knew?"

"What do *you* think?" Erin replied.

"Good point."

As they continued their strange exchange, I kept my mouth shut. If the truth about Paul's affair became public, it wouldn't be because I threw fuel on the gossip fire.

Besides, they were so fixated on Paul's infidelity, they were missing the bigger implication behind Bartlett's questions.

That Paul might have had reason to want Marylou dead.

———

"SORRY ABOUT THE ASSAULT," Rob said as we walked to our cars a short while later. "I tried to keep them from listening to your conversation, but once you spit out the coffee, all bets were off."

Wasn't my finest moment, I had to admit. "They would have eavesdropped, spit or no spit. Their ears are primed for gossip. Like everyone else in Woodbridge. Present company included." I gave his shoulder a nudge.

Red began creeping along the lines of his cheekbones. *Busted.* "Yeah, but I had a reason. I was trying to hear whether he was asking you out or not. Quite a specimen, he is. Don't suppose I'd be lucky enough for him to bat for my team."

"The way your luck runs? I'm sure he does." And wouldn't that make for one amazing looking couple. "Thank you, by the way, for defending my desirability to the posse."

"Well, I know you. You might not be having an affair, but that doesn't mean you don't want people thinking it's not an option."

"Exactly," I replied. He did know me. "Thank you."

Rob shrugged. "No sweat defending the obvious."

My turn to have a blush creeping across my cheeks. One of the reasons I loved Rob was because he was good for my ego. Always making me sound better than I was. Once, he even called me statuesque, an adjective I laughed over for about a week.

It wasn't that I was unattractive—there was a time when I could hold my own—but I was also a realist. In a town full of rich and pretty young women, an older woman who didn't work out or dress in the latest fashion was more background than head turner.

I frowned, thinking of what Detective Bartlett said. "Detective Bartlett called me memorable."

"There's my answer to what team be plays for," Rob replied. "And you are memorable. Not like me, obviously."

"Obviously." Sadly, he was right. Rob was one of a kind.

"But in a very Sadie-like way, you're very unforgettable."

"Oh." My pulse skipped a beat. "I'm not trying."

"I know. You don't have to try. Some people just are."

We reached my car first, and Rob leaned against the front quarter. With his hands stuffed in the pockets of his barn coat and his foot propped against the tire, he turned the moment into a magazine advertisement.

"What I don't understand," he said, "is why Bartlett cares who Paul's stepping out with. What does that have to do with Marylou falling?"

"If she fell," I said.

"Come again?" Rob's foot slipped to the ground. From the look on his face, this was the first time he'd heard Bartlett's suggestion. His eavesdropping skills were slipping.

"Hardly a surprise. I had four women squawking in me ear about your supposed affair," he replied when I said as much. "I may have missed a few things."

"Why would he make such a comment unless..." His blue eyes widened. "Holy... Was he suggesting someone might have 'helped' Marylou fall?"

I shrugged. "He claims he's simply being thorough and checking all the possible angles."

A car horn beeped. Detective Bartlett in his extra-large black SUV drove past us with a smirk and a nod. I nodded, making a point of maintaining eye contact until he'd moved on. Why, I wasn't sure. Only that I felt I needed to.

Meanwhile, next to me, Rob continued digesting my comment. "I can't believe he thinks Paul Paretsky might have offed his wife. He doesn't see the type for murder."

"He doesn't seem the type to have an affair, either," I said, "but prevailing wisdom says otherwise."

"By prevailing wisdom, I assume you mean Detective Bartlett?" He kicked at the parking lot gravel with his shoe. "Even if Paul was having an affair, murder seems a bit of a stretch. If you ask me, I think the good detective is doing a little wishful thinking. Looking for complications where none exist."

"So far as you know." Good grief. I sounded like Bartlett. In the good detective's defense, however, it wasn't that farfetched to think an unfaithful husband might also be capable of murder. "Everyone has a secret side they hide from the world. You, of all people, should know that."

This time, Rob's blush filled more than his cheeks. The red spread across his face and down his neck, before disappearing below his collar. "That's different," he said. "I'm not about to kill anyone."

"Good to know. I can stop sleeping with one eye open."

"Ha ha."

Seriously, though, while Rob's secrets might not drive him to kill, who was to say about others? When backed into a corner, people could do just about anything.

Including murder.

———

I LEFT Rob in the parking lot and drove to the neighborhood behind the middle school. Keith Koenig wanted to check out a Victorian that had recently come on the market. I already knew the showing would be a complete waste of time. Keith was, as people in the real estate industry liked to say, a tire kicker. Meaning he liked to look, but when it came time to buy, he couldn't pull the trigger. With the last house, I actually got as far as the inspection, only to have Keith decide the propensity of wildlife living near the house constituted a bacterial risk.

"There were chipmunks sitting on the patio wall eating. Not ten feet from the house," he said when he called to withdraw his offer. Because, God forbid, squirrels and chipmunks live near a house built on a wooded property.

Needless to say, he would find the Victorian equally undesirable for some reason, but if a client wanted to see a property, I was obligated to show it. Regardless. It was part of the Renee Drake Realty motto: *We won't stop until you find your dream home.*

Or in the case of Keith Koenig, we won't stop.

Keith was studying the flower beds on the side yard when I pulled into the driveway. He had one hand stuffed in his khakis' pocket, while the other was busy stroking his blond goatee.

I rolled down my window. "Morning, Keith. No Debbie today?"

"Had to work. I said I'd check out the property and let her know if it was worth taking time off."

"Her loss." My gut said Debbie already knew it would be a waste of time. "I haven't seen the property yet, but Renee tells me it's a great listing. A real steal."

I started to reach for the folder that contained all the house information only to feel a quick drop in my stomach. The seat was still pulled back from Sunday night. I'd removed Marylou's makeshift barf bag and wiped down the seat belt, but never readjusted the seat to its original position. There was a grease spot on the window where she'd rested her forehead.

One of the last things she'd ever done.

Shaking off the memory, I grabbed the folder and joined him outside. "I hope you weren't waiting long." I got tied up at Cuppa's."

"No worries. Gave me time to walk around the yard. Watch yourself. Those front steps look like they might be uneven. I don't suppose you have a level in the car so we can check?"

A level? This was either going to be the shortest showing on record or the longest. "Afraid not. If you decide you like the place, we can always make sure the inspector double checks."

"Oh, I would regardless," he replied. Thankfully for him, I was busy punching in the lock box code, so he couldn't see me roll my eyes.

"Do you know when the house was built?" he asked.

"Turn of the century. Last century, I mean. 1907 or '08."

We stepped into an entryway so newly waxed you could smell the lemon coming off the wood. The current owners, a brother and sister who'd inherited the place, had staged the property to move. Renee's coaching, no doubt. The walls were stripped and freshly painted white, and the windows cleaned to let in the October sunshine. They even left fresh logs in the fireplace to advertise its workability. The whole place oozed homey, old-fashioned character.

From the look on Keith's face, he wasn't feeling the magic.

"The essentials have all been modified," I told him. I began rattling off info about plumbing and electrical updates, doing my due diligence in case I was reading Keith's expression wrong. "Windows are fairly new too. Less than ten years old. Keith?"

He stood at the foot of the staircase, running a hand along the glossy white banister. "These stairs don't look level either."

"It's not unusual to find a few irregularities in houses this age, but that adds to their charm. Did you see the window seats in the dining room?" I pointed to the brightly cushioned nook. "One of the things I love about these old houses is all the nooks and crannies. So much architectural character."

"Hard to heat, though," he countered. "These steps are slanted. Look at the one second from the top. You can see the dip in the middle."

"They have seen a century of use, Paul. You can always install new stair boards if they make you nervous. I think you'll find that generally, the house is pretty solid. Construction from this era usually is."

"Mm, I suppose." He gave the railing a shake. Solidly installed, it didn't move. Thank goodness.

"See?" I said. "Strong as can be."

"I'm sorry. I don't mean to fixate on the stairs," Keith said.

I offered a smile, but said nothing. If not the stairs, it would be something else. "Would you like to see the kitchen? My notes say it was recently updated with counter tops and a new floor."

We started toward the rear of the house, where bright yellow curtains beckoned. "There's a half bath downstairs as well." I pointed to another recently painted room before our destination.

Keith poked his head through the door to check it out. "Someone I know lost his wife in a fall Sunday night," he said. "I think that's why I'm so focused on them. The stairs, that is."

"You know Paul Paretsky?" I stopped in my tracks.

Keith did the same. "You know Paul too?"

"I knew his wife."

"Oh. I'm sorry." Reaching up, he slipped the tweed cap from his head. I think, in a gesture of respect. Gripping it in both hands, he let his pale eyes drop to the floor. "Horrible, isn't it? I can't imagine if I came home and found Debbie. Poor Paul. On top of everything else." He shook his head. "Some people can't catch a break."

"It's hard losing a spouse," I agreed. "Especially unexpectedly." Unless the loss was actually a lucky break.

"The whole year's been a nightmare for the guy," Keith said.

"Really? How?"

He tipped his head. "I thought you were friends with his wife?"

"I am. I mean, I was," I replied. "But we hadn't known each other long." Or well, as it was turning out. "She only recently hinted about there being difficulties."

"Like I said, rough year. The worst part is that Paul was excited because he thought he'd be on his feet soon. Is this countertop quartz?"

"Granite." I propped a hip against the granite countertop and watched him open and close cabinet doors. Getting back on his feet. That implied financial issues. Paul did own his own firm. Maybe... I took a shot in the dark. "So his business was doing better?"

"That's the impression I got from Paul." Keith was on his hands and knees looking deep in the bottom corner cabinet. When he spoke, his voice echoed in the hollow space. "At least he was talking about giving his assistant a nice Christmas bonus to thank her for being such a loyal employee. And now here he loses his wife in a freak accident."

Backing out, he sat on his haunches and shook his head. "Hardly seems fair."

No, it didn't, although he and I probably had different ideas regarding the true victim. In the past forty hours, I'd discovered the Paretskys were hiding an affair, a possible drinking problem, and now financial difficulties.

Money and sex. That's what my Jack used to say. Crime always boiled down to money and sex. Paul Paretsky had connections to both.

Giving him two good reasons to shove Marylou down the stairs.

8

DETECTIVE BARTLETT's theory was looking more and more possible.

Then why did the notion feel off? Why was I having trouble buying the idea Paul may have pushed Marylou down a flight of stairs, even though he had two very strong motives for doing so? Was it because of the grief I saw in his eyes the other day?

Or my guilty conscience looking for an excuse not to feel guilty over leaving Marylou alone?

We ended up spending ninety long minutes touring the property. Keith was nothing if not thorough as he checked out every closet and cabinet. I swear the man had studied enough prospective homes that he could be an inspector in his own right. At one point, we went to the attic to check ventilation from the bathroom.

"I don't like how they have the moisture venting into the enclosed space," he said as we climbed down the attic ladder. "I think it needs to be connected and blow out of the house."

"I'll make a note," I told him. "I'm sure the inspector will say that's an easy fix."

"Mmm." He put his hands on his hips and gave the upstairs hallway one more look around.

We were never going to the inspection round. I could already tell from the furrows between his eyes. Today's tour was nothing more than going through the motions.

Finally, he shook his head. "I'm sorry, but I think Debbie and I would be more comfortable in a newer house. Something that requires a lot less renovation."

"Of course." I locked my jaw to keep from pointing out that last week, when touring a new development, he talked about wanting something with character. "I'll go to the office and check the listings. Sooner or later we will find you the right house."

I might be dying of old age, but I would find it.

The two of us walked outside. I waited on the front porch until Keith's car had driven around the corner, then took out my phone.

"No dice," I said when I got Renee on the phone.

On the other end of the phone, my boss sighed, and I imagined her rolling her eyes. "Did you push the updated kitchen and bath?"

"Pushed and pushed. He wants modern."

"No, he doesn't."

"This week, he does," I said.

"He only thinks he does," Renee replied. "Guys like Koenig don't know what they want. You need to tell them. Find a property and convince him he can't live without it."

Convincing Keith Koenig. That made me laugh. "Have you met the guy? He thinks they should pass a health ordinance against squirrels."

"So, throw some squirrel traps on the property before you show it. You need to be more aggressive."

"You mean be more like you," I said.

There was a reason Renee sold more houses than anyone in town. Inside her five-foot-two frame beat the heart of a killer and she was forever trying to make me one as well. As payback, I was sure, for letting her son, Hilton, spend much of his childhood playing video games in my family room.

"You'd be making a lot more in commissions," she reminded me.

True, but I'd also have to put myself "out there" more. Renee lived by the hard sell. She had her face on billboards and ads all over the place. I avoided the company holiday photo every year; that's how under the radar I preferred to stay.

"I do just fine," I told her. "I don't want more commissions."

"Liar. Everyone wants more commissions. Unless you're some kind of anti-money crazy person."

"All right, maybe I wouldn't mind more commissions, but I'm not trapping squirrels to get them."

Speaking of money, however... Renee was an active Chamber member herself. She always came back with dirt from the meetings. "Hey," I said. "You wouldn't know anything about Paul Paretsky, would you?"

"The guy whose wife just died?"

"Yeah. Marylou used to have coffee with us every morning."

"Wow, I didn't know. I'm sorry. If you need to take time off..."

I smiled into the phone. Heart of a killer, maybe, but there was some compassion in her sleekly styled shell.

"Thank you, but I'll be fine," I told her. "I'm curious though. Keith mentioned something about Paul having a lot of bad luck this year?"

"I'll say. The guy's business is hanging by a thread. That's why he and his wife moved here, you know. I'm friends with the Realtor who handled their sale in Braytonville. Said they had to downsize to keep the place afloat. If my ex had ever put us in that position, I'd have had his head on a platter. His wife was way too accommodating if you ask me."

After all I've done for him. Marylou's rant played in my head. Maybe not so accommodating after all.

"Keith said things looked to be improving," I told her.

"Really? First I've heard about it. I was under the impression the doors were about to close for good. But then, I don't spend a ton of time talking to people like him."

No, Renee would be too busy talking to the movers and shakers like Lindsay and Carlos. Paul Paretsky and his failing business wouldn't be worth her time.

She switched topics at that point. A new listing was coming on the market, and she wanted to spread the word. I promised to email the firm's current client list as soon as possible and made a note to give Keith a special phone call beforehand. I was capable of a little hard selling.

As I was plugging my phone into the car charger, I found my eyes drifting toward the empty passenger seat. Poor, nervous Marylou. Months of morning coffees and Night Walk meetings, and yet I'd had no idea she and her husband were in such bad financial straits. That she'd been forced to move to cut costs. That her husband paid her back by sleeping with another woman.

No matter what happened Sunday night, she deserved better than to end up at the bottom of a stairwell. I should have done better by her.

I let out a heavy breath. Maybe Renee had a point, and I should take an hour or so off. My head wasn't focused on selling houses today.

Leaning across the center console, I reached underneath the seat for the adjustment bar. Maybe if the seat was in position, I wouldn't keep picturing Marylou. Wishful thinking, but worth a shot. Instead, my fingers brushed a crumpled piece of paper. It was a torn piece of notebook paper covered with writing, and it didn't look familiar. Some client must have been taking notes.

Curious, I smoothed out the page to see what they wrote.

Whoa.

9

IT WAS a list of Night Walk Committee members. But not just any list. Next to each of our names, someone—Marylou most likely—had scrawled various words, such as *BobsBuynSell* next to Jenn's name. Erin's name had the word *Basement*, while Andrea earned two words, *Soccer Practice*. Lucky Lindsay got nothing more than a big thick dash that took part of her last name with it.

A chill ran through me. Clearly, it was some kind of shorthand. But for what?

Secrets. I realized as soon as I saw the words *Manchester RUR* written next to Rob's name. Only two people in town knew what that meant—Rob and me. Which meant...

Marylou had been collecting people's secrets.

Dear God. No. My hands started to shake as I, slowly, looked to the word printed next to my name.

Mercedes.

I was going to be sick. Stumbling from the car, I made my way to the edge of the driveway, doubled over and gasping for air. How did she know? It wasn't possible.

But there it was. In Marylou's precise handwriting. Twenty-five years destroyed by a black felt tip pen. No one was ever supposed to find out.

I tore the list in half. And in half again. Over and over until the page was nothing but shredded squares in my fist. What was I going to do now? Who did I call?

"Oh, Jack." My voice wavered as I said his name. What I wouldn't give for his steady presence, his calm voice. Problems were always more manageable when we managed them together. He would have...

Would have *what*? I took a deep breath. First thing he would have told me was to stay calm. Not to panic and react blindly.

"Start at the beginning," he would have said. "Let's think this through step by step."

I stared at the scraps in my hand. Why did Marylou have a list of secrets? What did she plan to do with them?

Only one answer made sense: blackmail.

People with things to lose would pay a lot of money to keep their dirty laundry buried. I know I would. Was Marylou compiling a record of our coffee klatch's secrets in anticipation of a windfall?

And Marylou's husband needed money. Marylou must have been planning to blackmail us to dig him out of his financial hole. Paul did tell Keith Koenig he expected the financial tides to turn. For the first time, I was relieved Marylou was dead. With her gone, the secrets could remain hidden.

If she had been working alone, that is. The question now was how much did Paul know? Could I sleep easy or did I need to leave town?

There was only one way to find out, and that was to talk to the man himself.

Hopefully, I wouldn't end up at the bottom of a staircase like Marylou.

———

"YOU'RE WHAT?" Rob practically screamed into the phone.

After much back and forth and pacing of my living room carpet,

I'd decided someone should know my plan—or at least part of it—in case Paul did turn out be a blackmailing murderous fiend. A regular murderous fiend I could handle. As long as I didn't imply that he killed Marylou, I doubted he would do anything. However, if he was in cahoots with Marylou and knew about the blackmail... Well, then we were talking motive to keep my mouth shut. So, I called Rob and told him I was stopping by to retrieve any files Marylou might have had regarding the Night Walk.

He reacted about as well I thought he would. "Didn't your detective friend tell you he thought the guy killed Marylou? Why would you go over there after dark by yourself?"

"Someone needs to pick up the files eventually," I replied. "Might as well be me, since I've already talked to the guy. Besides, if I recall, you thought Detective Bartlett was wishful thinking."

"If *I* recall, you weren't too impressed by my argument."

"Which is why I'm letting you know where I'll be. Just in case."

"In case of what? Needing to identify the body?"

"Ha, ha, ha." Briefly, I thought about telling him about Marylou's list. No sense freaking him out if there was no reason. Or risk having to explain what Marylou had on me.

I looked at the pile of burned paper in my sink. I wasn't sharing that with anyone.

Instead, I clung to my lame lie about Night Walk files. "We're talking about a fifteen-minute visit. Tops. I'm going to go in, give the man a meatloaf, see if Marylou left any paperwork we need, and leave. Hardly enough time for problems."

Then why call at all? I could hear him thinking on the other end. "Maybe, but I'd feel better if you weren't alone. I've got a thing, but I can cancel"

"Don't be silly." If Rob came, he'd wonder why I was asking questions. My hope was, by chatting, I'd be able to gauge whether Paul knew what Marylou had been up to. "You go do whatever it is you're going to do. I only called to let you know I was picking up the files.

"Besides," I added, "I doubt I'll be the only one visiting." When Jack died, I'd been inundated with visitors stopping by with casseroles and condolences. Since I doubted Detective Bartlett had told too many people about his suspicions, I imagined traffic at the Paretsky house would be the same, what with the neighbors and old friends from Braytonville stopping by. "I'll be in, out, and home before you know it."

"You better call me as soon as you're finished," he said. "If you don't, I'm calling your sexy detective friend to check on you."

"Don't you dare." Dan Bartlett was the last person I wanted to explain my actions to.

"You better report in, then."

"As soon as I'm in the car. I promise," I said. "I'll tell you everything."

Disconnecting the call, I turned on the faucet and watched the ashes flow down the drain.

10

I WAS wrong about there being people. The house was quiet when I arrived. If Paul had visitors, they walked. The only car on the street was a dark SUV parked a couple of houses down, its silver Woodbridge Youth Soccer sticker catching in my headlight.

Remnants of the police tape fluttered on stakes as I drove into the driveway. Someone, a neighbor perhaps, had attempted to reset Marylou's decorations that had been toppled by the police. One of the cabbages, however, was too far trampled for rescue.

Turning off my engine, I sat and stared at the garage door. Not twenty-four hours ago, I'd been kicking myself for not looking after her. Now my guilt had been replaced by nerves and anger. To think I'd actually felt a kind of connection during our last conversation. Every drunken word Marylou said took on a different meaning. Telling me I was a good friend when all the while she knew my deepest secret. Had she even liked me?

Do you ever wish you could change the past? Her drunken philosophical question echoed in my ears.

At the moment, I was far more interested in my future.

Taking a deep breath, I got out of the car.

Paul answered the door before I could even press the bell. Flung it open actually. When he saw it was me, his eyes widened with surprise. "Oh, Sadie, it's you."

"You were expecting someone else?"

"I heard the car door and thought... No, I wasn't expecting anyone." The way the words came out—strung together in one quick sentence—implied anything but. "It's nice of you to stop by. Would you like to come in?"

He stepped aside and I saw the stairway, its steps polished to the point of brilliance. The walls were gleaming white as well.

"I-I had a crew come by this morning," he said, confirming what the bleach-scented air already told me.

All I could think to say was, "They work fast."

"Thankfully. I couldn't stay here until they mopped up the..." He gestured at the floor. "I had to sleep at my assistant's house last night."

How convenient. In my anxiety, I'd forgotten about his supposed affair. "Kind of her," I said. You might even say, above and beyond.

"I'm not sure what I'd have done if she hadn't let me. This whole thing has been such a shock." His gaze drifted to the bottom stair. "Sorry," he said, clearing his throat. "Where are my manners? Why don't we go into the living room where we can sit down? There's no reason to stand in the doorway. Is that for me?"

"What?" I remembered the foil-wrapped container in my hand. "Yes. I brought you a meatloaf. To make sure you had something to eat."

"Thank you." He slipped the package from my hands. "I haven't been very hungry. Rita's been forcing me to eat."

"Rita. Is that your assistant?" Paul nodded. The man certainly was leaning on the woman, wasn't he?

"Not that I deserve her," he said. "She's propped me up more times than you can imagine and now..." His gaze drifted to the staircase again. "Please. Let's sit."

If I were going to describe Marylou's decorating style, I'd call it Farmhouse Chic meets Renaissance Faire. The furniture was straight out of an old Better Homes and Gardens article. I recognized the pink plaid sofa and oversize chair as being popular a few years ago. I'd also recently bookmarked a similar barnwood coffee table on a decorating site, thinking it'd look good in my family room. Seeing it up close, I mentally un-bookmarked it.

While the furniture was Farmhouse Chic, the artwork was strictly King Arthur. Dragons and gargoyles sat on every surface. There was a particularly ornate one sitting on the end table—a giant winged gargoyle gripping a glass ball.

Paul noticed where I was looking. "She searched months for that piece. Said it was the rarest one in the collection."

"Is that so?" I was embarrassed that I recognized the collection, or one like it, from ads that used to run in the Sunday circulars. "I didn't know she was so into mythical creatures."

"Oh, she wasn't. Not really. Just this particular collection. It was something she'd started in high school. She had nearly the entire set." Setting down the meatloaf, he reached past me and picked up the piece, cradling it in his hands as if it were a newborn baby. "I got so mad when she bought it. Told her we couldn't afford for her to spend money on useless junk." His eyes were wet with regret. "We had the biggest fight that night."

Hardly the reaction of a man who expected a blackmail windfall. Unless he was performing for me. Or I was wrong about the list, which I doubted.

Perching on the edge of the oversize chair, I tried to make my response sound as offhand as possible. "Marylou mentioned business was a little down."

In retrospect, leading with the money question might not have been the best strategy. Paul's eyes immediately narrowed. "Did she really?"

He began stroking the gargoyle's wings. "How unlike her. She didn't believe in sharing personal information."

"Only in passing. We were talking about the economy in general, and how things seem a bit sluggish. She only said business was off."

"Oh." The answer seemed to satisfy him. His shoulders relaxed.

"She's always been very observant when it came to trends. Was observant, that is."

"Yes, she was." More so than any of us realized, I almost added. "And I hope business isn't too bad."

Still petting the gargoyle, he shrugged. "Don't know why I'm acting like it's a secret. Plenty of people know. Business has been... well, it's been rough the past couple of years."

"I'm sorry."

"Me too. I'll probably close up shop now," he said, finally setting the dragon aside. "No sense sticking around. Marylou was the one who wanted me to keep trying to make it a go."

"She did?" Even though she suspected him of cheating?

"You know how Marylou was. Tenacious as a bulldog. Always fighting the good fight."

"She definitely believed in winning," I said. "And being a winner."

"She certainly did. 'We're not going to let them beat us,' she used to say." A sad smile played on his lips. "She even took on outside projects and gave me the money. Just to help me keep afloat."

I sat up a little straighter. "What kind of outside projects?"

"Freelance jobs, I guess. I'm not sure. Doesn't matter now anyway, does it?"

"Hey, Paul? I found a container of spaghetti sauce in the freezer. Why don't I thaw it out so you can— Oh, I'm sorry. I didn't hear the doorbell."

A woman appeared in the hall. She looked remarkably at home with a dishcloth in her hand and a fall leaves apron tied around her waist.

"Rita, this is Sadie McIntyre. She's a friend of Marylou's. Sadie, this is Rita DaVinci, my assistant."

"Nice to meet you," she said.

This was the other woman?

I'd been expecting someone different. Someone, I don't know, sexier. Younger. The woman standing before me was a bird of a woman, all angles and beak with streaks of dark brown running through her gray hair.

She looked old enough to be Paul's mother.

"Sadie brought meatloaf," Paul said.

"How nice. Vinnie and I've been trying to get Paul to eat all day."

Vinnie?

"I told you, Rita. I'm not hungry."

"Paul, you haven't eaten in almost twenty-four hours. I know it's hard, but you've got to keep your strength up. Marylou wouldn't want you making yourself sick."

His sigh sounded loud in my ear. "Fine. I'll have a few bites."

"Thank you. Would you like some too?" she asked me. "I told Vinnie I'd be home before eight, and I'd feel better knowing Paul had company."

"I'm afraid I can't. My son, Tim, said he might be stopping by." It was a tactic I'd learned many, many years ago. *When stuck, blame the kid.*

"I only dropped by to leave the meatloaf and tell Paul again how sorry I was about everything."

"Damn shame," Rita agreed. "Just when things might have started to turn around."

"Water under the bridge now," Paul said and there was genuine regret in his voice. "If only I'd..."

He shook the words away, frowning instead. I couldn't help thinking that with his face drawn into a grimace, he looked more like a woodchuck than ever. A sweaty, sad woodchuck. Not a blackmailer or a murderer.

"I'll go put a plate together," Rita said softly. "You'll feel better once you've eaten and gotten a good night's sleep." Reminded me of the voice I used with Tim when he was little and had a bad day. "Nice meeting you, Sadie."

"Your assistant certainly is dedicated to you," I noted once she was out of earshot.

"I'd be lost without her," Paul replied. "I'm always joking with her that she's my office wife, but it's true. The past year or so, she's been an absolute rock. If only Marylou wasn't...."

He shook his head. "Never mind. I don't want to bother you with my regrets."

"It's okay. I don't mind." I wanted him to bother me. What kind of regrets did he have regarding Marylou? "Regrets are only natural. When Jack died, I found myself wishing a lot of things had been different."

"Boy, do I wish that," he said, sighing. "I was going to say if only Marylou had liked Rita better. For some reason, she didn't."

The whole office wife idea seemed like a decent reason to me. "Maybe she was jealous of how close the two of you are. Women never like to think their husband is looking elsewhere."

His face fell flat. "Marylou never had to worry about Rita."

But she'd had to worry about someone. If not his faithful assistant, then who?

Didn't really matter. Not to me. My concern was the list Marylou left, and whether or not Paul knew about it. Based on our conversation thus far, I was happily leaning toward no.

A moist hand suddenly patted my knee. "Listen to me," Paul said. "Here you are, nice enough to come by, and I'm wallowing in self-pity. Marylou would be pleased to know you were thinking of her. Like I said the other day, she really liked you."

Yeah, I thought. She liked me so much she decided to dig into my life. Giving his hand a polite squeeze, I forced a smile in response.

"In fact," he continued, "meeting you all might have been the first positive thing she mentioned about Woodbridge. You and your friends at the coffee house. I don't know if she said anything to you, but she found the move from Braytonville...difficult."

"No," I said. "She never said a word." As a matter of fact, she'd barely said anything to us at first. It was only after a couple of weeks of her sitting nearby that Rob and I finally drew her into the conversation.

"She missed our old house. Marylou wasn't one for... Well, she'd never been big on change. But then she fell in with you all."

For the first time since I'd arrived, his eyes showed a little spark. "I remember how excited she was when she came by the office later. She had a completely different attitude."

"Did she now?" I fought to keep the edge from of my voice. When did excitement change into poking around everyone's lives? And why us? Unlucky coincidence? Or had she scoped us out on purpose?

A lot of questions that would probably never have answers.

"She told me she'd found her circle," Paul was saying. "I was so glad to see her excited. 'Everything's going to be right again,' she told me."

The light faded from his eyes. "At the time, I thought that meant she'd start letting go of some things."

"Things?" I asked.

"Long story. Marylou had a lot of anger. Life wasn't always fair to her, and she took the blows hard."

Didn't we all? Though most of us didn't keep coded lists about our friends.

I'd had enough. The heat from Paul's hand was beginning to seep through my pants, making my skin twitch. Forcing another smile, I pulled out my other reason for visiting. "I hate to ask this," I said, "but while I'm here, I was wondering if I could have Marylou's Night Walk files? I wouldn't ask except that with the walk taking place so soon..."

"Absolutely," Paul replied. "Marylou loved being on the committee. She would hate to think her not being there hurt the cause."

I let out a silent breath. "Thank you. I promise I won't take too long. If you log me on, I'll email the files to my computer at home." Along with, hopefully, deleting any information she had on me.

"No need for that. Marylou always did her committee work on paper. Said she spent enough time on the computer as it was."

"Everything?"

"Uh-huh. All the files are upstairs in her office."

"Great." My relief faded as fast as it arrived.

On the plus side, I was getting good at faking smiles. "I should have known Marylou would be organized."

"She always was." His touch vanished from my knee as he stood and looked to the front foyer. When he looked at me, his face was the picture of nervous expectancy. "I...um...I haven't been upstairs since I got home," he said, wiping his hands on his pants. "I don't suppose you'd"

"You want me to go upstairs with you?" The same stairs Marylou tumbled down.

"Would you? The idea of walking on those steps by myself... I need someone with me. At least the first time."

Just as long as it wasn't my last.

11

WE GOT AS FAR as the first step. Paul froze, his hand gripping the banister so tightly his knuckles bulged.

"I didn't realize what I was seeing at first," he said. "I wondered why she would curl up and go to sleep at the foot of the stairs. Then I saw the blood. On the walls. On her nightgown. Her head...."

A small noise sounded in his throat, like a strangled sob. The familiar-sounding anguish about broke my heart.

I had to admit, the man's grief seemed genuine. In general, I considered myself pretty good when it came to reading people—Marylou aside—and if you asked me, Paul Paretsky was clueless, possibly unfaithful, but blindsided by his wife's death.

On the other hand, I'd also say that Detective Bartlett didn't seem to be a man who threw suspicion around lightly. He wouldn't question Marylou's death unless he had a good reason.

Despite my concerns, I found myself reaching up to pat Paul's shoulder. "Try to block it from your mind," I said.

"You're right. I've got to do this sooner or later." Taking a deep breath, he started up the stairs and I followed, trying to take my own advice and not imagine Marylou tumbling toward us.

Another grouping of dragons and gargoyles greeted us at the top of the stairs, a trio of creatures set in a line atop the console table. Marylou definitely had the entire collection. As we turned to go into Marylou's office, Paul reached out and turned the figurine on the far left until the creature faced outward.

"Marylou always preferred them facing this way," he explained. "She liked the way their eyes watched you climb the stairs."

How soothing. Having your progress stalked by mythical creatures. Looking into their blood red eyes, I shivered. "Was there a reason this collection was so special to her?"

"Her friend Kim started her on them. From what she told me, Kim was into King Arthur when they were in high school, and the two of them started collecting stuff together. That's her, right there."

He was pointing to a photograph pinned to the bulletin board over Marylou's desk.

We'd walked into the spare bedroom that doubled as her home office. It wasn't fancy. A small veneer and particleboard desk with a wheeled desk chair and a couple of file cabinets.

The bulletin board was one of those craft-blog projects with cloth and ribbon. I leaned in to take a closer look at the woman who'd inspired the dragons. In the photo, a younger, thinner Marylou had her arm around a skinny brunette. Both of them had their hair cut in ear-length bobs and wore newer versions of the sweatshirt Marylou had on Sunday night. They looked so much alike that, if Paul hadn't told me otherwise, I would have assumed they were sisters.

What stood out most though, was Marylou's smile. I couldn't remember ever seeing her grin like that.

"They look like they were close," I said.

"Glued at the hip. Marylou said they used to be inseparable."

"Used to be?" *Not anymore?*

"She died their senior year," Paul replied. "Some kind of accident, I think. She didn't like to talk about it."

Explained the interest in finishing the dragon collection though. It was a way of memorializing her friend. Briefly, I thought of my own high school bestie, Donna Alford, and wondered if she'd kept photos of us from those years. We used to be glued at the hip as well. At least we were until Jack and I moved to Woodbridge.

"You know," I said, nodding to the photograph, "Marylou was wearing that same sweatshirt when I saw her Sunday night."

"She was? I didn't know she still owned anything from high school."

Odd. From its condition, I would have guessed she wore the damn thing constantly. Then again, given the level of Paul's cluelessness, he might never have noticed.

My eyes dropped from the photo to Marylou's desk. Neat as a pin except for a pair of scattered pens. Her laptop sat in the center, plugged in and open.

"Here's her file." Reaching around me, Paul picked up a thick manila folder. The words "Night Walk" were written in neat block printing across the front. Same lettering as the list.

"Thanks. Do you think everything is in here?" Probably; the thing had heft. "Or should we check the computer just in case?"

"I'm not sure I could log in. It's password protected."

"You don't know Marylou's password?" Jack and I always knew each other's as a matter of trust.

"Indian something or other, I think. To be honest, she told me, but I didn't pay close attention. No matter though. I'm sure everything you need is in the folder."

"Paul! Your meatloaf is ready." Rita's voice called up the stairway. "Come eat before everything gets cold."

Damn, but she was an incredibly maternal would-be mistress.

"I really would be lost," Paul murmured. There was no missing the fond smile playing on his lips. "You've got everything you need, right?"

"Hope so." My gaze lingered on the computer a second longer. What were the odds she left the machine on hibernate and had the resume setting bypass her password? If I could convince Paul to let me look around for more files...

"Are you coming, Sadie?" He waited in the door expectantly. "I'd feel better if we walked downstairs together."

Giving the laptop one parting glance, I followed him. This time, as we descended the stairs, it was impossible not to think of Marylou lying at the bottom. How had she come to lose her balance? There were banisters on both sides and yet she didn't grab either. Was that why Bartlett was suspicious?

When we reached the bottom, Paul opened the front door. "Thank you again for stopping by," he said. "Marylou would have appreciated it."

Before I could reply, he drew me into a one-sided hug, my arms still clutching the files against my chest. "It's nice to know Marylou had found a friend again," he murmured in my ear before he closed the door.

At least that's what I thought he said. A car chose that moment to peel down the street, making it hard to hear. No matter, my attention was still on the laptop upstairs. Paul seemed pretty clueless about Marylou's list at the moment, but what if he—or someone else— came across information on Marylou's computer?

What did I do then?

Lost in thought, I didn't notice the black SUV in the driveway until I was trapped in its headlights.

I shielded my eyes and blinked. Who else could be paying a condolence call? Half of Woodbridge drove black SUVs, myself included, so every vehicle in town looked vaguely familiar. Whenever there was a town function, the parking lot sounded like a symphony as people used their auto locks to determine which dark car was theirs.

At least this driver had the courtesy to park to the side, allowing me room to back out. I waved my thanks only to have him cut his headlights and open the driver's door. Immediately the dome light lit up the interior, revealing the driver.

Detective Bartlett stepped out of the car, one long leg at a time and sauntered toward me.

His eyes looked me up and down before settling on the file in my arms. I gripped it tighter, mainly to keep the internal ripple that followed his scrutiny in check.

"Don't tell me," he greeted. "You're here to pay your condolences. Again."

I smirked, but since his dome light turned off at the same time, it didn't have quite the same effect in the dark. "Actually, I was picking up Marylou's notes for the Night Walk Committee."

"Committee work is never done, huh?"

Was that an attempt at humor? Sounded almost flirty. "Life of a volunteer," I replied. "On the ready twenty-four seven."

Now I sounded flirty when I should be concerned about what had him visiting at this time of night. He was alone; you'd think he'd bring back up for an arrest.

"Little late for police work, isn't it?"

"What can I say? On the ready, twenty-four seven."

Oh my God, he *was* being flirty. Or sarcastic. Without being able to see his face, I couldn't tell for sure.

"Does this mean you still think Paul..." I deliberately stopped before saying the word *killed* out loud.

To no surprise, Bartlett didn't outright address the word either. "Needed to double check a couple of details in Mr. Paretsky's statement. To make sure the facts are accurate."

"How diligent of you."

"I believe in being thorough."

A second ripple passed through me, and it wasn't because the darkness made his second sentence sound naughty. "What kind of details?"

"Oh, you know how it is. People think they've told you everything, but they always leave out some small detail that falls through the cracks. You'd be amazed what people forget. Or decide they don't want to share."

Thinking of Marylou's list, I said, "I'm sure they have their reasons."

"People have reasons for everything, Ms. McIntyre. Unfortunately, in my business, reason can also mean motive."

I was hugging the file so tightly, I could feel the edge digging through my sweater and into my midsection. There was something about Detective Bartlett that left me off balance. Whether it was his voice, or how he smelled like soap and Old Spice, or the way his words always seemed to hold some hidden implication.

Although that might be more my nerves than reality.

"I should get going and let you do your job before it gets too late," I said, taking a step backward. My heel fell into a dip in the blacktop, causing me to step down hard. Because I was clutching the file, I didn't have a free arm to counter my equilibrium and I wobbled sideways. Detective Bartlett grabbed my elbow to steady me.

"Need to watch your step on these dark driveways."

"Yeah. Thanks. The...uh...garage light is broken." Not my most coherent response, but I was too distracted by how firm a grip the man had. Steady. Strong. His fingers stretched up to my bicep.

They didn't seem to be leaving anytime soon either.

"How do you know about the garage light?" While he was speaking, he guided me away from the dip and onto flatter ground. I could have moved myself—we weren't talking more than a foot—but I found myself not wanting to break contact, either. Having someone steady me was a nice change of pace.

"Marylou told me. I complained about the same thing to her on Sunday night."

"Interesting."

"It is?" He released my elbow. Without his grip, I caught myself swaying backward and had to lean into my car to steady myself. "Why?"

"No reason."

Of course there was a reason. Nothing was randomly interesting to a detective. But I also knew he wasn't going to tell me.

Made us equal since there were things I wasn't telling him, either.

Although, there was one other thing I could tell that he might find interesting for no reason. "Paul's assistant is here."

I was right. I could feel his body go alert a foot away. "Is that so?"

"Cooking him dinner. She's not what I expected," I added.

"Really? How so?"

There was the crinkle of leather as he folded his arms and joined me against the car door. I clutched my file tighter as the faint smell of Old Spice drifted toward me.

What was I supposed to say? That Rita seemed more interested in tucking Paul in with a bedtime story than going to bed with him? "She just isn't," I replied. "You'll see when you meet her."

"Trying to keep me in suspense, are we?"

"More like trying not to sway your objectivity."

"Appreciate the consideration. Although, you know..." He leaned in a little closer, bringing his scent with him. "You rushing over here to visit two days in a row makes me wonder if I shouldn't be giving you a second look."

Thank goodness I didn't have coffee this time or I would have spit it in his face. That is, I would have spit it if I could do something besides move my mouth like a goldfish. When I finally did manage a noise, it was a sputter.

Detective Bartlett chuckled. "Have a good night, Ms. McIntyre. Drive safe."

I swear I could feel him smirking as he walked away.

12

THEY HELD Marylou's wake on Friday. Rob, Jenn, and I drove to the funeral home together. Rob and me, because we always drove to things like that together. Jenn because her SUV was making "funny noises" and she didn't trust driving it in the dark.

Following their complete lack of sympathy the other day, I fully expected the members of the yoga posse to claim some weekend conflict, but to my surprise, as of that morning no one had. Ironically, it was the one time I wouldn't judge them for skipping out.

Unless that is, they didn't know what Marylou had been doing. Hell, I didn't know for certain. All I did know was that every time I pictured that torn page and the word *Mercedes*, I got sick to my stomach.

If only I'd been able to access her computer to see what, exactly, Marylou had uncovered. To think the information might be sitting there ready if—or when—Paul decided to turn on Marylou's computer...

Now, if the police arrested Paul, that might buy me some time; he'd be too worried about his defense to poke through Marylou's files. Unfortunately, I had no idea if he was still a suspect or not. I tried wheedling the information out of Tim, but all my son could do was shrug and tell me the case file was still open. After thirty-six hours of labor, you'd think the kid would throw his mother a little bit of a bone.

Instead, I was stuck in a holding pattern, waiting, with no choice but to carry on as if nothing was wrong. And that meant paying my respects at Marylou's wake. Thus, Friday night found Rob and me driving to Jennifer's house to pick her up.

"You didn't have to drive to my place," Rob said as I slid into the passenger seat of his SUV. "I could have picked you up on the way."

My headlights flashed as I pressed the button on my auto lock for a second time before dropping my keys in my bag. A neurotic habit, I know, but I liked double checking the locks for security's sake. "Except that you would have to pick up Jenn first," I said.

"So?"

"So, then she would have gotten the front seat."

He quirked an eyebrow in my direction. Wasn't quite as sexy as the way Detective Bartlett did it, but it was still pretty damn impressive. "Seriously? You're calling shot gun? Are you twelve?"

"You forget, I've ridden with you and Jenn before."

"We aren't that bad."

I shot him an eyebrow. Here's the thing about Jennifer and Rob. They were incorrigible flirts. Separately, they were bad enough. Together they made for a tsunami of coquetry. For my own sanity, I liked to put as much space between them as possible, and if that meant calling dibs on the front seat, then so be it.

"Why did she ask you for a ride anyway?" I asked. "She usually drives with Erin to these things."

"Dunno. I think Erin was tied up doing something or other at her mother's."

"Again?" Erin's mother lived in the Braytonville Assisted Living Facility. Lately she'd been usurping a lot more of Erin's time. "That's, what? The fifth time in three weeks? Do you know if everything's all right?"

"What makes you think I know any more than you?"

"Because she and Jenn like you more than me," I replied.

"Not true."

"Right, and Jenn just happened to decide her neighborhood football party should include her three yoga friends and the guy who lives two miles away. Wow, that sounded more sour-grapes than I meant it to."

"Yes, it did," he replied. "Keep it up, luv, and people will start thinking you want to be part of the posse."

"Oh, good Lord, no." I preferred our very surface friendship, thank you very much. Although an invitation still would have been nice. Everyone likes to be included.

Rob turned the corner, his headlights illuminating a corner mailbox as he did so. "Oh my God," I gasped when the address flashed. "We're on Daffodil Lane."

"Yeah. They're digging up the bottom half of Jenn's street, so I turned a couple blocks early," Rob replied. "I'll cut across Redwood Street."

"This is where I found Marylou. In fact, I think right there is where she got sick." I pointed to a gray colonial atop a sloping hill, spotlights angled at its front façade. "I never thought how close we were to Jenn's house at the time."

"Huh," Rob said. "Maybe she was mad about the party too."

"No. She was looking for Paul and his assistant."

"How do you know?"

"She told me," I replied. "Said she was going to teach them a lesson. I didn't tell you before, because I figured what goes on in a couple's bedroom should stay private."

"But now that rumors are out...."

"Doesn't feel like there's much a secret to protect," I replied with a shrug. "Especially since Paul's being pretty public himself."

We turned another corner and found ourselves two houses down from Jennifer's address. Jenn lived in an upscale, large colonial—a McMansion, as people liked to say—with a three car garage and built-in pool. Equally large, equally upscale houses sat on either side, although Jen's, with her stone faced façade and farmer's porch, was the winning property on the street. To no one's surprise, it was decorated beautifully. The swing hanging on the end of the porch looked lifted from a lemonade commercial.

Tonight, she had all the lights ablaze. Rob and I could see her walking back and forth in the front room, talking on her cell phone. When she heard Rob beep the horn, she waved at him through the glass. A few moments later, she came tottering out her front door in a painted-on pencil skirt and matching turtleneck sweater. A regular cover model for MILF magazine.

"Really," I said. "To attend a wake?" Glancing down at my ubiquitous black slacks, silk blouse and cardigan, I immediately felt like the dowdy spinster aunt. You know, the kind who owned seven cats.

Rob slapped my wrist. "Hush up you. Maybe she's looking to bag the widower. Steal him and get herself a rich second husband since Nick ain't payin'."

Good luck with that. Paul wasn't rich. "The widower is under suspicion for murder," I told him.

"Who knows how Jen's logic works."

"You caught me, Nick. I broke into your house and stole your First Edition whatever it was just to make you worry." With her cell phone tucked beneath her ear, Jenn yanked open the front passenger door. When she saw me sitting there, her face fell in disappointment.

I smiled. Not only was I childish enough to steal her seat, I was childish enough to be smug about it as well.

"What's that?" she said into the phone. "Give me a break, will you? Why would I want your stupid book? I don't know. Maybe one of your girlfriends used it to learn how to read."

She slammed the car door, reappearing at the rear. "Can you believe the jerk?" she said, sliding into place. "Fifteen minutes ranting about his antique book and not one word about the money he owes me. He's lucky I don't go over there and strangle him in his sleep. I've got a key. I could."

"Great sweater," I said, cutting off the rant. Threats of murder weren't the best of ideas, all things considered. "I don't think I've ever seen you wear it before. Is it cashmere?"

"Yeah. I saw it at the mall and couldn't resist the color, so I decided to splurge. I mean, if I'm not going to treat myself like a princess, who is, right?"

Pretty big treat for someone who was crying poor to her ex. Hope she hid it in the back of the closet when Nick came around to get the kids.

Rob looked over his shoulder and gave her one of his grins. "You'll always be a princess to me, luv."

"Awww, aren't you sweet?" she said, clutching her chest. "Does that mean I can call you my Prince Charming?"

"Anytime, luv. Anytime."

I rolled my eyes. The tsunami had hit.

It was close to eight o'clock when we pulled into the parking lot at McKinnon's Funeral Home. Usually when someone young dies—by young, I mean anyone under the age of sixty. A few years ago I would have said fifty, but as I creep closer to the mid-century mark myself, I've adjusted my thinking.

Anyway, usually when someone under the age of sixty dies, they have a lot of mourners. Co-workers, neighbors, friends of their children, etc. Seeing how they'd lived in the area awhile—not to mention the fact Paul owned a local business—I expected a fair-sized crowd. I was surprised when we found the lot only half full.

"Guessin' most people came straight after work," Rob remarked.

"Must have." Still, I would have expected a few more cars. I swiveled sideways in my seat so I could face Jenn, who was gazing distractedly out the passenger window. "Do you know if Marylou had a big family?"

"No clue," she said. "She never said anything to me."

"And people say we're private." Pulling into a front parking spot, Rob stopped the car to look at the two of us. "Do any of us know anything about Marylou? Besides the fact she drank decaf lattes?"

I bit my tongue.

"She had really boring taste in clothes," Jenn replied. "And she was really organized."

"She collected gargoyles," I said when he looked at me. *Among other things.*

"Wow. Three quarters of a year and that's all we know? Sweet little woman like her, you'd think we'd make a better effort."

"She wasn't all that..." Jenn stopped.

"What?" Rob's dark brows pulled together, the way they did when he frowned. "What wasn't Marylou?"

"I shouldn't," she said. "This is a wake."

"Oh come on. You can't leave us hangin' in the wind. What were you going to say?"

"She wasn't all that sweet," Jenn replied. "In fact, she could be kind of a witch when she wanted to be."

My senses went on alert. "How so?" Like with blackmail?

"Oh look. There's Andrea's car." She pointed to a black SUV in the next row, with a familiar orange school decal on the rear window. "She must be inside. Come on, we can cut the line and stand with her."

The parking lot was half empty; there wasn't going to be a line. I'd much rather have stayed and heard about Marylou's witchy tendencies.

Unfortunately, Jenn had already dashed out of the car. Avoiding both the question and her answer.

13

THERE IS an unwritten rule that funeral homes have to be stately Victorian homes. McKinnon's was no exception. A plaque next to the black lacquered door told visitors the building had been built by Colonel William Fitzhugh in 1868. He'd also been waked in the house, making him, in a roundabout way, the funeral home's first customer.

The smell of cut lilies enveloped us as we stepped inside. Someone had lit a pumpkin spice candle in the entrance to try to offset the pungent scent, but after years of funerals and services, the aroma had permeated the fleur de lis wallpaper.

"What is it about funeral homes that they have to be as warm and uncomfortable as possible?" I said to Rob as I shrugged out of my sweater. "I thought dead bodies were kept on ice."

He chuckled softly. "On ice. Listen to you sounding all gangster-like. Imagine it's because people wouldn't show if they had to stand around an ice box."

"Instead, we stand around in a sauna. *So* much better."

We followed Jenn, who had already gone into the main viewing room. The large room, selected, no doubt, in anticipation of foot traffic, mirrored the parking lot with only small clumps of people scattered here and there. Several rows of folding chairs had been placed in the middle of the room, but most of them remained empty.

Andrea stood with Erin in the corner furthest from the casket. Both looked like they would rather be anywhere else. I silently gave them points for being there at all. It was possible, I realized, that I'd misjudged the posse's ability to empathize.

"Have you gone up to pay your respects?" Jenn whispered to Erin when we joined them. The room's emptiness made speaking in a normal voice feel inappropriate.

"Not yet," Erin replied, giving a sniff. She looked like she might be coming down with the same cold Andrea had. Unless her red and bloodshot eyes were from crying, which I doubted. "We were waiting for you all to show up."

She turned her attention to the opposite end of the room where Marylou lay in a baby blue twin set, pearls resting around her neck.

"I wish people wouldn't insist on open coffins," she continued, giving a small shiver. "Dead bodies give me the creeps."

"I think she looks nice," Rob remarked. "For a dead person, I mean."

"Better than the last time I saw her, for sure." Well, maybe not *better*. Last time, she'd been alive.

"I think that's a new sweater set," Jenn said.

Erin wrinkled her nose, an act that made her eyes look puffier than they already were. "How would you know? She had a zillion of them."

"She was a creature of habit, wasn't she?" Rob remarked.

"Aren't we all?" Same things day in and day out. No wonder Marylou had been able to dig up dirt on everyone. Life in a sleepy little town turned us complacent. Any deviation from our routine would stand out like a sore thumb.

Going back to Marylou's appearance, I added, in a voice only Rob could hear, "At least she's wearing something better than her high school sweatshirt this time."

"True there," he whispered back. "I can't imagine fitting into the stuff I wore as a teenager. Or even wanting to, for that matter."

"Marylou didn't. Fit into it, I mean." The image of her swiping at her soiled front popped into my head. Then, realizing that must have been around the time she dropped her list of names, I shoved the image away.

A loud sniff sounded behind me. Although I would have said it wasn't possible, Andrea looked worse than ever. Her eyes were puffy and red, and there was a chapped patch beneath her nose from the tissue.

Like the rest of us, her attention was turned to the other end of the room. "S'not right,' she said, wiping her nose. It came out sounding like "snot rut."

"No, it's not," I agreed. Angry at Marylou as I was, death before a person's time was never right.

Paul stood to the right of his wife's casket, looking as lost as he had the other night. Every so often he would reach over and give the casket's rim a pat, not unlike how a person might absently pat a partner's leg while watching television, to reassure themselves they were still there.

Rita was there, too. Right by his side, her bird-like figure made sharper by her black wrap dress. She held a glass of water in one hand, while the other she used to rub his back.

"Who's the woman?" Rob asked.

"Rita DaVinci." Andrea answered him before I did. "She's Paul's assistant."

Rob's dark brows rose toward his hairline. "Isn't she the one Marylou said he was...?"

I nodded. "One and the same. I met her last night."

"Wow. Pretty ballsy, wouldn't you say? Bringing her to the wake? One would think he'd be a little more discreet, at least until Marylou was in the ground."

"Is it me, or does she seem more like a mother than a lover?" I asked as we watched her try to get Paul to take some water. They weren't acting like two people having an affair.

"Some blokes are into that. They are, you know," he added when I shot him a frown. "People have all sorts of needs. But I agree, it does seem a little odd."

Behind us, Andrea sniffed. Again. "Can we go through the line now?" she asked, her voice scratchy.

"But Lindsay isn't here," Jenn said. "Shouldn't we wait for her so we can go as a group?"

"Lindsay probably got smart and decided to stay home. Same thing we should have done."

"Keep your voice down, Erin," Jenn admonished. "Her husband's right over there."

The blonde waved a hand, dismissing Jenn's warning. "Puleeze. Bet he's wishing the same thing."

Jenn leaned in, and the two of them started talking in whispered tones. I was too far away to make out much of what they were saying beyond a couple of words, but sounded like Jenn said "Let it go,".

Let what go?

Whatever she said, it made Erin throw up her hands in defeat. "All right. Fine. Don't get your panties in a wad. Let's do what Andrea said and get in line. Sooner we get this thing over with, the sooner I can go home and eat."

"Sorry I'm late." Lindsay breezed up to our circle in a stunning black and white dress that immediately knocked Jenn off the MILF cover. "Today's been a total nightmare. First Liu Liu screwed up and switched my regular appointment to Mondays. Took me, like, fifteen minutes to explain to her that last Monday was an emergency only. Then Carlos asked me to run like a zillion errands. And then, as if that's not enough, Carter waits until five minutes before Sarah's dance class to tell me he has a history project due tomorrow."

"I know," she said, holding up a hand. "First world problems. But I have literally been in the car all day."

And yet, she managed to march in here looking like a cover model, with only a tiny flush to her cheeks to betray her "stress."

I should be so lucky.

There, in a nutshell, was the difference between the pretty, popular people and people like me. If I'd had that hectic a day, I would have looked like a crazed wild woman. All right, maybe not that bad, but I wouldn't come bursting in with the effortless elegance people like Lindsay possessed.

In some ways, I was like Marylou. Struggling to keep up in the sea of pretty people. Fighting the world just to keep two paces ahead, although I wasn't as angry. Or as malicious, I added, thinking of her list.

Lindsay's arrival erased the last of our excuses, and so we lined up to pay our respects. Lindsay took the lead—just because—while Erin and Andrea filed in behind. Jenn tucked herself next to Rob. That left me to bring up the rear. Because we were at a funeral, I felt compelled to behave nicely and therefore reached over and tucked the sales tag into Jenn's collar. Looking over her shoulder, she mouthed *thank you* with a hint of a blush rising in her cheeks.

Funeral etiquette dictated that the six of us queue up on the side of the room so we could walk by Marylou one by one and pay our respects. Along the route, someone—Bruce McKinnon, I guessed—had placed a set of easels, on which large poster boards had been set. Each board was a photo collage of Marylou's life. I remembered working with Tim on something similar for Jack's funeral. Making them helped us remember the good times we'd had as a family.

Whoever made Marylou's collage focused on childhood memories. There were a few more recent photographs, like her wedding photo and one of her standing with Paul in front of Fenway Park, but most were from when Marylou had been younger. There was Marylou posed awkwardly in a red gingham dance costume and another of her sitting uncomfortably on a horse, the expression on her face letting everyone know she'd rather be anywhere else. Her friend Kim was in many of the photographs. Wearing the same dance costume. Holding the horse's reins.

"Marylou sang?" Reaching over my shoulder, Rob pointed to a photo of a group of thirty young women posed sideways, hands on hips, and wearing matching bolero jackets. The sign propped at their feet read The Pennington Warblers, and bore the same logo that had been on Marylou's sweatshirt the other night.

"She must have," I replied, recognizing Marylou and her friend Kim standing together on the far left side.

"Not very well though, I'm afraid," a voice said.

An elderly woman joined us. "I'm Ruth Commeau, Marylou's aunt." I would have guessed her to be a relative without the introduction. She had the same stocky build as Marylou and wore a black twin set and pearls.

"You were friends of Marylou's?" she asked after we introduced ourselves. "I'm glad. My niece didn't always find it easy to get close to people."

It was the second time in two days someone had said that.

Ruth tapped the photograph with a stubby finger. "Oh, the concerts my sister would drag me to so we could hear her sing. Not that I ever did; Marylou mostly whispered her part. Now, Kim... Talk about a voice. Took everyone by surprise. No one expected her to have that kind of talent, she was such a quiet, mousy little thing." The older woman sighed. "Marylou knew, I guess. She was the one who pushed Kim into auditioning for the senior solo. Girl blew everyone away.She never stopped regretting twisting Kim's arm like that."

"I beg your pardon?"

Ruth offered Rob a sad smile before answering his question. "I think Marylou thought that if she hadn't convinced Kim to join the Warblers, she wouldn't have lost her best friend."

I didn't understand. "I thought Kim died in an accident." What did singing have to do with that?

My peripheral vision caught Rob's widening eyes. "Hello, what?"

"When I was picking up Marylou's files yesterday," I explained. "There was a picture of Marylou and her friend Kim in Marylou's office. Paul mentioned she died in an accident."

"Oh no, it wasn't an accident," Ruth corrected. "Kim died of an overdose. Such a tragedy, too. They found her in the woods behind the school. Marylou was beside herself."

Her brown eyes clouded over. "The two of them had been so desperate to be popular. Sad thing was, we always feared Marylou would be the one doing something foolish. We always thought Kim would be more sensible."

I looked at the photograph. Upon closer scrutiny, I noticed how the girl to the right of Kim had her back slightly turned, ostensibly separating Kim and Marylou from the rest of the group. They were outsiders within the club.

When I was in high school, popularity hinged on sports. Unfortunately, the team I joined, cross country, barely ranked on the jockdom scale, meaning I spent four years running in the woods with nothing to show for it beyond a pair of extremely muscular calves.

So, I could totally see Kim and Marylou thinking the choir could be their ticket to the in-crowd, especially if Kim had had as much talent as Ruth implied. I could also see them partying harder than necessary to prove their coolness.

Damn, I was feeling a little sympathetic for the woman again.

A thick silence settled among the three of us. I hadn't meant to dig up such a sour memory, although I had a feeling Marylou's life and her best friend's death were too tightly linked for it not to be mentioned.

"Is Marylou's mother here?" I didn't see anyone old enough in the receiving line, and it was only proper that we give her our condolences as well.

"Oh, no. I'm afraid I'm the only family left." Ruth replied. "Jackie died this past spring. Cancer."

"I'm so sorry. I didn't know. Marylou never said anything."

"I'm not surprised. She and her mother weren't very close at the end. For a while, really. Marylou wasn't the same girl Jackie raised. She'd grown..." The old woman frowned.

"Angry?" I supplied.

"At the whole world. It was as if she had a giant chip on her shoulder and was out to prove something to everyone."

They'll see. I'm a winner. A. Win. Ner. "Yes," I said softly, "she did."

Rob's fingers touched my elbow. "We better take our turn, Sadie. Didn't Lindsay say something this morning about the Night Walk

Committee talking to Paul in a group? About remembering Marylou at the Night Walk."

"That's our local charity event." I was about to explain to Ruth that Marylou had been a member of the planning committee when a motion near the door caught my attention.

The whole room's attention, actually. Dan Bartlett and his ever-present leather jacket were impossible to ignore.

14

THE DETECTIVE LOOKED INCREDIBLY IMPOSING STANDING in the doorway, his sandy head grazing the overhead molding. His eyes scanned the room, categorizing every person present. When he spotted me, his stare lingered a couple of beats extra.

I'm embarrassed to say I grew a little flushed.

Rob nudged me back to reality. "Is it me, or does he not look like he's here to pay his respects?"

But, that was exactly what the detective did, walking straight to Marylou's casket where he knelt and made the sign of the cross.

"Is he praying?"

"Looks like it." My opinion of him improved a little. You had to respect a man who respected the dead.

After a few moments, Bartlett crossed himself again and rose to his feet. Rob nudged me with his elbow.

"Don't look now," he said, "but Marylou's not the only one he's planning on acknowledging."

Sure enough, Detective Bartlett was walking our way. "We meet again," he greeted, wearing a weird half smile. "Our running into each other is becoming quite the habit."

I ignored the look Rob was shooting me, and pretended to be unfazed. "Good evening, Detective. This meeting is unexpected."

"I make it a point of paying my respects whenever I investigate a death. To let the family know I consider the victim more than a case file."

"That's decent of you," Rob said.

Yes, it was decent. Actually, it was quite sweet.

"Decent is a relative term," Bartlett replied. "I hear the funeral is private. Family only. I hope you're not too disappointed that you can't attend."

"We'll say our goodbyes tonight." I searched his face for a hint of a smirk or another insinuating expression, only to find nothing. Son of a gun looked sincere.

"Did you get the extra details you needed the other night?"

From the corner of my eye, I saw Rob turn and stare at me. I hadn't mentioned our encounter outside the Paretsky house. "What extra details?"

"Detective Bartlett came by to wrap up his report while I was getting the committee files the other night," I replied.

What I wanted to know was whether he still thought Paul had something to do with Marylou's death. If there was going to be an arrest.

"As a matter of fact, I did," Bartlett replied. "Mr. Paretsky told me everything I needed."

"I hope it was helpful."

"Very."

His smile was both polite and enigmatic. I should have known he wouldn't say anything concrete. My Jack used to do the same thing whenever he was working on an important case. It was infuriating then, too.

"Now, if you all will excuse me, I'd better get to the station." He gave a quick nod. "Nice seeing you again, Ms. McIntyre. As always."

"Don't say a word," I said to Rob as soon as Bartlett was out of earshot.

"Did I say anything?"

"No, but I can hear you thinking."

"Thinking what?" he asked. "About how the only two people he acknowledged in this room were a dead woman and you? I wasn't thinking that at all."

"He's Tim's boss. He was being polite," I replied. And, for some reason, he seemed to get a perverse amusement in chatting with me. Drawling my name like he was pouring a shot of whiskey.

Rob stared after the empty doorway, which looked suddenly barren without Bartlett's frame to fill it. "Pity," he said. "Your life could use a man like that."

"Use what? Another cop?"

"I meant handsome and straight. I can't play your arm candy forever, you know."

As if he ever played anyone's arm candy. We were all supporting players on his stage.

I grabbed his elbow. "Come on, Lindsay's waiting." On the other side the room, the blonde was giving us an impatient glare.

"Sorry to interrupt your flirting," she said when we stepped up to the group. The other three joined in by giving me the side eye.

"I wasn't..." It wasn't worth the bother. Instead, I turned to the grieving husband. "Paul, again, I'm so sorry for your loss." *Even if you did possibly kill the nosy, dirt-digging witch.*

"Thank you," he replied, his voice scratchy and raw. With the same lost, glassy-eyed expression he'd had a couple of days ago, he reached out and trapped my hands in his. "You've been such a good friend through all this." Beside him, Rita smiled and gave a concurring nod.

"It's the least I could do," I said.

Lindsay stepped forward, her shoulder wedging its way in front of mine. "We hadn't known Marylou long, but we want you to know she won't be forgotten. There's going to be a special luminaria in her memory at the Night Walk to honor the work she did on the committee."

"Thank you. That's sweet," Paul replied.

"Marylou made an impression on all of us."

"She certainly did," Erin added. "A very big impression."

Andrea reached out to touch his arm, thankfully drawing his attention away from holding my hands. "If there's anything you need," she said, sniffing. "Call."

"Thank you," he said, glancing at her before letting his eyes roam past the rest of us. "Thank you all. It helps knowing Marylou had such good friends who cared about her."

Jenn coughed. "Sorry. Think I'm getting Andrea's cold."

Our entire group departed shortly after that, thank goodness. Besides the fact that none of us wanted to spend longer than we had to milling around a funeral home, I didn't want to spend what time I did linger listening to comments from the posse. Bad enough Lindsay made that remark about flirting with Detective Bartlett, but Erin and Andrea had to weigh in on Paul's hand holding. "He didn't grab anyone else's hands like that," Andrea had sniffed.

"I wish people would stop suggesting there is something going on between Paul and me," I grumbled as I trailed behind Rob and Jenn.

"It does strain credulity. Especially when you think about the competition." Rob winked at me from over his shoulder.

"*Et tu*? Dan Bartlett isn't competition." I wished they'd stop implying there was something going on with him, too.

"No kidding. The man would win hands down," Jenn said. "Goodness knows, I wouldn't mind getting to know him better. Not that you're not still my number one," she added, leaning her head on Rob's shoulder.

"Of course, I am. I'm irreplaceable. But," he said, looking at me again, "you're right. He's impressive."

"Nice of him to stop by, don't you think? Considering he didn't know Marylou. Beyond studying her dead body, that is."

"He wanted people to know he cared about her," I said. "But then..."

We had reached Rob's car. I paused to grab the front door handle only to have Jenn beat me to the punch. "But what?" she asked, commandeering the bucket seat.

What the heck? Bartlett wouldn't have said anything to me if he wanted his suspicions kept secret. "Detective Bartlett isn't sure Mary-lou's death was an accident."

"Of course it was. She fell down a flight of stairs."

"Yes, but what caused her fall?" Rob replied. "Sadie's sexy detective friend is wondering if she might have been helped along."

"Like someone giving her a shove?" In the glow of the dome light, I caught Jenn's wide-eyed surprise. Wow, but she was a beautiful woman. I don't know why that was my first thought, but it was. I bet Dan Bartlett would like to know her better.

"So he was at the wake checking out suspects? Who does he think did it?"

She answered her question in less time than it took for me to buckle my seatbelt. "Ohhhh. Wow. And I thought things were bad between Nick and me."

"Have to say, I have trouble imagining the man we saw tonight offing his wife," Rob said. "Guy looked genuinely broke up."

"He certainly did." It was the one consistent piece that made Bartlett's suspicions feel off. "But you know what they say, it's always the person you least expect."

"You'd be surprised what desperation makes people do," Jenn added. "And he had to be desperate, right? To resort to murder?"

"Or he didn't mean to kill her," Rob said. "Could be they were fighting and she pitched a header down the stairs."

"She was spoiling for a fight Sunday night."

"She usually was," Jenn said.

"Wanna clarify that, luv?" Rob got the question out before I could.

Jenn's silhouette shrugged in the darkness. "Like I said before, Marylou wasn't as nice as she seemed. She could be nasty. And demanding."

"Demanding how?" I asked, leaning forward so I could look over the seat. "Did Marylou want something from you?" "She..." From the waver in her voice, Jenn knew she'd backed herself into a corner, and was now rapidly trying to think of a safe answer. "She wanted money. A loan to help with Paul's company."

"From you?" Rob asked. "Why on earth would she ask you for money?"

"I know. Crazy right?"

Not really. I kept my mouth shut and let Rob ask the questions.

"Did you give her any?" he asked.

"A little. Enough to cover her for a month."

"That's nice of you," I said. "Considering how poor you are."

"I didn't feel like I had a choice. She made the situation sound pretty dire."

No kidding. As in speak up or your secret's public knowledge.

Good thing Paul was Dan Bartlett's number one suspect, I thought settling into the darkness. Because whether she realized it or not, Jenn had just hinted at her own motive for murder.

15

ROB DROPPED me off with a reminder that I owed him a latte for driving. "A large," he called through his driver side window. "Don't cheap out."

"I wouldn't dream of it," I called back. Soon as I told Jose who it was for, the drink would be free anyway.

The neighborhood was quiet. Kids running around until all hours stopped on Labor Day. Now they were inside doing homework or watching videos on their laptops or both. There was a black SUV parked in front of the Roybinski residence. Honestly, people needed to be more original with their car choices in this town. If I were inclined to turn heads, I'd buy a red sedan next time around to shake up the status quo.

The new neighbors, I noticed, had finally put out their fall decorations. There were strands of orange lights on the front railings and miniature ghosts hanging from her trees. A giant inflatable jack-o-lantern held court in the middle of the front yard.

Personally, I preferred a less-is-more approach. Ornamental corn on the door and a trio of pumpkins leading up the steps. If they survived mischief night, they would become a family of jack-olanterns. A signal to the neighborhood that the house with the full-sized candy bars was open for business.

It was a tradition Jack started when Tim was a baby.

"I want people to come to our house," he'd said. "I'm part of the community. I want people to know they're welcome, and that I'm proud for them to meet my family."

That was Jack. Where I kept people at bay, he embraced them, no matter how prickly or laden with baggage they might have been. With a heart that big, it was impossible not to embrace him back. I couldn't have asked for a better husband, or a better father for Tim.

Two decades plus after he had carved his first pumpkin, it appeared I was carrying the mantle. Completely unintentionally, I assure you. I told Jack when I moved to Woodbridge not to expect me to put down roots in a place where they hosted mommy and me jam making classes. Little by little, though, a soccer game here, a parent-teacher night there, my resolve fell away. Before I knew it, I'd embraced Woodbridge as much as Jack had. For better or worse, this town had become part of my life. I thought I knew it. Knew the people who lived in it.

Now we had a murder and potential blackmail to go along with the stellar school system.

Made me realize that as much as I thought I knew my adopted hometown, I didn't know it at all.

———

I woke up the following morning to a good old-fashioned nor'easter. The kind with driving wind that forced rain sideways and kept everyone except the obligated and the desperate inside.

Normally, being a Saturday, my day would be booked with showings, but as luck would have it, both my morning appointments decided that they were neither obligated nor desperate, and canceled before I finished my first cup of coffee. That meant I could stay curled on my sofa until noon. A most heavenly prospect, considering the long week.

"Looks like we have the morning off, Buffles."

The Maine Coon responded with an unimpressed yawn. He had every morning off. Along with afternoons and evenings. The cat had been a present from Tim who apparently decided I would need someone to wait on while he was away at college. An arrangement Mr. Buffles embraced wholeheartedly, I might add.

At the moment, he was weathering the storm on the sofa, atop my chenille throw. Not wanting to disturb him—because he did look comfortable—I settled for tucking myself into the corner. My usual spot.

If you were to rank Woodbridge interiors from dumpy to super luxurious, mine fell somewhere in the middle. Suburban lived-in, I liked to call it. The sofa and chair were the same striped set I bought when Tim was in middle school. The coffee table bore nicks from years of teenagers propping their feet and playing video games. I'd decorated the walls with collages in antique frames. As I looked around the room, scenes of my life with Jack and Tim looked at me. Jack, Tim, and I at the beach. Jack and Tim camping. The last collection featured Tim's recent milestones: his National Guard commissioning, college graduation, graduation from the academy. My son, the picture of honor and integrity. Just like Jack.

Curse you, Marylou. If she needed money, why didn't she just say so? Why did she have to go digging into everybody's business?

I ought to get my explanation ready for when the other shoe dropped.

Instead, I reached for my laptop. I was nothing, if not excellent at procrastination. After my obligatory scan of the Midwest headlines, I pulled up the latest Woodbridge Weekly Gazette; the town didn't generate enough major news to warrant a daily newspaper. No surprise that Marylou's death made this week's front page.

The article didn't say much I didn't already know. Marylou had been found at the base of her stairs by her husband, and was pronounced dead at the scene by paramedics. There was also a quote from Dan Bartlett saying the incident was still under investigation. I almost smiled. He truly was a man of few words.

Marylou's obituary was almost as brief. Forty plus years summed up in two brief paragraphs. She was a graduate of Pennington High School and Rensselaer Polytech and her mother was dead. There was no mention of her father. Ruth appeared to be her sole living relative.

Interestingly, whoever submitted the information included the fact that Marylou had been a lifelong friend of the late Kim Rivard. I thought of Marylou's house filled with a collection continued in tribute. Decades later, and the two of them were still being connected. This time in print.

Must have been some friendship.

Curious, I typed *Kim Rivard, Pennington, NH* into the search engine. Only a handful of relevant results came up, most from subscription newspaper archives.

There was one site, though. A blog called Strange Deaths in North County, of all things. The site summarized all the odd and unsolved deaths that had occurred in and around Pennington since the 1800s. There had been four, Kim Rivard's being the last one listed.

According to the site, seventeen-year-old Kimberly had been found dead in Huntley Swamp, which had been a popular party location in the late eighties. Friends at the time said Kim had been partying at a nearby house party, gotten upset over a fight with her best friend, and stormed off to be by herself. Police speculated she went into the woods, got high, and lost consciousness, a theory backed by a coroner's report that found Ecstasy and alcohol in her system.

The website, however, noted that despite the police's ruling, there remained questions surrounding the death.

For instance, Kim's best friend, Marylou Commeau, reported leaving the party a half hour before Kim. Why, the site asked, would she wait thirty minutes before storming outside?

Moreover, despite being mid-November, and one of the coldest nights of the fall, the body had been found sitting against a tree and wearing only a T-shirt and a pair of jeans. Forensics discovered traces of blue cotton fibers as well as traces of vomit on the body, but nowhere else on the scene. According to the party's host, Brian

Jorgusen, Kim had complained of being sick at the party, but that only accounted for the vomit, not the fibers.

Finally, the site noted, Kim had recently been selected to sing a prized solo at an upcoming school function, an honor that reportedly upset many of her more popular classmates. Marylou told police that Kim never did drugs and insisted one of the popular kids did something to her because they wanted the solo for themselves, but the police didn't consider her charges seriously.

I scanned to the comment section. For an obscure website, there were a lot of comments. Proof that there were a lot of arm chair detectives in the world. All agreed that while the circumstances surrounding Kim's death were odd, murder for a school solo seemed a pretty farfetched theory.

More likely it was about a boy, one poster wrote. He had a point. If a crime wasn't about money, it was probably about sex.

Has anyone checked out the best friend? wrote another. *Maybe she was the jealous one.* There was a reply posted directly underneath. From MC.

Hey, loser. Don't comment on stuff you know nothing about. Kim was the best friend I ever had. Without her, I never would have survived high school. There was no way I could ever be jealous of her. If anything, she didn't realize how awesome she really was. Instead of posting stupid comments about me, maybe you should ask the losers at the Pennington police about why they never busted Jorguson and his skank cheerleading girlfriend for throwing the party. Because they didn't want the town star to lose his scholarship and ruin his future. That's why. Meanwhile, the kindest, nicest person in town gets left for dead in the woods.

Seemed Marylou read the comments too. Scrolling down, I saw that MC had posted replies to several comments. Her response to the theory Kim was killed by a copycat version of the Oregon Trail Killer was particularly sharp.

"There's always at least one person blaming a serial killer, isn't there?" I said to Buffles, whose spine had somehow become a Slinky and whose body was now stretched from the throw all the way to my corner of the sofa. His paw rested on my ankle.

I dug my fingers in his long fur and got a low rumble in return. "Wonder if Detective Bartlett has seen this website?" How would he have handled Kim Rivard's death? Bet he wouldn't be accused of brushing things off. I imagined him being very, *very* thorough.

And yes, my insides fluttered a little at the image.

The back door sounded. "Hey, Mom? You home?"

Slipping free of Buffles's paw, I walked to the kitchen where I found Tim shaking rain from his dark blue overcoat.

"Let me guess. Just got off shift, and you're hungry."

He grinned. "Starved. We have any sandwich meat left?"

"What's with this 'we' stuff? Shouldn't you be buying your own groceries?" The kid moved out a year ago after graduating the academy.

"Haven't had time this week. Bartlett's had me running all over creation. Besides, you know you always buy enough for two."

With good reason. I swear, he eats home more since moving out than he ever did when we shared an address.

"There's a half a pound of buffalo chicken in the drawer," I replied. "Leave me enough for lunch."

"Don't I always?"

"One slice of chicken doesn't constitute *some*. You're here earlier than usual. Working the night shift again?"

"Yeah, but I hear they're hiring someone new next month so I won't be low man anymore," he replied, his head in the fridge. "At least this shift went by fast."

"That's good."

"Even better? Bartlett actually said something nice to me."

"He did?" At the mention of Bartlett's name, I stood a little straighter. "What did he say?"

"Nice job. Do you mind if I have this?" He held up the key lime yogurt I'd planned to have with my lunch. I nodded. "What did you do to earn such an effusive compliment?"

"Dug through the trash. Literally. He had me Dumpster diving, looking for evidence. What's up with the two of you anyway?"

"What do you mean?"

"When we were heading to the station, he started asking questions about you."

"Questions?" The muscles between my shoulder blades started to tighten. Too many thoughts about Marylou and her list. "About me?"

"Unless I have another mother I don't know about."

He emerged from the refrigerator, arms laden with lunch fixings. "He asked a lot of them too. If I didn't know better, I'd say I was being interrogated. What'd you do, Mom? Kill someone?"

"Ha, ha, ha. Very funny."

With luck, he didn't notice the nerves lacing my sarcasm. Tim tended to be observant when I least wanted him to be, even before he entered law enforcement. My fingers wrapped a little more tightly around my mug. I hid behind a sip while Tim piled his food on the kitchen island and commenced making a sandwich.

"So what kinds of things did Detective Bartlett want to know?" I asked.

"What didn't he want to know? He asked how you felt about my being a cop, about your friendship with Uncle Rob. Whether I knew if you were dating anyone."

He stopped spreading mayo mid-stroke. "Please tell me you're not going to go on a date with my boss."

"I'm not going to date your boss."

"Sure sounded like he planned to ask you on one."

"Hardly. The two of us have had a total of four conversations." One during which he lectured me on being a helicopter mom and two where he implied I might be having an affair.

Tim frowned. "You've counted how many times you spoke?"

"No! I... They were memorable occasions." That didn't come out right. "I mean, they were about Marylou's death. Speaking of which, how is that case going?"

Tim waved the butter knife in my direction. "You're trying to change the subject,"

"Yes, I am. To one that's far more interesting to me." And pressing. "Does Detective Bartlett still think Paul pushed Marylou down the stairs?"

"You know I'm not supposed to tell you that stuff."

"Oh please." He was going to throw police regulation at me? "Your dad talked about his cases all the time. Right there, at that same table."

"He talked about his arrests, Mom. Big difference."

"He talked about his open investigations too." Not a lot—Woodbridge didn't have that many major crimes—but he talked enough. Sometimes you need a spouse's view to help sort out the information and let you sleep.

"Some of the stuff you were too young to hear, so he didn't share it with you," I added. Above all else, Jack wanted to protect Tim from the darker side of life; it was one of the reasons I loved him so much.

"But he did talk about them. Besides, I was the last person to see Marylou alive. If she was murdered..."

"All right." In the middle of opening the pickle jar, he ended his sigh with the pop of a lid. "It's going to be public information soon anyway. But, if anyone asks, you didn't hear it from me."

"My lips are sealed," I said.

"Well, your friend Marylou didn't fall down the stairs on her own. But we've suspected that from the start from the blood splatter at the scene. There was too much distance between the top step and where the blood first appeared. If she tripped, she would have hit her head farther up the stairwell."

"Unless she was halfway down when she fell," I said. "She was plastered. That would make her unsteady no matter what stair she was on."

"True. But the crime scene guys are pretty sure she was standing near the top. And, if so, then she would have had to have some momentum behind her for the blood to appear where it did. Laws of physics and all.

"Apparently Bartlett noticed something was funky right off, and that's why he kept us at the crime scene so long."

"He knew he had a murder on his hands," I said.

"Strongly suspected. And now that the coroner's report is in, we know he's right." There was a hint of admiration in his voice. "They found a bruise on the back of your friend's skull."

A bruise. "You mean someone hit her from behind?"

"Uh-huh." He paused to take another bite of sandwich. "By something heavy too."

Like a big old gargoyle statue maybe? Killed by the collection she assembled to memorialize her best friend's life. Little irony there.

"Does this mean you'll be arresting Paul soon?" With him in jail, I wouldn't have to worry about his stumbling across any information while I figured out what to do about it.

Tim shook his head before stuffing the last of his sandwich into his mouth. "Nope."

Nope? A chill ran across the back of my neck. I was getting a bad feeling.

"Why not?" I asked.

"Because Paul Paretsky didn't do it. His alibi checks out. The bartender remembers him being there until after ten."

The chill traveled down my spine to my stomach and turned into a big ball of dread. "What about his girlfriend? The assistant?"

"Says she's not his girlfriend. Even so, her alibi checks out too. She was at her daughter's house, watching the game. Which means we've got to come up with another reason why someone would want to kill your friend."

Like a list of people's secrets? I should have known. This was so not how I intended for him to find out. "Tim, I think I might—"

My words were cut off by his phone's message tone. "Shoot. I've got to go," he said, looking at the screen. "Hilty locked himself out of his car again. Third time this month."

"Yeah, but Tim—"

"Sorry, Mom. You know how Hilty gets when he's frustrated. Thanks for lunch." He grabbed his overcoat, then leaned in to kiss my cheek. "Remember, you didn't hear any of this Marylou stuff from me."

"Tim—"

"I'm kidding! I know you can keep a secret."

Couldn't I though? I watched him shrug into his coat. My law and order son. "Tell Hilty we're going to start tying his keys with a string around his wrist, like we did balloons when he was a kid," I said, as his fingers closed around the door handle.

"He always lost those too, remember?"

And just like that, he was out the door, leaving me with a dirty plate, one lone slice of buffalo chicken, and one very knotted stomach. Paul Paretsky having an alibi was not the news I'd expected to hear.

Bet Bartlett hadn't either.

Caffeine wasn't the best choice for a churning stomach, but I poured a fresh cup anyway, wincing when I remembered I'd used Cuppa's signature blend. The fragrant aroma teased my nostrils as I took a sip.

If Paul didn't kill Marylou, and Rita didn't kill Marylou, then it had to be someone on that list. Someone from our coffee klatch who had a secret they wanted to keep hidden. But who?

I needed to find out. And before the police found out about Marylou's potential blackmail schemes. Because, once they did, and added my name on the list to the fact I was the last person to see Marylou alive?

I would be their number one suspect.

16

1. CHECK FOR INFORMATION ON MARYLOU'S COMPUTER.
2. FIGURE OUT WHO KILLED MARYLOU.

BACK IN THE corner of my sofa, I stared at my short to-do list. Easy enough. Soon as I climbed Kilimanjaro and beat Renee in real estate commissions, I'd check those items off, no problem.

Where did I even start?

"You'd know, wouldn't you?" I looked at my end table, where Jack smiled at me from his brass frame, his Scottish cheeks pink and pudgy. First time I'd talked aloud to him in years. "Damn your love of fast food. I could use a shoulder about now."

For some reason, mentioning shoulders made me think of Detective Bartlett. Jack would appreciate his doggedness. No doubt the man was, right now, doing the same thing I was. Probably not exactly the same—he wouldn't be talking to a photo—but he would be wondering where to focus, now that Paul was no longer a suspect.

Who had the most to gain? That's what Jack would ask. Who has the most at stake, be it money, love, or something else?

I considered the names on Marylou's list.

Me, obviously, but I was innocent.

Rob?

No way. While he wanted his past to stay secret, he couldn't kill over it. I wouldn't even call it blackmail worthy.

That left the other four. If only Marylou's notes weren't so cryptic. Basement? Soccer Practice? And what about the slash next to Lindsay's name? Did she have nothing to hide or could Marylou simply not come up with a code word?

The only way to know anything for sure was to find Marylou's files.

Which brought me back to item number one on my to-do list: check out Marylou's computer. But how?

———

SUNDAY MORNING, Keith Koenig called and asked if I would attend an open house in Braytonville with him and Debbie. Since, I still didn't have a solid plan for talking my way onto Marylou's computer, I said yes. Maybe contemplating the finished basement would provide some inspiration.

If ever two towns were separated by birth, Woodbridge and Braytonville were it. Other than the fact that Braytonville preferred lacrosse over soccer and had a country club, the two towns were amazingly similar. The colonial Keith and Debbie wanted to view was in a particularly desirable leafy neighborhood, two miles from Braytonville Elementary. Five years old and meticulously maintained by its upwardly-mobile owners, the house would be the center of a bidding war by the end of the afternoon.

The Koenigs would not be participating.

"Excuse me, but we're not comfortable spending a half million dollars within minutes of seeing the property," Keith said as we stepped off the farmer's porch. Our umbrellas bounded off one another as we simultaneously covered our heads.

Beside him, his wife, Debbie, nodded in agreement. "We want a chance to think the decision through."

I took back my theory that she was as frustrated with his nitpickiness as I was. "Up to you," I said. "Keep in mind, though, we're in a seller's market and properties are going to move fast."

"But..." He started in about hidden flaws when a flash of blonde from across the street caught my eye. It was Jenn, pulling a plaid blanket over an object in the rear of her dark SUV. Per usual, she looked better in Sunday afternoon casual than I did in my work clothes. Her skinny jeans and navy trench coat were exquisite. Envy stabbed at me. She really could be a model for MILF magazine, couldn't she?

And a murderer. I needed to remember that. What was she hiding in her SUV?

"Will you excuse me one second?" I cut Keith off mid-sentence and headed across the street, waiting until I was just feet away before I spoke.

"Got rid of the noise, did you?"

"Wha—?" Sucking in a squeal, she whipped around, her eyes wide and nervous. At least until she recognized me. Then she let her lids drop as she sighed. "Oh, Sadie, it's you. You frightened me. I wasn't expecting anyone to talk to me."

"That makes us even then. I wasn't expecting to see you either. You got your car fixed, I see."

"Fixed?"

"Friday night. At the wake. You said it was making a funny noise. I take it you got it fixed. Hope it wasn't too expensive."

"Not really," she replied. "Fortunately."

"Good for you." There wasn't a funny noise. I could tell by the way she turned away when answering. She'd made up a car problem so Rob would drive her, and she didn't have to arrive at the wake alone.

"What are you doing in this neighborhood?" I asked. "Don't tell me you are thinking of dumping Woodbridge."

All the while I was talking, I craned my neck to try and see past her to scope out whatever it was she'd put in her car. All I could see was several lumps covered by the blanket.

Jennifer followed my line of sight. "Don't be silly. I'm not uprooting my kids unless I absolutely have to," she said, shutting the hatch. "And if I did have to, it definitely wouldn't be to move to this neighborhood. This is Nick's house."

"Really? I knew he moved to Braytonville, but I didn't realize he'd moved to such a family neighborhood." Definitely didn't look like he was hurting for money either. No wonder she was angry about the alimony. "Are you dropping Brandon and Emma off?"

"No. I... That is..." She looked up the driveway. "Brandon left his shin guards last time he stayed here and he needs them for his game."

What was she rearranging in the back of her vehicle then? Last time I checked, shin guards could be tossed in the front passenger seat.

"I don't miss those days," I said. "Tim always forgot his equipment. I'm surprised he doesn't forget his gun and badge now. Probably does and just doesn't tell me. But, doesn't travel league play on Saturdays?"

"Rain out. They pushed the game to today because of the storm."

"So they're playing in the rain today instead."

"Go figure, right?" I wasn't sure if her laugh sounded awkward, or if I was over analyzing.

What I wasn't over analyzing was her fidgetiness. She hadn't stopped moving since I approached. Hopping from one foot to another, folding and unfolding her arms.

Looking around.

"Everything all right?" I had to ask. Her nervousness was that obvious. "You seem a little..." I searched for a good, non-threatening word. "Stressed."

"Everything is fine," she replied with a shake of her head. "I need to go is all. Brandon's waiting for me at the field and if I'm late..."

"Right. Don't want a pre-teen freak out on the sidelines."

If there was a pre-teen on the sidelines. My gut didn't think there was. Today's weather was no better than yesterday's. What then, was Jenn up to?

"I better go too," I said. "The Koenigs want to drive past another house they aren't going to buy. See you tonight?"

She blinked. "Tonight?"

"The Committee meeting at Lindsay's house." The final meeting, in fact, before the Night Walk.

"Right. The committee meeting. Of course. You're going?"

"Absolutely." I'd just said as much. I planned to bring up Marylou's list and see what kind of reaction I received. Maybe get a hint as to who among them had the biggest secret. After this conversation, Jennifer was near the top of the list.

"Wouldn't miss it for the world," I said with a smile.

17

IT WAS after five when I finally said good-bye to the Koenigs and made my way to Marylou's neighborhood. Officially, Daylight Savings Time didn't start for another week or so, but that didn't stop Mother Nature from pushing her own agenda. Therefore, it was once again dark—or nearly dark—when I arrived at Marylou's house. Like before, the neighborhood was quiet. There were a couple of sedans parallel-parked in front of houses—friends there to watch the four o'clock game. Odd seeing them outnumber larger cars. There was only one SUV parked among them. Large and black like the one I saw the other night. Had to be a teenager driving their parents' vehicle; who else would park in the opposite direction of the others? The headlights nearly blinded me when I stepped into the street.

To my surprise, Rita answered Paul's door. Check that. I wasn't that surprised. She again had an apron wrapped around her boney frame.

"If you're here to see Paul, I'm afraid you're out of luck," she greeted. No hello. No what can I do for you. Just straight to the point. "He took a sleeping pill and conked out on the couch about a half an hour ago. Poor man needed the rest. I'm just pulling a plate together for him to heat when he wakes up."

"How sweet of you," I said.

"It's the least I can do. He's had such a horrible luck the past couple years. Between the business and now this. I worry about him."

She stepped away from the threshold. "Will you look at my manners? You're going to get soaked standing out there. Come inside."

"Thank you. Hopefully, I won't need to stay."

Shaking the rain from my umbrella, I slipped through the front door, and for the second time in a week, found myself staring at the spot where Marylou died. I glanced to the right, and saw Paul sprawled face down on the sofa, a gray coverlet draped over him. His snoring could be heard in the empty foyer.

My umbrella was dripping on the hardwood. Rita slipped it from my hand and laid it on a nearby boot mat. "Why don't you take off your coat? Do you want something warm to drink? You look cold."

"Thank you, no. I've been drinking coffee all day."

When I didn't move to take off my coat, she looked at me and then at the droplets forming on the floor, a single eyebrow raised with the same kind of imperious look I used to give Tim. Shame actually crept into my cheeks. Last time that happened, I was seventeen years old and my father had caught me making out on the living room sofa.

I slipped the raincoat off my shoulders. "Is your husband here with you?" I had to ask.

"Vinnie? Good heavens no. He won't leave his La-Z-Boy until football season ends. I came by myself."

"He doesn't mind?"

"Nah. He knows how much Paul needs me."

"Sounds like an understanding man. A lot of husbands might be jealous."

The door clicked shut behind me. "You sound like that detective. He said the same thing. Even asked if Paul and I were having an affair. Talk about a laugh riot."

Only Marylou hadn't found the idea quite that funny.

"I told him Paul and I had been together since the beginning of the agency. Anyone can see that he's like a son to me."

"Marylou didn't. She thought you two were a couple," I said. "Told me the night she died."

"The detective told us that too. Did you know I've been behaving the same way around Paul since he hired me seven years ago? It's the mother in me; I can't help myself. Seven years and suddenly I'm the other woman.

"But then, that was Marylou. Ignoring Paul until the last minute. Forget I said that," she rushed to add, pressing a fist to her lips. "It's not nice to speak ill of the dead."

"Even if it's true?" I asked.

Rita looked away, her cheeks pink. "Marylou was a funny one, that's for sure. Once she got an idea in her head, she wouldn't let go. She'd focus on it to the exclusion of everything else."

"You mean like an obsession?"

"Obsession is the perfect word," Rita said. "Take those statues for example. She would spend hours on the computer trying to track down this statue or the other. Paul said some nights she'd be up past midnight and never say a word. Just scroll through the computer."

My eyes took in the dragons and gargoyles lining the shelves in the other room. I swore some of them were staring through the doorway at me. "Paul said she was completing the collection in her friend's memory."

"That was another obsession," Rita said. "Her dead friend. She couldn't let it go." Apparently, we were over our reticence about speaking of the dead, because the woman was on a roll. "I mean, what happened to the poor girl was a tragedy, but at some point you need to let things go and move on. Pay attention to the living, you know?"

"By living, you mean Paul."

"Poor man worked so hard. Bad enough with the business. Would have been nice if he could come home to some comfort and car. Instead, he got..." She waved her hand as if to say "nothing." "It's no wonder he..."

"Looked elsewhere?" So Paul *was* having an affair. If not with Rita, then with whom?

"If he was, he didn't tell me, but I certainly wasn't surprised when that Detective Bartlett asked. Would you listen to me," she said, switching topics abruptly. "Talking away and I've barely let you get a word in. What was it you wanted to talk to Paul about?"

In other words, I wouldn't get an answer from her. Hopefully, I'd have better luck with my main task. "Well…"

Before I launched into the spiel I'd rehearsed, I tossed another glance toward the living room. Paul was still asleep, dammit. Something told me Rita would be a tougher nut to sell.

"I was hoping Paul would let me look on Marylou's computer."

Rita's eyes narrowed. "Why?"

Yep. Tougher nut. "Do you remember the last time I was here, when Paul gave me Marylou's files for the Night Walk?"

"I remember."

"Turns out there were a few items missing. I'm thinking Marylou might not have had a chance to print hard copies before she, you know." Inwardly I winced. In my head, those words had sounded far less harsh. "I thought, maybe, if I could get on her computer, I might be able to find the files. I'm sure they're labeled accordingly."

"I'm sure they are too," she replied. "Marylou was nothing if not meticulous about her notes."

"Exactly. I'm sure finding them wouldn't take long at all. I could probably be in and out in less than fifteen minutes." I hoped. God, but did I hope.

I tried to sound as casual as possible, as if the answer didn't matter one way or another. On the inside, it was taking all my effort not to bounce up and down on my heels.

Rita's thin lips flattened into a straight line. "I don't know if you've heard, but they're investigating Marylou's death as a murder."

This was where, if I were a decent actress, I could feign surprise so as to look a little less suspicious. Since acting wasn't my forte, however, I figured I was better off going with the truth.

"I know. My son told me yesterday morning. It's shocking. I can't imagine why anyone would want to hurt Marylou."

"You were the last one to see her."

"I know," I repeated. "I've been sick about it, too. I keep thinking that if I'd insisted a little stronger about going inside with her, she might not be dead." This time, I didn't have to feign anything. Mad as I was at Marylou, the idea that I could have prevented her death continued to plague me.

"Or been killed too," Rita replied.

That thought had occurred to me as well. "I just don't understand any of it..."

"None of us do. The police have been in and out all weekend looking for answers. First thing they did was take Marylou's computer."

"Oh?" My stomach hit the floor.

Of course, they would take the computer. They would search anything they thought would help find Marylou's killer. Her emails and files would be the first place they would look.

"Apparently Marylou locked everything with double passwords or something. Paul told me that Detective Bartlett told him they would have a computer expert work on the machine."

"Oh," I repeated. That bought me a little more time. "Those guys can usually crack anything."

"Paul said that Detective Bartlett told him the same thing. There's no guarantee that what they find will help find Marylou's killer, but—"

"It might reveal a suspect or two," I completed for her.

"I hope so. For Paul's sake." Letting out a long breath, she looked with maternal fondness at the man sleeping in the other room. "He deserves closure."

"Don't we all," I said.

We talked for a few more moments. I thanked her for her time, and told her to let Paul know I'd stopped by. To my credit, I kept my nerves at bay the entire conversation.

Wasn't until I got inside my car that I let out the groan that had been trapped in my throat. Great. The police had Marylou's files.

I was cooked. Cooked. Cooked. Cooked. I banged my forehead against the steering wheel in between words.

Okay, so what now?

I took some deep breaths. In the overall scheme of things, Detective Bartlett reading my secret wasn't the end of the world—provided he was the only one who did and Tim didn't see anything.

However, if Detective Bartlett decided I was a suspect, then any information Marylou dug up would be shared with the rest of the investigative team. And, in turn, the department grapevine. Everything Jack and I worked for would go up in a flame of gossip.

Therefore, it was back to item number two on my list. If I wanted to avoid becoming a suspect, I had to find Detective Bartlett a better one.

Looked like it was time to shake things up at the Night Walk Committee meeting.

18

LINDSAY AND HER HUSBAND, Carlos, lived on Cartwright Street. Better known in our office as Billionaire's Woods—the B used to differentiate it from neighborhoods with regular old million dollar homes. Believe it or not, there once was a time when Woodbridge had more land than people. Of course, that was before the housing boom, when the farmers and orchard owners realized they could leave their children a far more lucrative legacy if they sold off their land to real estate developers, making the town the leafy suburb it is today.

The Cartwright land represented the final frontier. Space but with wetlands, pine trees, and some kind of endangered newt. For a long time, that newt made the land undevelopable. But then, out of the blue, the newt stopped being an issue. The zoning laws changed, and Ben Cartwright—yes, like the TV character—decided to cash in. Billionaire Woods was born.

Pulling into Lindsay's circular driveway, I did my best to swallow the envy rising in my throat. Usually, fancy real estate didn't bother me. I'd long grown content with my modest little house and what it represented, but there was something about Lindsay's place that left a longing sensation in my chest.

It wasn't that her place was overly large or fancy. Jennifer's house took the crown in both those categories and her house didn't affect me in the least. No, it was that Lindsay's house was freaking idyllic. A custom built post and beam, it looked like it had been sitting in Cartwright Woods for two hundred years, just waiting for someone to discover the modern luxury hidden within.

And naturally, Lindsay had been the one to find it. Honest to God, there were days when I was certain her purpose on earth was to make me and the rest of the world look inferior.

"Absolutely not," Lindsay said when she answered the door. I was about to look over my shoulder when I realized she was talking into her Bluetooth earpiece. "I don't feel like dealing with those PC nut bags screaming we're disrespecting the Cherokees or whatever. Bad enough you screwed up the invitations. Use the new logo so we don't get any complaints."

She motioned with beige acrylic-tipped fingers for me to come inside. *I'll just be a minute*, she mouthed. "And order at least a dozen extra. In case people change their minds and decide to show at the last minute."

As she carried her conversation toward the kitchen, I hung up my damp coat on one of the hooks that lined the entryway wall and made my way to the great room where we held our meetings. Again, the place was perfect. With its giant stone fireplace and glass windows, the room could have been taken from the pages of a design magazine. Had been, in fact. Lindsay all but admitted as much once after too much Chardonnay. I couldn't help thinking how Marylou had done the same thing with her living room. Only while Marylou's room came across as looking staged, Lindsay's did not. Another one of those gifts that came from being a pretty person.

Taking advantage of being first, I helped myself to a pair of prof-iteroles—Lindsay never hosted a meeting that wasn't stocked with the best pastries—and snagged the coveted spot by the fireplace while my hostess finished her call.

"...do you think it's necessary? This is supposed to be a happy occasion. Why get all maudlin by bringing up dead people? Besides, it's not like people don't know..."

Without pausing a beat, Lindsay waltzed in and handed me a glass of wine. *One more minute,* she mouthed, before sashaying off again. I felt another pang of envy at how her skinny jeans didn't overemphasize her thighs like they did on mere mortals. I sucked a dap of whipped cream from my index finger and wondered if she'd secretly done that cool sculpting thing they advertised in magazines. It would certainly make me feel better about going back for seconds on the cream puffs.

"Sorry about that," Lindsay said a few seconds later. She threw herself onto the leather sofa, managing to plop back without spilling a drop of wine. "My high school class reunion is coming up."

"Oooh, fun." I'd never attended one myself, so I had no idea if they were fun or not, but it seemed like the right thing to say.

"I hope so. I'm still trying to decide if I want to bring Carlos with me. My high school boyfriend is going to be there, and well," she combed through her hair, making the blonde locks fall in soft curls around her face, "you know how awkward those kinds of situations can be."

I thought about what it would be like running into my old sweetheart. Awkward wouldn't begin to cover it.

"We were so hot and heavy in high school. All four years." She leaned forward as though telling me a secret. "There was this one little bump senior year, but that didn't last long. I thought he was the one. But then college and, you know. Life."

Yep. I definitely knew about life. "Maybe you'll luck out and discover your ex got fat and bald."

"He didn't. BJ and I are friends on Facebook and he looks as hot as ever. Besides, I was the one who broke up with him. I told Carlos he has nothing to worry about, but you know. Men."

"Right," I replied. Jack would have said that whenever a spouse said there was nothing to worry about, there usually was. Maybe that was Lindsay's secret, the one Marylou didn't have the chance to write down. Chatting up an old flame would certainly tick off Lindsay's rich husband.

"Anyway, the more I think about it, the more I think it'd be better if Carlos stayed home. I'm going to be running around all night, and won't have time to keep him company. I swear there isn't a single useful person on the reunion committee. I have to do *everything*."

Have to or wanted to? From the sounds of that phone call, I was guessing the latter. My experience with the blonde was that she had definite ideas regarding how things should go.

"Thank goodness you don't have to do everything on this committee," I replied with a smile.

"I know, right? You guys are, like, rock stars. I love working with you all. Well, almost all of you. By the way, I heard you picked up Marylou's files. Speaking of useless members," she added with a roll of the eyes.

More true feelings revealed. I pretended interest in a dab of leftover whipped cream. "What do you mean by that?"

"I'm not one to speak badly of people who can't defend themselves," she said, missing the fact that she'd done exactly that. Seemed to be a theme when it came to Marylou. "But Marylou didn't gel with the rest of the committee. She tried, but she isn't—wasn't —like us."

"Like us? You make us sound like we're a country club." Certainly the way she said the word gave it an elitist connotation. Either that or being in Billionaire's Woods was making me self-conscious.

She waved her glass. "You know what I mean. She wasn't savvy. She didn't grasp how we did things."

"Well, she had only lived in town nine or ten months. I'm sure she would have caught on by next year."

"I'm not so sure. Not if rumors are true."

"What kind of rumors?" I asked.

Again, I was treated to her leaning forward, as though we were two girlfriends sharing gossip. "I heard she drank a lot."

Oh, *that* rumor.

Finishing her drink, Lindsay stood, and headed toward the table where the wine sat chilling. "She was drunk the night she died, you know," she added, refilling her glass.

"I know. I drove her home." And, if you asked me, someone else might want to slow down on the drinking, if she didn't want the same rumors started about her.

"You did, didn't you? That's why the detective came to see you at Cuppa's. Man, he's hot."

I smiled. No sense in disagreeing with the obvious.

"From what I heard about Marylou, being drunk was par for the course. I don't imagine it took much of a shove for her to fall down the stairs.

"Jenn told me what you said the night of the wake," she said, sitting down again. "About Paul pushing her."

She shuddered. "I can't believe I had a murderer in my house. Remember how he skulked around here that night I hosted the committee mixer? He followed me into the kitchen, and then later he had Andrea practically cornered on the deck outside the kitchen. Remember?"

"Not really." I didn't know Lindsay had a deck outside her kitchen.

"He was so creepy. I knew something wasn't right. When you think about it, we're lucky he didn't snap then and there."

Bit melodramatic, but I let it pass.

The desserts called, and I stood. If Lindsay could overindulge on Chardonnay, I could have a third or sixth pastry. Besides, my being busy filling my plate would make my remarks sound that much more offhand.

"Actually, I heard that the police think Paul might not be the killer," I said, reaching for the lemon squares.

"What?" Her glass hit the coffee table with a sharp clack. "You're kidding! Who else could have done it?"

"Done what?" Rob and Jenn stepped into the room. Swear to God, they looked almost coordinated in their jeans and cashmere sweaters. Was that another new outfit on Jenn?

"The door was open," Rob said, "so we let ourselves in." Behind him, I caught a flash of bright blue nylon indicating they weren't the only ones.

A second later, Erin strolled in. "Hey," she greeted with a sniff.

"Sorry, I'm late. Got tied up at Mom's. Ooh, are those mini cheesecakes?"

"They are, and no worries, we're still waiting on Andrea," Lindsay replied, snatching back her wine. "We were talking about Paul Paretsky. Sadie heard the police might not arrest him."

"You don't say," Rob said, setting himself on the arm of my chair. Reaching over, he took one of the lemon squares and broke the pastry in half. "Not too big a surprise, really. When you think about it, the man hardly looks like a killer. Too nerdy."

"Don't they always say it's the quiet ones you need to look out for?" Erin asked from her place at the dessert display.

"They who?" Rob asked.

She shrugged. "Psychologists. Cops."

"Speaking of," Lindsay asked, "where did you hear the news about Paul? From your sexy detective friend?"

"Tim, more likely," Erin answered for me. She was building a perilously high pyramid of mini cheesecakes on her plate. "No offense, but he's not the most reliable source. He's a rookie. They're not going to tell him anything."

"That's not true. He's as active in this investigation as anybody."

Forgetting I wasn't supposed to reveal Tim as my source, I swiveled in my chair and glared at her. "Besides, he wouldn't say anything unless it was true."

"Unless the police knew he'd say something, and want Paul to think they're looking elsewhere."

Cheesecake pyramid teetering, she made her way to the sofa, and plopped herself next to Lindsay. Amazingly, the pyramid didn't topple. "I watch television. I know how these things work."

"That is not how the real police work," I said.

Erin's response was to pop an entire cheesecake in her mouth.

"And, they went through you," Rob said, nudging my shoulder, "because of how Paul and you are getting all hot and heavy."

"You suck, you know that?" I moved my plate out of his reach.

"Who's getting hot and heavy with who?" Andrea had arrived.

She stood in the doorway, looking damp and disheveled, like she'd spent the afternoon in the rain.

"Paul Paretsky," Jenn answered. "Don't tell me you went to all three games." So she'd been telling the truth after all.

"Last one ended in a shoot-out. Kids were miserable but Matt insisted they finish it out." Andrea's husband was soccer coach for all three kids. Now that I thought about it, I could see him insisting on playing, rain or no rain. Guy was a bit intense when it came to soccer.

"Let me get you some wine. That will warm you up." Lindsay stood only to have Andrea wave her off with a cough. "I took cold medicine. What is this about Paul and Sadie?"

"Ignore him, Andrea. Rob's joking."

"I'm not so sure I was. Awfully touchy feely at the wake, he was. And, you have been taking to visiting him late at night." Lucky for him, he managed to swing his legs out of range before my foot could connect with his shin.

"Could we get on with the meeting?" Jenn asked. "I'm paying a sitter."

"I couldn't agree more," Lindsay said. "Fascinating as this conversation is, we have a ton to do, and not a lot of time to get things done."

For the next hour or so, she herded us through her checklist of event tasks. Having done this event for a number of years, we pretty much all had our jobs down pat. I would be in charge of placing luminaria bags around the high school track to light up walkers' first and final laps. It was supposed to be Rob and me, but if tradition prevailed, Jenn, who oversaw the rest of the luminaria course, would radio in with some emergency that required his assistance. Erin and Andrea would take care of refreshments and registration respectively.

"...and then, after I sing the national anthem—"

"Why don't we skip the anthem this year? To save time?"

Erin should have stuck to eating cream puffs; Lindsay cut off her suggestion with a glare. "People expect the anthem. It's tradition."

"God knows we wouldn't want to break tradition," I muttered into my glass.

"Or pry the microphone out of her hands," Rob muttered. "Maybe this year she'll at least be in the neighborhood of the high notes."

"What's that, Rob?"

"Nothing, luv. Just agreeing you should do the anthem."

"Appreciate the support. As I was saying, after the anthem, I'll announce 'Light up the Night' and the event will be underway. Any questions?" Lindsay flipped the papers on her clipboard into place, the challenge underscoring her question clear. There were to be no questions. "Good. I'll send you all a copy of the time table by email. I think—"

"Didn't we promise Paul that we'd do some kind of special thing for Marylou?" Jenn piped up.

You know that look you get when you step into verbal dog poo? The hard-eyed frozen smile letting you know your comment was decidedly unwelcome?

That was the look Lindsay shot Jenn.

So did Erin.

And Andrea.

"She was on the committee," Jenn pressed on. "Aren't people going to expect us to do something? Especially since she was, you know, murdered?"

"Lady's got a point," Rob said. "It'll look awfully strange if we don't do something."

I watched with interest as Lindsay's smile grew tighter and she tapped her fingers one deliberate fingertip at a time. You could almost see her thinking how honoring Marylou might take the spotlight off her.

Or was her reluctance the result of something more?

"What if we created a special spot on the track, off to the side, as a memorial?" I suggested.

"I like it," agreed Rob. "Somber but not over the top. We can print a little sign and put it in the ground nearby to explain."

"What a good idea, Rob. Sadie." The still-frozen smile on Lindsay's face said she thought it anything but. "I'll let the two of you hash out the details."

"Sure," I replied. Since Rob and I—and Jenn—were the only ones who seemed interested in remembering Marylou at all. The others seemed content to forget she ever existed.

"Now, does anyone else have anything?" Lindsay asked again, looking around the room.

"Actually..." I started.

Lindsay's cheeks had to ache from being frozen in her smile. "Yes, Sadie?"

Time to mention Marylou's list and see what kind of reaction I might get.

19

"I FOUND the oddest thing when I was cleaning my car the other day,"
I said. "I think Marylou dropped it when I drove her home."

Andrea sneezed. "What kind of thing?"

"A list," I replied. "About all of us."

"Really? How so?" Jenn asked. She set down her glass and leaned
forward. In fact, they all leaned forward, even Rob.

"That's the thing," I replied. "I'm not sure. She used some
personal shorthand. Next to each of our names—or rather most of
our names—she wrote a random word or words. She wrote
Manchester next to your name," I told Rob.

His gray eyes widened, but the rest of his face remained placid.
"No kidding."

"No code there," Jenn replied. "Isn't Manchester your
home town?"

"Not much of a code then, is it?" he replied. "More like a biog-
raphy guide."

"Why would she list people's home towns? That's stupid. Does
anyone need more wine?" Lindsay rose and headed toward the table.
"I can open another bottle."

"They weren't all hometowns," I told her. "They were random

words. Soccer Practice. Basement. BobsBuynSell." I watched Jenn and Erin exchange a look.

"Sounds like a lot of gibberish to me," Andrea said. As though seeking confirmation, she looked across the room to the sofa to where Jenn and Erin sat. The two women nodded.

Despite my not asking, Lindsay appeared and topped off my wineglass. "You said she dropped this Sunday night?"

"Uh-huh."

"There's your answer then." Erin popped her final cheesecake into her mouth. "She was drunk and being stupid. Stupider. More stupid."

"I don't think so," I replied. I also thought she and Jenn were trying way too hard to try to brush the list aside.

Maybe if I shook the tree a little harder. "I think these words had very specific meanings for each of us."

"Specific?" Erin's eyes locked with mine. Not for the first time, I noticed a hardness behind her red rimmed eyes. "How so?"

"You tell me," I said. "What's 'basement' mean?"

"In my house? Means we've got to tackle our mold problem." Continuing to meet my gaze, she reached for her wineglass and took a long, slow sip. "What did it say next to your name, Sadie?"

Four more pairs of eyes turned in my direction. I too took a long swallow of wine. "Speeding tickets," I replied once I had swallowed.

I had considered saying "nothing" but no one would believe me. That would only turn the conference into my defending my answer. Hardly useful in getting information.

As it was, all of them were waiting for me to elaborate. "I had a bunch I forgot to pay," I said. "I owed a small fortune."

"And you didn't have your son fix them? Stupid you." Lindsay said from her spot near the sofa. She was still topping off wineglasses.

"Are you kidding? My son was the one who flagged me."

"Sounds like our Mr. Red, White, and Blue," Rob said. "Kid's a walking, talking, pillar of ethics. But why would Marylou be keeping track of that, or anything about us for that matter?"

"Because she was obviously a drunken weirdo, that's why," Erin said. "I don't know about the rest of you, but I'm sick of talking about her. She's all we've talked about for a week."

"She was murdered. Don't you think it's interesting that she was digging up dirt on people around town?"

The thud of a wine bottle coming down hard on the table made us start. Lindsay had returned to the serving table and stood with her hands wrapped around the neck of the bottle. "What are you suggesting, Sadie?"

"Nothing," I replied, "Just trying to figure out what Marylou was up to that might have made someone want to kill her. Aren't any of you curious?"

"Only thing I'm curious about is who makes it to the next round on *Singer Searchlight*," Erin said. Rising, she wiped the graham cracker remains from her sweater. "It starts in twenty minutes."

"I'll join you," Jenn replied. She tossed her ponytail. "Better than wasting my sitter fees talking about crazy Marylou."

The two blondes left together to retrieve their coats.

"How about you, Andrea?" I asked. The brunette remained alone in the high back chair tucked slightly off center from the rest of the conversation circle. She still had on the windbreaker she'd been wearing when she arrived. "Any idea what Marylou meant by all her weird comments?"

"Not in the slightest." Standing, she brushed her damp hair away from her face. "If you don't mind, I need to talk to Lindsay a moment before I leave."

"And then there were two," Rob murmured. Leaning against my chair, he looked down from his perch. "Did Marylou's paper really say 'Manchester' next to me?"

"It actually said Manchester RUR."

His handsome features fell. "You think that means..." He motioned with his eyes across the room.

"That the others know? Doubt it. They'd have said something by now." Pictures of Rob in guy-liner would be way too good to let pass without comment.

"Then why the blazes would Marylou write it?" Might as well

have T-shirts made with the question, it being the theme of the last ten minutes. I waited, let him put the pieces together himself. "You think she was looking to use the information somehow?"

"That is exactly what I think. I think Marylou was going to use what she found out to try to make some money. She never mentioned knowing about Manchester to you?"

"No. Although..." He chewed his lower lip. "She did suggest we grab a drink at Gilroy Tavern once the Night Walk was over."

"Same place I spotted her with Jenn and Erin a couple of weeks ago."

"Aren't many other places to go in town."

"But why did they go out with her in the first place?" I asked. "When I asked Jenn, she said it was for committee stuff, but—"

"Since when do those two do committee business without Lindsay overseeing the show?

"Precisely." Speaking of, I checked to make sure our hostess was still distracted. She was. "Add in the fact that Erin clearly has no love lost for Marylou, and it makes you wonder if maybe they were meeting about something else."

"Such as whatever it was Marylou had hanging over their heads." Slinging an arm across the back of the chair, he leaned in, bringing his head closer to mine. "Certainly would explain the animosity."

"It would also explain why she was wandering around Jenn's neighborhood that night." The mysterious "they" Marylou had been rambling on. At the time I assumed she meant Paul and Rita, but could it have meant Jenn and Erin? And if so, could one of them be responsible for Marylou's death?

I really needed to learn what Marylou had on them.

Meanwhile, Rob had shifted his attention to the upholstery seams on Lindsay's winged back chair. "Who would have guessed?" he mused, his elegant fingers tracing the curves. "All these months thinking Marylou bland and rather forgettable, when in reality she was quite the underhanded little spy. If only I'd realized she was this interesting when she was alive."

I cocked an eyebrow. "She was a potential blackmailer."

"Better than being a nervous chipmunk. In a way, it's almost intriguing. You've got to admit, the idea of mousy little Marylou nosying around our pasts? Little amusing."

To him, maybe. But someone out there didn't think so. They'd killed to keep her quiet.

20

WHEN I WAS A KID, we had this board game where you needed to put different shaped pegs in the correct hole before your time limit ran out. If you failed, the game "exploded" and shot the pieces at you. No matter how well I knew the pieces, hearing the tick, tick, tick of the timer made my heart race.

Marylou's murder felt like that game. A lot of jumbled pieces and an impending explosion. Revealing Marylou's list didn't do much. I still didn't know anyone's secrets. Although, seriously, what did I think was going to happen? That my bombshell would be so shocking, the killer would jump up and confess?

At most, I confirmed that three of the people on the committee—Lindsay, Jenn, and Erin—disliked Marylou. Erin really disliked her. And, I was pretty sure Jenn and Erin knew what Marylou had been up to.

Was that why Marylou had been wandering on their side of town the night she died? Were the two of them the "they" with whom Marylou vowed to get even? Blackmail provided one heck of a motive for a killer.

But was it enough of a threat to kill over? Were either of them capable of clubbing Marylou?

I didn't notice the car approaching from behind me until the headlights filled my rearview mirror. Blinded by the glare, I checked my side view mirror and saw a dark SUV bearing down on me. Someone was in a hurry to get home.

I hated tailgaters. They always insisted on riding your bumper on impassable roads. Didn't they get that people drove slowly on winding country roads late at night for a reason?

Growling under my breath, I sped up.

The SUV sped up too.

In a perfect world, there would be a shoulder where I could pull over and let the jerk pass. Unfortunately, this was Cartwright Road. Residents paid millions of dollars to live on a narrow winding road. Only things on the side of this road were trees and dark undergrowth.

The car behind me drove closer. He was pushing his luck now. I sped up some more.

So did he. The headlights were practically on top of my rear bumper at this point.

What now? I squeezed the steering wheel with both hands. We were both already going way too fast for a wet country road and there was no place to pull over.

Without street lights, it was impossible to see beyond my headlight beam. I flicked to high beams. White light lit up the trees. Not that it helped. Not when the car behind me seemed intent on riding up my behind.

Ahead, the trees turned into a wall of foliage. A turn in the road. Heart in my throat, I sped up one more time, and hoped there was space on the shoulder wide enough for two.

The speedometer inched rightward.

I inched the car right as well.

The SUV pulled to the left.

Thank goodness. I breathed out and was loosening my grip on the steering wheel when suddenly the SUV swerved right again.

Straight into my lane.

Straight for my car door.

There was nothing I could do but yank the steering as hard as I could. A squeal, a fishtail, and my car pitched off the side of the road, bumping along in the darkness until it jolted to a stop with a loud bang.

The sound of my breathing filled the car as I sat frozen, my hands still squeezing the wheel.

The SUV's taillights disappeared into the night. The driver never so much as slowed.

What. The. Hell?

When I finally finished shaking, I got angry. At the driver. At myself. For not getting a license plate or a good look at the driver. I could practically hear Jack giving me a lecture about awareness.

To which I would have told him that awareness takes a back seat when you are busy trying not to crash your car. Later, once my heart rate settled, details hopefully would return.

Taking a deep breath, I went to ease my car back on the road. There was only one problem.

The car didn't move.

The engine ran, and I could hear the tires spinning, the car stayed put.

"Stupid, son of a..."

Throwing every name I could think of at the other driver, I stepped out of the car.

Ankle deep into the mud.

Shoot me now. I had cold ooze seeping into my shoe, and rain coming down on my head. The wind whipped a shock of hair across my mouth, and I combed it away, noting the quickly mounting wetness weighing the rest of the strands. If I ever saw that SUV again, so help me God, I was going to slash their tires. What kind of maniac runs cars off the road and doesn't stop?

The kind who is sending a message, that's who.

I froze in the mud. Could it be my announcement shook things up more than I thought?

Now I was even madder I didn't get a look at the driver. I might have nailed Marylou's killer. Soon as I got home, I was going to write down everything I remembered. Everything.

But first, I had to figure out how to get home.

Sludging my way around the front of the car, I discovered the right wheel wasn't touching the ground. No wonder the car didn't move. The bang I heard must have been something catching the undercarriage.

Awesome. Using my flashlight app, I squatted in the bushes, and attempted to access the damage, but there was nothing overtly visible. About the only thing I was managing to accomplish was ruining my best black slacks by sitting in the wet ferns.

"Hello? Everyone all right?"

The deep, gravelly voice came out of nowhere. Soon as I heard it, I did what every normal person would do when facing a faceless, sexy-voiced stranger.

I screamed.

Then I dropped my phone, cutting off my only light source. Needless to say, my stomach dropped with it.

"I heard the bang. Is everyone all right?"

A beam of light bounced across the hood of the car and caught me in its glare. I raised my hand to keep the light from blinding me.

"Sadie?"

A hot shiver ran down my spine as recognition kicked in. Unbelievable. Why was it always him?

"What happened?" he asked.

"What does it look like? My car went off the road."

"How?"

Despite my being blinded by the flashlight, I could feel his stare scrutinizing me.

"Do you think you could lower the flashlight? It's hard to concentrate with the glare." Not to mention the fact my thighs were killing me from being pinned in a squatting position.

He obliged and at the same time, reached out a hand. I didn't need help getting to my feet, but I accepted the offer anyway, after snagging my phone from where it glowed in the wet plants. His hands were cold, but dry, like they'd been in his pockets. They were also remarkably soft. I don't know why, but I'd imagined his hands to be calloused. He looked like a man who liked to use his hands as well as his brain.

"Better?"

Much. I could see him now. Even in the rain, Dan Bartlett managed to look good. Like one of those movie-version first responders. Not many men could pull off a reflective neon-yellow rain hood, but he made it look natural. Some men had natural panache. Rob did. Dan Bartlett did too. In comparison, I felt like a dumpy, wet idiot with mud covered shoes and her bangs stuck to her forehead.

"Don't suppose you have an umbrella hidden in your pocket too?" I was going for humor, but the question came out more desperate than playful.

"Hold on a second."

The flashlight disappeared completely this time. I heard a pair of snaps, and then warm nylon settled over my head and shoulders. His rain jacket. I immediately flushed from head to toe, appreciative and certain I didn't look nearly as good as he did.

Lack of attractiveness didn't stop me from slipping my arms into the sleeves though. It was large, despite my wearing a trench coat underneath. "I'd offer a protest, but we both know I'd be pretending."

"Appreciate the honesty," he replied with what looked like a smile. Hard to tell in the shadows. "Now that your head's covered, do you want to tell me what happened? Before *I* get completely soaked."

"A car came up on my left, cut in too soon, and I had to swerve to miss him." I decided to leave out my Marylou-related thoughts, since they were, at the moment, only thoughts.

"Someone tried to pass you? On this curve?"

"No, the curve a half a mile back. I just kept driving in the ditch because I felt like it. Of course this curve."

I pulled his rain jacket tighter. His question might have annoyed me, but his coat was heavenly.

"I tried to reverse, but the car won't move. I'm hoping it's just stuck on something."

"That would definitely be the best scenario. Let's take a look."

Kneeling, he aimed his flashlight under the car. I knelt beside him. Might as well. My pants were already ruined.

"The right wheel is in the air, so I'm thinking there's a rock or branch wedged against the axle."

He adjusted the flashlight angle. "Close. Tree Stump. Looks like you might have punctured something. Your rear tire looks blown, too."

"Lovely."

"Could have been worse. You could have struck the whole tree. And the driver didn't slow down at all after he ran you off?"

"No." Would they have stopped if I'd struck a tree? A voice said no, leaving my insides suddenly cold.

Bartlett stood and wiped his hands on his pants. While we'd been talking, the rain had intensified. His T-shirt was molded to his body, like blue cotton Saran Wrap.

"You're going to need a tow," he said. "And probably a loaner car for the next day or two."

No sooner did he say car then it dawned on me that I didn't see his. The side of the road was as dark and deserted as ever.

When I asked, he pointed across the street where, through the trees, a light glowed softly. "I was taking out the trash when I heard your tire blow."

"You live on this street?" I shouldn't have sounded quite so surprised, but not even the police chief could afford to live in Billionaire Woods.

"Temporarily. The owner had to go out of town for a few months, so Renee Drake arranged for me to rent the place while he was gone. She was very accommodating."

I bet she was.

"You're welcome to wait out the tow there."

"In your house?"

"Beats sitting in a dark, cold car, doesn't it? Night like this, probably going to take at least thirty to forty minutes before the truck gets here."

If not longer. Sunday night, and Woodbridge only had one garage.

"Might as well dry your feet by the fire," he added.

My feet were wet. And I was cold. "Hot beverage too?"

"Keep us standing out here much longer, and it'll be hot showers."

Well, wasn't that just the image I needed to temporarily chase away thoughts of Marylou's murder.

I let him lead the way.

21

TWENTY MINUTES later found me stretched out on Dan Bartlett's floor, my bare feet propped on the hearth, my skin happily drying out in the scorching sensation of nearby flames.

"You can sit on the furniture, you know," he said, walking in carrying a pair of thick black socks and a hand towel. While in the other room, he'd ditched his wet T-shirt and jeans in favor of a Woodbridge PD sweatshirt and gray sweatpants. He wore them well, too.

"Didn't want to get the sofa wet," I replied. It was a more polite excuse than admitting I didn't feel comfortable sitting on it.

While he looked appealingly casual, Bartlett's living room did not. Apparently, when it came to design, his landlords were fans of modern minimalism. Unfortunately, they weren't good at it. Instead of clean and simple, they went with cold and stiff. White leather furniture. White accessories.

I patted the thick patterned rug beneath me. "This is more than comfy."

"Bought it last week. Better than the hardwood, for sure. I couldn't stand listening to my shoes clack on the floor another second."

"I should have guessed this was your addition. The style doesn't go with the rest of the house."

"The fact it's got actual color, I'm sure was a major clue."

He tossed the socks and towel in my lap. "Here. I thought you might want these."

"You have no idea. Thanks." Picking up the towel, I started squeezing the rain from the ends of my hair, damage done before he let me wear his rain coat. "I must look like a drowned rat."

"More damp than drowned. I think your shoes are ruined though."

My pumps sat drying on the hearth. Good thing I kicked them off in the kitchen. The insides and outsides were caked with thick, wet mud.

"Another pair bites the dust," I sighed. "One of these days I'm going to start buying backup pairs so I don't have keep shopping for new ones."

"Had a case once where the killer bought backups of every single piece of clothing he owned. We nailed him because he was missing one backup polo shirt."

"Note to self, make sure the closets are in order." Adrenaline depletion combined with toasty warm feet had me relaxed and a feeling a tad loopy. "You know," I added, leaning back on the carpet, "whenever Jack talked about a case and said 'we,' he usually meant himself." In his mind, good cops could afford to share credit.

Bartlett ducked his head, but I managed to catch the barest hint of a grin nevertheless. "Do you want something to drink? I don't have coffee, but there's tea."

"Nothing stronger?"

"No."

Short and clipped, his answer said a lot. His house was dry, and it wasn't because he forgot to make a run to the package store. I waited to see if he'd say more, knowing he wouldn't.

I could respect the need for privacy.

"Tea will be great."

"Black or green?"

Like there was a choice. "Black." If I had to drink tea, I wanted caffeine.

While he made his way to the black granite bar that divided the living and kitchen spaces, I sat up and folded the towel.

"I have to say," I heard him say from behind me, "you're pretty calm for a woman who was run off the road."

Only because I was too exhausted to work up a freak out. The panic from when the car first swerved was still there beneath the surface.

"Don't worry. I'll be ranting up a storm to the insurance company tomorrow."

A cupboard opened and closed. "I called the station and told them to be on the lookout for an erratic driver in a dark SUV. Too bad you didn't get a closer look."

No kidding. "Unfortunately, I was too busy freaking out. Only thing I noticed was that it was a dark colored SUV."

"No worries. Only seventy-five percent of the town drives dark SUVs."

It was hard to tell if he was being serious or making a joke. Tipping my head as far as I could, I found myself looking at the stainless steel tubing from the pendant lights that hung above the bar. "At least you can eliminate the minivan drivers," I told him.

"A fact that all fifty of them, I'm sure, will appreciate."

He *was* joking. The effort made me smile way more than the joke.

"Would it be too much to hope you recognized the make and model?"

"Sorry. All I saw was a big, blank rear window as it sped by me. So much for cop's wives being observant, huh?"

"Even cop's wives and mothers miss details now and then."

"Tell that to my son. I can hear his lecture already. *Mom, it's important to stay alert.*"

"Gotta love the arrogance of youth and inexperience," Bartlett replied. "Always certain they know best."

Footsteps sounded behind me. The soft thud of bare feet on hardwood. Bartlett appeared in my line of sight bearing two steaming mugs.

"Hope you didn't have your heart set on sugar or milk because I'm out of both," he said.

"No problem. When the grid goes down we won't have them anyway."

"Excuse me?"

"Sorry," I said, taking my cup. "Just something Tim drags out whenever I give him a hard time about drinking black coffee. He's big into disaster survival."

"I know. I've heard many a conversation at the station."

"I feel your pain."

He shrugged. "Nah. Never hurts to be prepared."

"Being prepared, and suggesting I buy tampons in case I need an emergency water filter are two completely different things."

I sipped my tea and watched as he settled himself, legs extended, on the floor beside me. He cradled his mug with both hands; the beige porcelain dwarfed by his palms. It dawned on me that he was one of those men who filled every space he entered, no matter how large. Not because of his size, but *because he entered.*

Only one other man that I knew of entered the room the same way. Although he cut a much more distressing swath.

Funny. I wasn't used to finding men attractive. Rob, for all his handsomeness, barely blipped my radar. Dan Bartlett, though... I don't know if it was the leather jacket, the blue eyes or just...him, but I found myself feeling decidedly female around him. Like a woman instead of a mom or a friend. I hadn't felt that way since Jack died.

The sound of his rough voice called my attention back to the present. "You two seem to have a good relationship," he was saying. "Tampons or no tampons." He smiled at that. "I know I called you a helicopter mom before, but it is nice you're close."

"Apology accepted. Again," I replied, smiling back. "I'm glad we're close too. With Jack gone, he's the most important thing in the world to me."

"Spoken like a true mom."

"Is there any other kind?"

"Suppose not." His voice grew softer and he looked into his mug. "Tim said your husband died of a heart attack."

I nodded. "When Tim was in high school. Poor guy wasn't even fifty." That was always one of my biggest regrets. God knows I had many, but Jack not getting the chance to see Tim become a man sat toward the top of the list.

"I'm sorry."

"Me too. He was a great guy."

"A good cop too, from what I hear." When I eyed him, he ducked his head. "I might have asked around about you a little."

Considering we'd been talking about my husband two sentences earlier, the fluttery sensation in my stomach should have felt inappropriate, but it had been so long since any man had shown interest, let alone a man like Dan Bartlett.

"So my sources tell me," I replied.

He let out a soft groan. "I take it back; you and Tim being close isn't a good thing."

"He's being protective of his mama. Although I'm sure there's some self-preservation involved as well. Got to make sure he's not going to be embarrassed by my personal life and all."

"Kids," Bartlett replied. "You'd think we exist solely to make their lives miserable."

"You mean we don't?"

When we finished chuckling, I rolled onto my side, so I could look him straight on. "Why were you asking about me?" I asked him.

"You really want me to answer?"

"Uh-huh."

The red creeping into his cheeks was enjoyable to watch. Wasn't often I could say I flustered someone who presumably couldn't be flustered. I had a feeling my next comment might redden him even more. "There are a lot of women in town who are younger and better looking."

Like Jennifer, for example. Who could be a killer. I didn't want to spoil the moment my thinking about Marylou and her secrets, so I shoved the thought—and Jenn's name—aside and focused on the fun of watching Bartlett blush.

His eyes were locked on his tea cup. He was still steeping his bag, the way he had in the coffee shop the other day. Since there was no string, he poked the bag with his finger, submerging and unsubmerging it, each dunk turning the water a new shade of green.

"I wouldn't say a lot of prettier women," he murmured. "I mean, Woodbridge has a pretty small pool to start. And there are even less with spunk."

"You think I have spunk?" That was something I hadn't heard before.

"Spunk isn't the right word, maybe, but you've definitely got a backbone. I like a woman who gives as good as she takes. Plus," he added, leaning in a little, "I've always had a thing for brunettes."

Now it was my turn to blush. Compliments were foreign enough. Having his long frame stretched out beside me made them downright awkward. "Is this where I tell you I've always had a thing for cops?"

"Have you?"

I felt pinned. What on earth made me open that can of worms? Naturally, he was going to ask a follow up. "Not always. They were an appreciation I acquired later in life. Like switching from beer to wine. How about you?" I asked, changing the subject just as he was about to sip his drink.

"Do I have a thing for cops?"

He deliberately misconstrued my question. "More like did you always want to be one?"

"Actually, no. I wanted to play pro ball. Even played a little A-ball."

I could see that. "Infield or outfield?" He looked more like an infielder. Not that I knew what an infielder looked like, but I imagined them to be sleek and strong.

"Wherever they put me," he replied. "After a summer, I realized the only place where they weren't going to put me was the next league up. So, I moved on to option two. Turns out I'm a lot better cop than I am a shortstop. Go figure."

"Go figure," I repeated. How on earth did he end up in Wood-bridge? That was the next obvious question. He seemed far more big city cop in bearing and mannerism.

Then again, lots of cops took jobs in smaller towns as they got older. For their families. Or their health. I wondered if Bartlett's move had anything to do with the fact there was no alcohol in his house.

I wanted to ask, but that was one of those topics a person had to want to share, and like I said, I could respect his desire for privacy.

There was a pair of photos on the mantel that didn't fit with the décor. I got up to get a closer look. Two young girls in school uniforms with dark blonde pigtails and serious blue eyes.

"Are those your daughters?" I asked, gesturing toward them.

"Lainey and Brenna." His face lit up with pride. "Those were taken a couple of years ago when they were in second and third grade."

"They're adorable."

"Thanks. They're older now. Lainey's practically in middle school."

"Let me guess. Acting far older than you're ready for."

"My ex... She has custody. I don't see them often."

Explaining the dated photos. But he wished he saw them. I could tell from his expression. My stomach ached on his behalf. Not being able to see your kids... More than once I'd stayed awake wondering what I would do if someone took Tim away. What possible reason could Bartlett's ex have for keeping his girls away from him?

"Last time I saw them, Lainey was asking if she could wear makeup."

"Everything starts so young nowadays," I replied. "Middle school was the worst. I was pretty sure Jack and I were going to kill Tim by his fifteenth birthday."

"Girls? I was a fifteen-year-old boy once," he added when I looked at him from over my shoulder.

"My sympathies to your mother. Although you turned out all right."

"Thank you. For the record, so did yours."

"He grew up a lot after his father died. Became the man of the house. I didn't even have to say a word." I studied Bartlett's daughters and wondered how much they were missing with their father out of their lives. It was obvious, even during our brief conversation, that Bartlett missed them.

Enough with the maudlin. Tonight had had too much of it already.

Bartlett seemed to think so too. He came up behind me, bringing his warm body to the side of mine that didn't feel the heat from the flames. "Don't go letting Tim know I said good things about him," he said. "We can't have the rookies thinking they know what they're doing."

"No worries there. Tim thinks you hate him."

"Good. Means my evil plan is working."

He flashed a smile before taking another sip of his tea. Peppermint. The aroma mingled with the smoke and dampness to create a strangely enticing scent. Made a woman want to drop her boundaries.

"Does he know what he's doing?" I asked. "Being a cop is something he's wanted for a long time."

"Like I said, he knows what he's doing. In fact, he found a key piece of evidence this morning in the Paretsky case."

"He did?" Just like that, the warm moment ended, and Marylou's death was once again front and center. "Does that mean you have a lead on who killed her?"

Bartlett didn't answer. No matter. He might have a poker face, but I'd been married to a cop, and they got a very distinct gleam when the puzzle pieces started coming together. The same gleam flashed in Bartlett's baby blues before he put his mask into place.

"You do, don't you?" I said.

"We're looking at a number of possible scenarios."

Scenarios meaning suspects.

I leaned forward. "Like who?"

22

"You know I can't talk about an open investigation."

Nor could I use the argument I gave Tim. I doubted Bartlett cared about how the McIntyre family discussed crime at dinner. "Worth a shot though, wasn't it?"

"You definitely get points for trying." He propped his elbow on the mantel. "For what it's worth, if it was my friend, I'd be curious too. All I can tell you is that we're looking at who, in Marylou's life—besides her husband—would benefit from her death."

"Like the woman Paul was really having an affair with?" I asked.

Bartlett frowned.

"Rita filled me in when I stopped by yesterday. To make sure I had all of Marylou's committee paperwork," I added, in case Rita mentioned I wanted the computer.

"That is one busy committee you're on," he noted. The peppermint aroma lacing his remarks kept them from sounding too suspicious.

"Charity events take a lot of work, if you want them to go right. Any idea who the real girlfriend is? Rita didn't know her name."

And he wasn't going to share it either. "Former girlfriend.

According to Paul, they broke things off a few days before Marylou died."

Paul had ended the affair? Marylou had been wrong there too. "Hell hath no fury..." I muttered.

Bartlett contemplated his cup. "So they say."

"You don't sound convinced."

"We're considering a number of theories."

I knew that comment. Jack used to say the same thing whenever he had a bothersome case. It meant that despite the facts, his gut had doubts.

Jack always had a great gut. I imagined Bartlett did too.

Letting out a long breath, he returned to the carpet and stretched out again. There, he switched from studying his tea to studying the flames.

"Are you sure you can't think of anyone who might have wanted to hurt your friend?" he asked.

Think of? I had an entire list. Once his computer people hacked Marylou's computer, so would he. Probably within a day.

Was it obstruction if you postponed providing information you knew they were going to obtain eventually?

Even if it wasn't, I couldn't lie. Not to his face.

Not completely.

Pretending to take a long sip, I listened to the wood crackle and thought of how to best begin.

"I'm learning that Marylou might not have been the person I thought she was," I said.

Bartlett sat up. "What do you mean? How so?"

"Well... I always thought of Marylou as meek and mousy— everyone did, actually. Then last Sunday, when I was driving her home, she rambled on and on about losers and being a winner, and how they were going to be sorry."

"She was drunk."

"And angry. At the time, I figured she was letting off steam regarding Paul and Rita. But now..."

I took a real sip this time, trying to wet my tongue. "Now, I find out that most of the people in our coffee klatch disliked her."

"They did?"

"Uh-huh. In fact, they've been pretty blunt about their feelings ever since she died. Tonight they all but said they couldn't stand her. I had to talk them into doing a memorial for her at the Night Walk."

"Interesting. Did they say why?"

I shook my head. "No, but..." Here it was. "I think Marylou was..."

A knock on the door interrupted us. "Ambrosia Auto Repair. Did someone call for a tow?" a gruff voice called from the other side.

"Looks like you've been sprung," Bartlett said, getting to his feet. "Wait here where it's dry, and I'll go show him the car. "

"Thanks." I smiled, grateful to avoid the rain for a few more minutes.

Confession time would have to wait.

———

AN HOUR LATER, the tow driver—a very nice man named Tony—dropped me off in front of my house. Detective Bartlett offered to drive me instead, but as appealing as the idea of being tucked in a car with him sounded, I politely declined. Partly because I'd already imposed on him enough, and largely because I was afraid he'd ask more questions about Marylou.

Thing was, I'd told him about Erin and the others disliking Marylou, information I knew he would quickly follow up on. Anything else would be speculation on my part. If those words meant something important, he would learn what soon enough. If my theory turned out to be incorrect, then no harm done. Everybody's secret would be safe. If I was correct, then he could investigate without knowing what Marylou had on me.

At least until he looked on Marylou's computer. Even then, maybe he'd be focused enough on someone else, that I could talk to him about burying the information.

And, if I were really lucky, Paul's girlfriend—ex-girlfriend—would confess, rendering the entire investigation moot.

Because that hope had worked well when it came to Paul being guilty.

The entire line of thinking was a horrible attempt at rationalization and I knew it. By the time Tony pulled into my driveway, I knew what I had to do.

First thing in the morning I'd call Bartlett, tell him the *entire* story, and hope he would be a friend. After all, he was a parent too.

At least the rain had let up to a light drizzle. I had that going for me as I stepped out of the truck. My shoes squished as I made my way along the brick walkway. Both they and my pants were ruined. I was too exhausted to care. All I wanted was a hot shower and to collapse in bed.

Funny, those were the same things I'd wanted last Sunday night as well.

Something was off when I reached my front porch. My brain couldn't quite figure out what, but I felt it on my neck. Tiny pin pricks of discomfort.

It hit me as I reached the top step. The porch light was off. I could have sworn I'd flipped the switch on my way out the door. Maybe I didn't. But...

My foot slipped. I grabbed hold of the column to keep myself from losing my balance. What the hell?

Pumpkin. I smelled raw pumpkin.

You had to be kidding me. Could this night get any longer? Nearly two decades in this house without incident and the neighborhood kids pick this night to pull a mischief night prank? So help me, if they made a gigantic mess, I was going to bang on every door on the street until I found them, and make them clean it up.

My trusty cell phone, still in my pocket, had barely enough battery for me to use my flashlight app one last time. I turned it on and surveyed the damage.

This was no ordinary Halloween prank.

The pumpkins were smashed all right. All three of them had been thrown against the front of my house, including one right next to my porch light. That too had been broken. Shards of shattered light bulb lay mixed with the pumpkin pulp. There was pumpkin smeared on the walls and on the doorframe.

But it was my storm door that captured my real attention. In the center of the window someone had left me a message written in soap:

BACK OFF.

23

IT HAD to be either Jenn or Erin.

After thinking about it most of the night, I decided they were the most likely suspects. Erin, because out of everyone, she'd been the most vocal about her distaste for Marylou, and Jennifer, because she had definitely been hiding something when I saw her in Braytonville. Something she didn't want me to see when I approached her car.

I called Detective Bartlett first thing so I could finish telling him about Marylou's list, and relay my suspicions. His voice mail picked up, so I left a quick message thanking him for help and asking him to give me a call back.

Then I headed to Cuppa's for my regular Monday morning coffee. I was eager to see how I would be greeted.

"You're late," Rob said when I walked in. "And, you owe me a latte."

He was sitting alone at our regular table. I wasn't the only one running behind.

"Could you explain to me again why we bother with this pretense of me buying you a drink?" I asked, as I set his drink on the table. "Jose never, ever charges you."

"Principle. I don't want you thinking you can use me as a chauffeur willy-nilly. Are you drinking peppermint tea?"

"I woke up with a craving." For the aroma as much as anything. Every time the mint liquid hit my lips, my stomach did a double back flip with a twist. The smell, however, left me feeling warm all over. It was very soothing. Which, considering the night I'd had, was a welcome sensation.

The bell over the front door rang, and Jennifer and Erin walked in. Instead of joining us, they took a table by the front window.

Rob and I exchanged a look. "Something I said?" I asked.

"Definitely unusual," he agreed. "Guess your news last night hit a nerve after all."

"Oh, it hit a nerve." I told him about what happened with the SUV and about the message on my window. His eyes nearly popped out of his head.

"Bloody hell! Did you tell your detective?"

"Some of it," I replied. "I wasn't one hundred percent sure about the SUV until I saw my porch. I left a message for him this morning."

"Good." He sat back in his chair and reached for his latte. "Suppose this means me secret is going to get out," he said, his features falling a little.

"Would it be so awful if it did?" I asked.

He shrugged. "Some things you like to pretend never happened, is all. I'd grown used to being the proper professor."

"You mean the sexy, mysterious British millionaire."

"That too," he said with a grin. "I do love having people wondering if I'm a member of the nobility or something."

I hated to tell him the sharp Manchester accent killed that theory years ago. "If it's any consolation, you'll still be sexy and British."

"True. Neither of those will be fading anytime soon, will they?" he said, giving a wink.

You had to respect the man's ego; it was definitely robust.

"At least I know you wouldn't kill to keep your secret. Now, if we only knew what the other words on the list meant?"

"Nothing earth shattering, I hope. I'd hate to think one of our immediate circle is a killer."

"Me too," I said. "But, even if the SUV last night was only a crazy driver, we can't ignore the fact someone left a clear warning on my front door the same night I mentioned Marylou's list."

Cradling my tea, I raised it to my nose and inhaled. Across the table, I could feel Rob watching but didn't care. The smell cleared my head.

"Would be nice if we knew exactly what those words meant. I'd like to know who we can trust and who we can't," he said.

He'd read my mind. After last night's soapy warning, I was more determined than ever to find Marylou's killer. Not only had they upended my life, they'd nearly killed me and vandalized my property.

Plus there was the whole keeping-myself-off-the suspect-list thing.

"Same here," I said.

"Question is, how? We can't go up to people and start playing *Guess my Secret*."

"Who says we're going to talk to them?" I'd already done that. "We need to jump in with both feet."

Rob leaned forward. "What are you talking about?"

"How do you feel about playing detective?"

———

NATURALLY, Rob took to the idea like a duck to water. He was always up for an adventure.

"Okay," I said, figuring we'd start with the most recognizable clue first. "Marylou wrote BobsBuynSell next to Jenn's name."

"Hardly a mystery there," he said. "She's always selling stuff online. What could Marylou possibly blackmail her about over that? Unless…" Grabbing my laptop, he went to the site and started typing.

I tried to see what he was up to. "Sometimes people use Bob's to sell stuff other than merchandise," he said.

"What kind of... Oh!" Stuff. "You think Jenn is selling herself on the Internet? I know she's desperate for money, but she's a mother."

"Mothers can't be sex workers?" He kept typing. "In fact, you'd be surprised what mothers—and fathers—do for cash. They can't all sell real estate."

"And you know this how?"

"I know this, is all. I searched the site for her cell phone number. Only listings that came up were for a designer handbag, an oversize driver, and an underwater camera. A nice one too. I didn't know she scuba dived."

Me neither. "Must be from when she was married. She mentioned that Nick liked to go to the islands."

"Well, if she's selling anything else, she's using a different cell phone."

Made sense. Less chance of a child accidentally answering the call.

If Jenn was selling herself. I glanced at the window table where Jenn and Erin were still having coffee. Jenn was her usual perfect-looking self. Today's yoga outfit was one I recognized. Blue top. Black spandex bottoms. Bright white sneakers. She'd probably be wearing the same thing when she picked the kids up at the bus stop.

I couldn't see her as a prostitute.

"What do you want to do now?" Rob was asking. "Call every massage ad listed until a familiar name answers?"

Before I could answer, Jose approached.

"Noticed you needed a refill." He looked at Rob through his dark lashes as he set down a fresh latte. "Didn't want you to have to get up and interrupt your work."

"You treat me so well. Keep it up, and I'll be having to take you home."

"Well, I don't like seeing my favorite customer go without."

Honest to God, it was worse than watching Rob and Jenn. The two of them thickening their accents and making bedroom eyes. "One of these days, you're going to meet someone who doesn't want to flirt back, and it's going to be glorious."

"Never going to happen, luv. I'm too darn adorable." Taking the lid off his drink, he lapped the extra foam. "Back to my question. What do we do now?"

"I can't do anything at the moment. I have to meet a client. We're going to have to divide and conquer."

My tea, which hadn't been monitored or refilled, was cold so I set it aside. "While I'm hopefully selling my fixer upper, why don't you put your charm to work and see what information you can get out of Jenn."

"Sounds easy enough."

"Just, for goodness' sake, don't book a 'massage.' With her or anyone else. That'll only put thoughts in my head I won't be able to erase." I began packing my things. "I'll call you as soon as my appointment is done and we can work on step two."

"Which is?"

"I'll call you," I replied. No sense mentioning my idea until I absolutely had to.

While Rob waited for Erin and Jenn to wrap up their conversation, I got up and headed to the register. Both Jenn and Erin looked in my direction, so I nodded hello before ordering a second peppermint tea.

"What's up with the new drink?" Jose asked as he rang up the order. "We had your usual order all made."

"Sorry. Woke up with a bit of a sore throat this morning." Out of the corner of my eye I saw Erin glance up from her cell phone so I added in a slightly louder voice, "I got caught in the rain last night. Some idiot ran me off the road."

"Bummer," he replied. "That'll be $3.25."

I handed him a five-dollar bill, adding, just for fun, "What's a person got to do to get free refills like Rob?"

"Look like him."

Ask a stupid question.

They were still watching me when I walked by their table. Erin looked more herself this morning. Less puffy-eyed than last night. I noticed she too had skipped her usual latte and muffin. But then, who wouldn't if they'd gorged on cheesecake the night before? A small black coffee sat next to her phone.

Jenn, on the other hand, had her usual muffin and soy latte.

"Did I hear you say you had an accident last night?" Jenn asked as I walked by.

"Some jerk in a dark SUV tried to run me off the road," I replied. "Gave me a flat tire and punctured my oil tray."

"And he didn't stop? Unbelievable," she said when I shook my head.

Was that her real opinion? I tried to read her expression, but couldn't tell if her reactions were authentic, or just well-practiced.

"Did you call the police?" Erin asked.

"Didn't have to. The accident happened in front of Dan Bartlett's house."

"You're lucky," she said. "You could have driven into a tree and been seriously hurt. And, wouldn't that have been a shame. Especially right on top of what happened to Marylou."

"Wouldn't it though?" I replied with a smile. Two could play the passive aggressive game. "Goes to show, we never know what's in store for the future. Enjoy your coffee, ladies."

I headed out the door.

24

"STRUCK OUT," Rob reported when I called him from the office a little while later. "I must be losing my touch."

Poor baby. Much as I wanted information, it would do him some good to learn he wasn't completely irresistible. "Did you find out anything?"

"Not much, although she did offer me a great deal on the dive camera," he said. "I waited around until Erin left to see her mom at the retirement house, then chatted Jenn up while she walked to her car. She told me you mentioned your accident."

"Did she mention anything else? Did you ask her about Marylou?"

"I tried. Shut me right down, she did. Wanted no part of the subject. Told me she had an appointment and jumped in her car."

"Did you follow her to see what kind of appointment?" I asked.

"Of course I did. What do you take me for?" On the other end of the line I heard the whirr of his coffee grinder. "She went to the nail salon. The one in the plaza next to the bank. Did you know Paul Paretsky's office is across the street?"

"It is?" Interesting. Although it could be only a coincidence. Most of Woodbridge's businesses were clustered within a few miles of each other. Plus, everyone in the posse went to that salon, it being the best, according to Lindsay. "Did she go anywhere near it?" I asked. "Or anywhere else?"

"Nope. Soon as she was finished, she went home." He paused. "If she's doing something we aren't supposed to know about, she isn't doing it today."

I expected as much. It could take days of following her around town before we caught her doing something suspicious. "Worth a shot," I said. "Maybe we'll have better luck with Plan B."

"That's the second time you've mentioned it," Rob said. "What exactly is Plan B?"

———

"I CANNOT BELIEVE we're doing this."

"Oh, shush," I said, shoving my mini flashlight in my pocket. "How else are we supposed to figure out what Erin has in her basement? We can't very well go up and ask her."

It was late afternoon. Not completely dark, but gray enough that lights would be coming on soon. The two of us were parked in Rob's car a couple houses away from Erin's colonial, waiting for her to start round two of the afterschool shuttle.

"What makes you think you'll be able to see into her basement in the first place? If she's truly doing something scandalous, do you honestly think she's going to leave the evidence lying on the middle of her floor?"

"Of course not. But maybe I'll spot something that will give me a clue." What else could I do? Short of breaking and entering, peering through the windows was my only option. "Anyway, it's not like your counter-suggestion was any better."

Rob had wanted me to pop over for a spot of tea, excuse myself to go to the bathroom, and then sneak into the basement. That wouldn't be suspicious at all, given I'd never visited Erin's house. Ever.

"At least you'd have been in the house instead of peering through the window," he muttered.

I refrained from noting his skepticism hadn't stopped him from dressing for the occasion in a black cashmere turtleneck and black jeans. My outfit was similar but less expensive. "You're welcome to stay in the car and wait," I told him.

"I would, but then I wouldn't be able to scoff when I'm proven right."

Having helped Renee host open houses in the area, I was pretty familiar with Erin's neighborhood. The houses were on the newer side—not as new as on Lindsay's street, but new enough—and set closely together. Every backyard had the same three accoutrements: a sprawling deck, a built in pool, and an underground fence for the family dog. In the summer, the street would be loud with the noise of kids running from one yard to another. Thankfully, though, now that school was in session, those same yards would be empty until dinnertime. Thus, Rob and I cut across Erin's front yard to the back of her house unnoticed.

"Whoa," he whispered when we came around the corner. Talk about Jekyll and Hyde.

He was right. While the front of Erin's house was pristine and landscaped, the backyard was a chaotic hodgepodge of toys, yard equipment, and bags of soil. "Looks like she planned on putting in some kind of container garden, then changed her mind," he said, examining the two by four he tripped over.

"Either that or she didn't have time," I said. Kids had a way of sucking the summer days right out from under you. You start out every May with great plans, and before you realize it, August has arrived.

I heard a low humming noise coming from the deck. "Is that an air conditioner making that noise?" I asked.

"This time of year? Doubt it."

I clicked on my flashlight and let the beam play across the deck. Dan Bartlett's flashlight had done something similar the other night. He'd be pretty angry if he knew what I was up to right now. I was surprised at how badly I wanted his approval. The idea of disappointing him made a heavy weight in my stomach.

Strange, you'd think I'd be more worried about disappointing Tim.

Unfortunately I didn't have a choice but to let both of them down.

While I was flashing the beam looking for the window, Rob had climbed onto the deck to look around. "Whatever that humming is, it's coming from beneath the deck," he said.

"Odd. They must have some kind of equipment there. I once showed a house where the guy had an entire print shop in his basement. For his underground magazine."

"Something tells me Erin isn't the underground magazine type," Rob replied, raising the top of a storage bench.

"Hardly seems an earthshattering secret if she is. Your be-bopping around Manchester is racier."

"Unless she's printing subversive, anti-government stuff. And it wasn't be-bopping; it was synchronized dancing."

"Tomato, to-mah-to." Anyway, Erin subverting the government made even less sense than an underground magazine. "Hard to picture radicals living in a four-bedroom colonial."

"Really? Where do you picture them?"

"I don't know. On television, they're always in burned-out apartments with mattresses on the floor."

"This is Woodbridge, luv, not Serbia."

"Even so, I figured they lived a little more austerely."

I found the window I was looking for behind an ungainly Rose of Sharon. Squatting, I fished my light at the glass and tried to look in. "Crap. There's some kind of paper taped to the windows."

"Told ya," Rob said. "Who leaves their mysterious secret exposed for anyone to see?"

I hated when he was right.

The humming was louder at ground level. Looked like he was also right that the sound was emanating from under the deck. Pivoting, I flashed my light through the holes in the lattice surround and saw a box.

"We can scratch printing press off our list," I told him. "It's an air conditioner."

"For the basement?"

"Uh-huh." A small portable unit tucked in the basement window. "The only rebelling Erin's doing is running her air conditioner way past season."

"Sadie."

"Maybe she's got an apartment there." Zoning laws prohibited tenants in this section of town. Again, hardly earth shattering, but something she wouldn't want public. "What kind of tenant tapes black paper over the window? That's creepy."

"Sadie." Rob's voice sounded sharper this time.

"What?"

I stood to find him standing by the sliding glass door. When he saw me, he gave a gentle push and the door slid effortlessly along its tracks. "She forgot to lock the slider," he said.

In every person's life there comes a time when they find themselves confronted with an ethical dilemma. A fork in the road of virtue, so to speak. It's up to you to decide which path you're going to take. I'd reached that fork the night before when I failed to mention Marylou's list to Dan Bartlett. Even with that, I could still claim a mental lapse for my behavior. There was no plausible excuse for crossing this threshold. At least not one I could share. A smart woman would tell Rob to close the door and go home.

There was only one problem. That air conditioner and black paper had made me curious.

"We're definitely going to hell," I said as I crossed the threshold.

"At least we'll be together," Rob replied. "Let's find the basement door."

We headed toward the kitchen. Thankfully, the builder hadn't been one for originality and built all the houses in the neighborhood with the same basic floor plan. As we crossed her living room and I noticed Erin's house had been recently updated with fresh paint and carpeting. The kitchen was new too. Marble countertops, new cabinets. She even had one of those indoor grills.

Rob whistled softly when he saw it. "Aerospace equipment sales must be going well," Rob replied. "Remind me to buy some stock in the company her husband works for."

Just as I expected, the basement doorway was right next to the pantry door. Same as in every other house on the street. "Let's do this quickly and get out," I said. The hair on my neck was on full alert, now that I'd taken up breaking and entering. I turned on the light and started downstairs, not realizing until I'd gone down the first two steps that if there was a downstairs tenant, he or she might be home.

"Hello?" I called out before peering over the railing. Rob turned on his flashlight app.

Holy crap.

It was an indoor garden. And not just any indoors garden. A twenty by thirteen indoor marijuana factory. Rows of spiky green plants in pots lined the floor. The paper we thought was black was really silver reflecting paper, hung to enhance the artificial light.

"Well, this certainly explains last night's cheesecake binge," Rob said.

As well as the red, puffy eyes. Jeez, the clues had been right in front of us, and we missed them. Talk about being blind to the obvious.

Except for Marylou, apparently.

"Awful lot of plants for a personal stash," Rob remarked. "Maybe she got one of those medical permits from the state?"

"Right. The state always hands out permission to grow drugs in your basement." He did have a point however. There was way too much Mary Jane down here for personal use. This was an indoor farm. "Marylou must have figured out what Erin was doing," I said, "and..." And what?

Used it to push her way onto the committee? Gain an in with those she decided were the popular girls? Or had she wanted more?

They think I'm a loser, but I'll show them...

One thing was for certain. Whatever Marylou's motives, Erin had cause for wanting to keep her secret quiet. Enough to push Marylou down the stairs?

My stomach churned. "You know what this means, don't you?" I asked, looking over at Rob. I was going to have to give the details about Marylou's list to the police.

"Yeah, I know." He frowned for a bit, before straightening himself and delivering one of his typical shrugs. "Oh well, like you said, it's not the most horrible secret in the world. Hell of a lot better than being a suburban drug dealer, right?"

"Trust me," I replied as my hands squeezed the chair rail, "there are far worse secrets." All he risked was a little embarrassment. Some of us faced far bigger consequences.

Like being caught breaking into someone's house. Someone had opened the door upstairs.

Crap. "Someone's home," I whispered. "We've got to get out of here."

"How?" Rob whispered. "We'll be spotted if we go upstairs."

I looked around the basement and its covered windows. There were no exits. "Get under the stairs," I said. "We can hide there until whoever leaves."

"What if they don't leave?"

Then we were stuck there until bedtime. Or worse. We headed down the stairs. "Jesus Christ," Rob hissed, "How many bloody plants are there?"

He was right. The floor was thick with foliage. It was like cutting through a jungle.

Then, two feet from the stairs, Rob's foot hit an empty pot. The plastic container clattered as it tipped over.

I held my breath. Maybe the noise wasn't as loud as it seemed, and whoever was upstairs didn't hear.

Or not, I thought as the basement suddenly flooded with light.

25

ERIN APPEARED at the top of the stairs, her face glowering. She looked angry enough to kill. "What the hell do the two of you think you're doing?"

I silently gave thanks I was standing at the floor and not on the stairwell.

"Oh hey, Erin," I replied. "Nice set up. This what paid for the kitchen?"

Her face darkened. "Get upstairs," she growled. "Now."

When we got to the kitchen, we found Jennifer at the kitchen cabinet, a steak knife in her hand. "Really, Sadie?" she said when she stepped into the kitchen. "Breaking into other people's houses?"

"Technically, we didn't break in," Rob replied. "Erin left the slider door unlocked."

"Dammit," Erin muttered. "I told Ian to put the security bar down when he came. Kid never listens. One of these days I'm going to strangle him."

Not literally, I hoped.

"I told you something was up," Jenn said. "Rob was being way too flirty."

"Too flirty?" I couldn't help myself. I didn't know there was a tipping point.

"Plus, I saw his car following me all over town."

"You aren't much better, Sadie," Erin said. "I could see your car from the kitchen window."

Obviously, we had a lot to learn about playing detective.

"We suspected you might try to poke around, so I picked up Jenn and we doubled back here to see if we could catch you in the act." She pointed at the kitchen table. "Sit."

Rob and I looked at each other. The slider was less than twenty feet away to my left. Moving in sync, we took a step in that direction.

Jenn stepped in front of me. "Nice try," she said. "But you've got some explaining to do."

We needed explaining? We weren't the ones with Mary Jane Valley in our basement.

Erin locked the basement door, then joined Jenn at the counter. The two of them stood side by side. A natural-fiber clad inquisitor panel.

"What are you planning to do with the knife?" Rob asked Jennifer.

"This?" She looked down as though suddenly remembering she had it in her hand. "I couldn't find the corkscrew. I was going to try and pry the cork out with it."

Oh thank God.

"For crying out loud." Erin opened the drawer behind her. "Here," she said, thrusting a corkscrew at the blonde. "Before you hurt yourself."

"I'm telling you, I read it on the Internet. In one of those Life Hack articles."

"I don't care where you read it," Erin snapped. "You weren't going to use one of my good steak knives. I paid a fortune for those."

Jenn shrugged into her glass. "Whatever."

With Jenn disarmed and happily uncorking her Chardonnay, Erin turned her attention back to Rob and me. "I can't believe you two. I should have known when you mentioned Marylou's stupid list last night that you were going to poke around to find out what her code words meant. Why else would you bring up the subject?"

"The woman was murdered," I said. "And it's not as though you did a bang up job of dissuading me. Letting everyone know how much you disliked Marylou.

"Paul told me Marylou had figured out a way to make some extra money to help get them out of financial trouble. Doesn't take a rocket scientist to figure out that her new job was tied to those words on her list."

"So you decided to break in to my basement."

"Only because we found the door open," Rob reminded her. "We had planned to simply look in the windows. Which, for the record, I said was a bad idea."

"Remind me not to walk near a bus with you," I snapped. "You're the one who found the unlocked door. I would have gone home after we found the air conditioner. Why is there an air conditioner in your basement window?" I asked her.

"Temperature regulation. The reflective walls tend to heat up the room."

She grabbed the bottle Jenn had opened and poured herself a large glass. "I can't believe this," I heard her mutter. "So how much are you two going to want to keep quiet?"

"That's what happened with Marylou, isn't it?" I asked. "She found out about the marijuana and asked for money?"

"A thousand dollars a week," Erin replied. She drained her glass in one impressive swallow and poured another. "Four grand total."

Next to me, Rob let out a low whistle.

"Who knows how much she would have bled me for if she wasn't killed."

"Why didn't you tell somebody?"

"Who was I going to tell, Rob? The police? Sadie? Did you not see what I've got downstairs?"

"Why do you, anyway?" Cop's mother or no, I wasn't a prude; I understood growing a few plants for personal use. What Erin had downstairs was a business venture.

"Why do you think?" Erin replied. "For the money."

"You're a drug dealer." What the heck? Our little coffee klatch had a blackmailer and a drug dealer and possibly a murderer and I didn't know? Talk about wearing blinders.

"It's not like I woke up one morning and decided I wanted to peddle weed. We always smoked, but I bought the stuff from a supplier. We didn't start growing until he went to college."

"That's your personal stash? What are you doing, chain smoking it?" Rob asked.

"No, I'm not chain smoking it." For the first time since our conversation began, Erin looked embarrassed. She ducked her head and stared at her running shoes. "I accidentally brought a pan of brownies to my mom's place, and her neighbors went crazy over them. They kept asking me to bring more. Originally, I gave them the stuff for free, but it started getting expensive. Half of them are on special diets so I was buying special flour and organic chocolate. Not to mention, I needed more plants which meant more equipment...."

"Wait a minute." I interrupted her laundry list of expenses. "You're selling marijuana to the residents at your mother's assisted living facility?"

"And at the senior center. Who knew seniors were such party animals? Then again, they did live through the sixties...."

She finished her wine, and set the empty glass on the counter. "The money is good, too. Paid for this kitchen."

I had to admit, her custom cabinetry was lovely. "What about your kids? Weren't you worried about exposing them to your activities?" Or getting into the product? Ian was eleven years old, and his brother nine. Old enough to think about experimenting.

"That's why the cellar door is kept locked," Erin said. "We told the boys there were poisonous chemicals in their father's workshop, and they needed to stay out. Plus, I always make sure to do my baking when they're out of house. So far, it's worked."

Yeah, but for how long? I kept the question to myself. Now wasn't the time for a talk about the dangers of drugs and children. "How did Marylou find out?"

"No clue. She came to me one day, said she had something important to talk with me about, and asked if I'd meet her for dinner at Gilroy's Tavern. It was there she lowered the boom."

"To you as well," I said, looking at Jenn. That was the night I saw the three of them together. "She had something on you too."

Rob spoke up. "Please don't tell us you're selling pot over the Internet."

"What? No! The pot is all Erin's business. I would never sell drugs."

"Then what are you selling?" I asked. "You are selling something you shouldn't, right? That's what Marylou meant when she wrote BobsBuynSell."

"Stupid Marylou. No one would have ever known if she weren't buying those stupid dragons."

"Know what? I saw your listings. Last time I looked it wasn't illegal to sell your own stuff."

"Unless it wasn't your own stuff."

I looked at Rob. "The driver," he said. "Didn't think about it at the time, but you don't play golf."

"Or scuba dive," I added.

Bits and pieces started coming together in my head. The driver. Jenn's hiding objects in the back of her car outside Nick's house. Nick's missing book.

"You're selling Nick's stuff, aren't you? That's what you were doing when I saw you yesterday morning. You're breaking into Nick's house, stealing his things, and selling them online."

"Wrong," she said, swatting her ponytail. "I don't break into Nick's house. I have a key."

"But you're still stealing his stuff."

"Stuff that I bought him. That stupid book was an anniversary present." She reached for the Chardonnay. Between the two of them, the wine had to be almost gone, a fact that could work in Rob's and my favor.

"Bastard drags his feet about paying alimony, then turns around and takes his girlfriend to Turks and Caicos for a spa weekend?"

Snorting, she rolled her eyes. "Give me a break. He's lucky I didn't sell his car."

"Instead you started helping yourself to other stuff."

"Not on purpose. At least not at first," she said, hanging her head. "Brandon left his school book at Nick's house the weekend he took the skank away. I went over to retrieve it.

"Brandon has a key," she explained. "Anyway, I'd never been in his house beyond the front door, so I decided to snoop."

As would we all.

She squeezed her goblet stem. So tightly, I was afraid it might snap. "You wouldn't believe how good he's living. He's got a sixty-four inch flat screen. Brandon has a game system in his room. I mean, for crying out loud. I get to spend Monday through Friday playing mean parent because money's tight, and he goes out and buys a game system? And goes on vacation? I saw the book on the shelf, so I grabbed it. Figured if he wasn't going to pay me what he owed me by check, he could pay me another way."

She was breaking the law, but damn if I didn't sympathize with Jenn's position. Anyone who knew her, knew Nick was a self-centered, arrogant, unfaithful jerk. There was an element of poetic justice to her making ends meet by selling his things, wrong though it may be.

"The night she met you for dinner, Marylou told you she knew and started blackmailing you as well."

Jenn nodded. "She said she saw the ad for the book while looking for her dragon statues and recognized the phone number."

"Blackmailing a person who's selling her things to pay the bills," Rob mused. "Not decent at all."

"Told you she was a bitch," Erin said. "She cut Jenn a break by only charging her a couple hundred dollars."

"We used to pay her after coffee klatch," Jenn added.

"Sitting in her car looking all smug. I can still see her face."

"And hear her smug little voice." Jenn twisted her mouth into a smirk. "Must be hard being on the losing end of things," she said, in a high pitched, nasal voice.

"I'm a winner." That's what Marylou had meant. In her drunken brain she'd merged Paul and Rita with the people she'd blackmailed, turning them all into a crew of losers.

And her into a giant winner. Until someone clubbed her in the head.

On the other side of the table, Rob sat fiddling with one of Erin's salt and pepper shakers. A ceramic rooster. He ran his thumb up and down along the edge of its plumage. Under different circumstances, I would have made an inappropriate joke about fondling. "What I don't understand is why she went after the two of you for money, yet waited on asking me," he said. "No offense, but if she needed cash, I've got way more money than either of you."

"Who knows what the hell Marylou was thinking," Erin replied. "Maybe we were her practice cases. To see how much she could get away with before hitting the big bucks."

"Or she wasn't sure she wanted to..." Something Paul said popped into my head. About how Marylou said Rob made her laugh. "She liked you," I said. "She might have been dragging her feet about blackmailing you because she considered you a friend."

"Well aren't you special," Erin drawled. Sounded like the wine had kicked in. "What did she have on you anyway? You murder someone back in Manchester?"

"Nothing so dramatic, I assure you," he replied.

"Then what? You know ours. It's only fair we get to hear your dirty laundry in return. Especially since you broke into my house." She narrowed her eyes at me.

Rob's cheekbones turned bright pink. An attractive pink, of course, because it was him. "RUR stands for R U Ready."

"Are you ready for what?" Jenn asked.

"No RU Ready. With the initials. It's the name of a band."

Jenn and Erin stared at him with blank expressions. "You sang in a band?" Jenn asked.

A boy band, if you wanted to be precise.

That's right. Woodbridge's suave British lit professor made his fortune singing Auto-Tuned bubble gum music in a manufactured pop act.

"Remember the song 'Be-bop-alicious'?" I asked. The insipid song tormented the charts for eighteen months. *Be-bop-alicious. Your lips look delicious.* Musical torture at its finest. I wouldn't be surprised to hear they played the song to torture prisoners of war.

"Oh my God, that was you?" Erin twisted her face in disgust. "You guys wore gold lamé baseball caps."

Rob grew indignant. "So? It were part of the costume."

"I thought you inherited your money," Jenn said. "I had no idea you...you were in a *boy band*." She winced worse than Erin. "And I flirted with you. I need more wine."

Wow. She had zero problems flirting with him even though he was gay, but boy band membership was a deal breaker. Who'd have guessed?

"And, what about you?" Erin said, directing her attention to me. She folded her arms. "What did Marylou have on you?"

"I told you. Unpaid parking tickets."

"The real question is what are you going to do to now?" Rob asked. "Can't very well push us down the stairs. People would find your Magical Mystery Garden."

"Why would we...?" The blondes exchanged looks. "You think we pushed Marylou down the stairs?" Erin exclaimed.

"You two did have the most to lose," I replied.

"We also weren't the only names on the list," she shot back. "What about Rob? Or Andrea and Lindsay?"

"My secret is embarrassing, not murder worthy," Rob replied. "I'm not breaking the law."

At his mention of the law, Erin's demeanor shifted. She paled. "Are you planning to tell the police about us?"

"You wouldn't do that, would you?" Jenn asked. "I wouldn't have done anything if Nick hadn't screwed me first."

Much as I hated to say so, I did sympathize with her position. "But..."

"I swear I'll take the other stuff off the market, and return it. Nick will never know."

"And I'm closing the business anyway," Erin said. "The seniors are getting way too demanding. Plus legalization is going to put me out of business."

"See?" Jenn said. "We're both stopping, so there's no reason to say anything to anyone."

As though promising to stop mitigated the fact they broke the law.

The sad thing was, I wasn't the one they needed to worry about. "Doesn't matter if I say anything or not," I told them.

"Why not?"

I waited, knowing Erin would realize the reason soon enough.

"Because the police are still looking for Marylou's killer." Erin slid to the floor where she sat, hugging her knees and glaring up at me. "You already told the police about the list didn't you?"

"Not yet. But I did tell them you three weren't getting along."

She spat out an obscenity.

Jenn sat beside her. "I don't want to go to jail."

"No one's going to jail."

"Easy for you to say, Lamé Boy. All you did was sing a crappy song." Erin's glare grew sharper. "I thought we were friends."

Were we? I wasn't so sure anymore. Didn't stop a guilty pang from stabbing my stomach though.

"Instead the two of you break into my house because you thought I might have killed that bitch. That is why you broke in, right?"

Someone should tell her that continually referring to Marylou as "that bitch" wasn't helping her case.

"I'm simply looking for answers," I told her. "Someone tried to run me off the road last night as a warning, and it was right after I mentioned Marylou's list. I want to know who."

"And naturally, you decided it had to be me or Jenn. What about Andrea and Lindsay? They were on the list too."

"They aren't telling everyone how much they hated Marylou and how glad they are she's dead," I spat back. Guilty conscience or not, she had to know that would raise a flag.

Erin spat at me again. This time with literal spit. I was seeing a whole new charming side to her. "You're as big a bitch as Marylou," she said. "Both of you. Get out of my house."

"Erin..."

"I said get out of my house, Rob."

Without another word, Rob and I stood and slunk toward the slider. Showed how angry—or drunk—Erin was that she didn't insist we use the front door. As we passed them, Jenn looked up with watery blue eyes. "You two really suck, you know that?"

"Safe to say, our coffee klatch is officially over," Rob said when we were finally on the sidewalk.

No kidding. I'd definitely torpedoed a couple of friendships this afternoon, if, like I said, they ever were friendships. I could live with Jenn's and Erin's anger if it weren't for my conscience calling me a hypocrite. After all, I'd investigated them to keep myself out of the suspect lineup. Made me as bad as they were.

Almost.

I didn't break the law.

"I'm sorry Jenn ripped on the gold baseball cap," I said to Rob.

"Me too," he replied. "I rocked that sucker."

26

WHEN I WALKED into Cuppa's the next morning, our entire section was empty. No surprise. Erin and Jenn were no doubt hunkered down, plotting their legal defenses. Andrea and Lindsay had been missing the past couple of mornings as well. If Andrea was part of their blackmailed circle, I wouldn't be surprised if the duo called her as soon as Rob and I left.

I wondered if the police had contacted any of them as well. Detective Bartlett still hadn't returned my message.

Rob was at the counter flirting with Jose. "Hey!" I said as I joined them. "Looks like we're no longer part of the cool gang."

"Speak for yourself. I am the cool gang. Those other four were posers. You want a latte? On me."

On Jose, he meant. The barista was going to get himself fired one of these days. "Thanks," I said.

"Anytime, luv."

Gosh, but he was a good friend. In all the back and forth yesterday, the fact it was my fault his past had been outed against his wishes had kind of fallen by the wayside. By all rights, I deserved the cold shoulder too.

Instead, I was getting a free coffee. Leaning in, I kissed his cheek.

He looked at me, surprised. "What was that for?"

So many things. For pulling me out of my depression after Jack's death. For standing by me when I needed a friend.

"For being awesome," I said.

"Can't help it. Comes naturally."

That was my Rob. "You going to be okay? With the whole RU Ready thing?" Once they got over their anger, Jenn and Erin would spread the story all over Woodbridge.

"Don't have much choice, do I?" he said with a shrug. "Would have had to tell your Detective Bartlett soon enough. Besides, it was silly of me to think I could hide. Sooner or later, the past always catches up with you. You found the CD. I'm sure others got copies. Someone's bound to recognize me face, despite the cap and eye makeup."

"But you wanted to start fresh." I remembered our conversation the day I found the CD. *Worst four years of my life,* he'd said. *I want to pretend they never happened.*

Clean slates could be hard to keep.

"Eh," he said with a shrug. "I'll deal. Like we said yesterday. T'ain't all bad. Still got my money and my looks, right?"

"And free coffee," I said as Jose returned carrying two cups.

"Here you go," he said, sliding them across the counter. "Rob was telling me about how he used to be a professional singer. That is dope."

Yep. Rob would be fine.

Leaving them to their banter, I took my coffee and headed toward a table by the window. I got about half way when a leather mountain blocked my path.

"Morning." I looked up at him through my eyelashes—a total Jennifer move—before remembering I had serious business to discuss with him. "Did you get my message?"

"I did. I'm sorry I didn't call you back. Things have been a little crazy."

So I could see. He looked uncharacteristically disheveled, his shirt wrinkled and lived-in looking. Someone had been up all night.

"Is everything all right?" I asked.

Immediately, he let out the longest, slowest sigh I'd ever heard. "I shouldn't tell you, but seeing as how she's your friend…"

"What are you talking about? Do you mean Marylou?"

"Afraid not," he replied. "It's Andrea Baronelli."

A sudden bout of foreboding washed over me, chilling my insides. My blood froze. "What about Andrea?"

"I'm sorry. I hate to have to tell you." His ruddy features grew paler. It was the first time in our brief acquaintance that I'd seen his control slip.

"Tell me what?"

He washed a hand over his face. "God, it's been a long twenty-four hours."

"Tell me what?" I repeated. Why was he talking about Andrea? Without thinking, I reached out and touched his forearm. "What happened?"

"Your friend, Andrea…."

He was interrupted by Lindsay, who came rushing across the coffee shop. "Oh my God, did you hear? I can't believe it."

Whatever "it" was, had to be pretty terrible because she was shaking like a leaf. "I was at the middle school picking up supplies for the walk and the vice principal told me."

I looked from her to Bartlett, waiting for one of them to explain what was going on.

"Told you what?" Rob asked, voicing my frustration.

"About Andrea," Lindsay replied. "She's dead."

27

ANDREA WAS DEAD?

I looked up at Bartlett for confirmation. His eyes said everything. "How?" I asked.

Two friends in two weeks. This sort of thing wasn't supposed to happen to people my age. Granted, Marylou's involved extenuating circumstances, but Andrea? "We saw her on Sunday and she was feeling fine. Battling a cold, but fine."

"They're saying she killed herself," Lindsay said.

Again, I looked to Bartlett. "I'm afraid I can't..."

"Please, Dan." It was the first time I'd ever used his first name. "Andrea was a friend." Not a close one, perhaps, but a friend nonetheless. "If she killed herself..."

He nodded. "It certainly looks like a suicide. We won't know for certain until we finish investigating."

I couldn't believe it. "We didn't even know she was unhappy."

"A lot of depressed people keep their feelings to themselves," Lindsay remarked. "Afraid to be a bother. You know how quiet Andrea was."

Very. She barely said two words most days. Still, she had friends. Why hadn't she reached out for help?

"Who found her? Not her boys?" Her youngest was only nine. I couldn't imagine coming home from school and finding your mother like that.

"Actually, I did," Bartlett said. "I stopped by her house to ask some questions and found her in the living room. Looks like an overdose. We can't be sure though, until we get the tox screen."

"At least she went peacefully." Lindsay said. Small consolation.

"And you're sure it was suicide?" I was still in shock. "Maybe she took too much cold medicine."

Bartlett shook his head. "She left a note."

Oh God. Even as I digested the awful news, I sent him a grateful look for breaking protocol and letting me know.

"Her poor family." I couldn't imagine how her husband was going to tell her boys.

Had there been clues? I tried to remember, and came up blank. Andrea had always been the quietest of the four, but I never thought her depressed. If anything, she'd seemed incredibly chipper this summer. Briefly, I thought of Marylou's list. Andrea's name had *Soccer Practice* written next to it. Had her secret been why she seemed so happy this summer? Or the reason for her suicide?

The things people keep just below the surface. I wouldn't be able to look at the people in Woodbridge the same way again. Hell, mornings at Cuppa's would never be the same.

"Maybe we should cancel the Night Walk." I thought aloud. We had two committee members dead. I know I didn't feel like hosting an event, even one to raise money for charity.

"We can't cancel," Lindsay said. "It's tomorrow night. People are planning on it. Besides, there are permits and things to consider. We cancel, and there's no guarantee we'll be able to get a date that doesn't clash with the holidays."

"I guess."

"It might actually be good for people," Rob said. "A night about hope and all."

"You can never have enough hope." From a man who prayed over his crime victims, Bartlett's quietly spoken sentiment wasn't surprising.

"I'm going to take a lasagna over later," Lindsay said. "The boys will need to eat and I imagine Matt's in too much shock to think, let alone cook. If you want, we can go together. So he's not inundated."

"Good idea. Maybe we could also add a special luminaria. Next to Marylou's."

"Ummm..." Bartlett interrupted. "That might not be the best idea."

"Visiting Craig?" Lindsay asked.

"No, the side by side luminarias."

And like that, the hair on my neck started to prickle. A second expression of extreme discomfort crossed his face. Only briefly, but while it lasted, he looked like a man about to ask a very uncomfortable favor.

Police detectives didn't ask favors.

"Would you mind taking a seat?" he said to Lindsay. "There are questions I'd like to ask the three of you."

NOW WE KNEW what Marylou meant when she wrote *Soccer Practice* next to Andrea's name. Andrea had been skipping out on soccer practice. And soccer camp. And a few other things.

Andrea had been having an affair.

Unfortunately, Marylou had one detail missing: Andrea's adulterous partner. If she'd known the answer, our ride together on Sunday night might have gone differently.

A whole lot differently.

"So none of you ever saw her and Paul Paretsky together?" Bartlett asked. "Not even once?"

"Maybe once," Lindsay said. "We had this committee get together last spring and everyone brought their spouses. The two of them probably talked there."

"I remembered that party," Rob said. "Most of us went downstairs to watch the baseball game."

"Most of the guys," I corrected. "We stayed upstairs and gossiped."

"Except for Andrea," Lindsay said. "She was downstairs with the guys."

"No, she wasn't," Rob said. "She came down, but Matt was being Mr. I Know Sports—he doesn't know a thing, by the way—so she went outside on the deck. Come to think of it, Paul might have gone outside too. The air was getting a mite stuffy."

"But that's the only time you saw the two of them together?"

"Yes, but it's not like we monitored her activities," I said. "After morning coffee, we go our separate ways." To very separate lives, I wanted to add, but didn't. "Marylou didn't even realized. She thought Paul was sleeping with Rita." She must have known Andrea was up to somethinghence the words *Soccer Practice* on her listbut hadn't had the chance to figure out what.

I was still trying to wrap my head around the idea myself. Paul and Andrea. Bartlett didn't say how he knew, but the information must have been what took him to Andrea's house yesterday.

"This explains why she was outraged when the detective here suggested you were having a thing with Paul," Rob said.

"Here I thought she was outraged on my account," I replied.

"She was also adamant that he didn't kill Marylou, remember?"

"Because she knew he didn't," Lindsay said. "Or should I say, believed he didn't."

"Would you? No one likes to think the person they're sleeping with is a killer. At least I wouldn't." Rob drained the last of his coffee. Behind the espresso bar, Jose moved to make a new one, but he waved the barista off. This wasn't a time for flirting.

"Actually," Bartlett said. "Paretsky claims they broke up before his wife's death. He also said that she didn't take it well. Did you notice a change in her behavior?"

"She'd been sick," I said. "A heavy cold. We didn't see her for a couple days."

Including the day after Marylou's murder.

A very unsettling idea had started to take shape. If you took the affair and coupled it with Marylou's blackmail schemes—because who's to say she didn't try to blackmail Andrea without knowing the whole story—as well as Andrea's absence Monday morning... Suddenly things didn't look good for Andrea.

"She was outside Paul's house," I said, as yet another piece fell into place. "The night I stopped by to pick up Marylou's files. She drove right by me."

Bartlett leaned forward. "Are you sure it was her?"

"I saw the sticker on her car."

Her black SUV.

Like the one that ran me off the road.

Could it have been Andrea who ran me off the road? Seemed unbelievable. But then, if you told me one of my morning coffee mates had a marijuana farm in her basement, I wouldn't have believed that, either.

"There's something else. I didn't think it was a big deal at the time, but the other night at our meeting..." Lindsay paused to give Rob and me a look, as though her comment might jar a memory for us. "She made this big deal about seeing me near Paul's office this week. Asking why I'd gone to visit him. It was weird."

Bartlett arched his brow. "What were you doing at his office?" he asked.

"That's the thing. I wasn't at Paul's office. I was at the nail salon next door. When I told her that, she said she thought it was odd I would visit him. The whole conversation was really weird."

"Indeed," he said.

"Seriously. When I asked her what she was doing there, she said she was booking a nail appointment herself."

"Andrea didn't do her nails," I remarked. She barely wore makeup.

"I know, right? That was the other weird thing. Now that you said you saw her outside Paul's house, I'm wondering. Do you think she was stalking him?"

Sounded like it.

The picture came together in my head. Paul and Andrea had an affair. He broke it off, and she handled it like any unhinged woman would. Following him around and suspecting him of replacing her. Meanwhile, Marylou tries to blackmail over the missing soccer practices. They argue. Andrea loses her temper...

"Oh my God, she killed her." I said the words aloud without thinking, drawing the remaining three's attention. "Is that why she killed herself? Because she killed Marylou?" I looked at Bartlett, hoping for a clue that I was on the right track.

He looked at his notes.

Oh, Andrea, Andrea, Andrea. My heart dropped into my stomach.

Meanwhile, Bartlett was stuffing his notebook into the breast pocket of his jacket and getting to his feet. "Thank you all for your cooperation," he said. "If you remember anything else, don't hesitate to give me a call. Oh, Sadie." He turned to me. "What was it you wanted to talk about?"

In the shock of the news about Andrea's death, I'd forgotten about my phone message. If Andrea killed Marylou, then Jenn and Erin were no longer suspected. Meaning the list was no longer important.

"It's nothing," I said.

He frowned. "Are you sure?"

"Yeah. We can talk later." I felt my secret receding once more. As for Jenn and Erin, I'd deal with them later.

28

THE DAY of the Night Walk, talk of the town-wide event took a back seat to the bigger news of the day. On its eleven o'clock broadcast, one of the Boston TV stations broke the news that Andrea Baronelli had left behind a suicide note confessing to the murder of Marylou Paretsky. While the reporter didn't know all the details, it appeared Andrea had apologized for what she called a terrible accident, and that she couldn't live, knowing Paul would hate her for what she had done. The Woodbridge police declined to comment, but more details were expected soon.

Overnight, Cuppa's became not only the best source of local gossip, but also a place where a torrid love triangle had unfolded. The shop was crawling with reporters. I wanted nothing to do with them so I immediately turned around and went across town to the pricey name-brand chain. Rob was in line when I arrived. He greeted me with a nod. "Saw the mayhem, did ya?"

"Are you kidding? I nearly collided with the truck from Channel Seven trying to make a U-turn."

"Same here, only it was Channel Four. That reporter you think looks like a porn star was in the passenger seat. She was teasing her hair." His grin faded. "You see the report?"

I had. "They made Andrea sound like she was some kind of unhinged lunatic."

"I wouldn't call stalking and murder the act of a hinged person."

No, they weren't. Neither was blackmailing your neighbors into being your besties. I was still trying to wrap my brain around the chain of events. The pieces were lined up, but something felt off. Maybe it would make more sense when the shock wore off.

"I wondered what Paul Paretsky is thinking," I said. "His being the reason two women are dead."

Rob shrugged. "I'm too busy wondering how he got two women."

"Three, if you count his doting assistant."

"Lord knows, they saw something the rest of us missed. Maybe one day we'll figure out what that was."

"Maybe," I replied. "Or maybe it'll be one of those things we'll never know." Right along with how we never noticed our coffee klatch included a pot peddler to geriatrics and a thief.

The barista at the counter motioned that we were next. I took out my wallet. "My treat," I said. "I still owe you."

"You owe me way more than one."

"Well, excuse me for not rushing to buy a coffee for the man who gets his drinks for free."

"Hey, not my fault I'm irresistible." His trademark grin lifted some of the heaviness from my spirit. At least one thing in my life remained constant.

"You know what else we'll never know?" I asked after we placed our order. "Besides Paul Paretsky's appeal to women."

"Why this place insists on charging more for a large latte?"

"No. What was Marylou doing that night, wandering around town in her high school sweatshirt?"

THANK GOD for short news cycles. When I left the office early that afternoon, the trucks were gone, off to chase another news story. Other than the management at Cuppa's, only two people were sorry to see them go. Renee, who'd headed over to the shop with her Renee

Drake Realty tote bag strategically hung on her shoulder only to discover she'd arrived too late, and Lindsay, who sent me a text saying, "Wear last year's Night Walk T-shirt if you plan to get coffee."

Personally, I never wanted to hear the words Night Walk again. I wanted the day to end, so I could go to sleep and process everything that had happened. It had been one hell of a week and a half.

I don't know why I turned onto Hemlock. I was driving down Edgewater, past the spot where Marylou fell in front of my car, and my subconscious took over from there. As I approached Marylou's house, I saw that the flowers on her front step were drooping from lack of water. I was surprised Rita hadn't watered them. Then again, she was the office wife. Flowerpots might not be in her purview.

So busy was I, looking at the flowers and thinking about various wives' duties, that I nearly missed the movement to my right. I slammed on the brakes, coming to a jerking stop just as the man himself appeared in my windshield.

Paul looked horrible. His skin was gray and pasty. He had dark circles under his eyes. His shoulders were hunched as though carrying a heavy weight. Which they probably were, metaphorically speaking.

He frowned at the windshield for several moments, before realizing who I was. Immediately his features softened. "I didn't recognize you," he said, coming around to the driver's window. "I thought you drove a different car."

"It's a loaner. Mine's in the shop. I was looking at your flowers and didn't see you. Sorry about that."

"I was getting the mail. It's been a couple of days." He held up the stack of envelopes in his hand. "Bills mostly. Hardly worth the walk."

"They never are," I said.

"Very true. Would you like to come inside? For a cup of coffee?"

"I..."

Sensing my hesitation, he looked to the ground and I imagined him shuffling his foot in the gravel. "I suppose you heard the news. About Andrea," he said finally.

"Last night. I'm sorry."

"Thanks." You could almost hear the words "Me, too" hanging in the air. "I couldn't believe it when the police told me about her note. She took the break up hard, but I never thought her capable..." He frowned again, pained. "It was an accident. I don't think she meant for Marylou to die."

"I'm sure she didn't." Maybe if he hadn't dragged her into an affair in the first place, neither of them would be dead. I hoped he felt like shit.

"She...uh... We didn't mean to get...that is, we weren't looking to get... It just happened. I think that's why she took it so badly."

If he was looking for sympathy for his justification, he was talking to the wrong person. I said nothing.

"Matt's kind of a douchebag, you know," he continued. With that, I had to agree. "He never pays—paid—attention to her, and Marylou..." He finished with a shrug. "It can get lonely when your spouse is obsessed with other things."

Like drinking, collecting dragons and blackmail. Or your kids' sporting careers. "I imagine it can," I said, a tiny kernel of understanding finding its way into my heart.

"I tried to explain to her that I had no choice. Marylou was trying to save my business. I saw that as a sign we might be able to get back... I owed it to her to try. But she—Andrea—didn't want to let go."

Of course not. Breaking up meant going back to being lonely and ignored. I'd take the break up hard, too.

"Did the police tell you what Marylou's plan was?" I asked. I was wondering how much he knew.

He shook his head. "Nothing. I guess we'll never know either. The plan died with her."

I'm ashamed to say the muscles in my shoulders relaxed for the first time in days.

Paul, on the other hand, was defeat walking. "What are you going to do now?" I asked.

"What else can I do? Rita thinks I should fight to save the business for Marylou's sake, but my heart's been out of it for a while.

Besides, whatever chance I might have had died with the scandal. No one's going to want to work with a man responsible for two women's deaths."

He had a point there.

"Maybe I'll move to another state," he said. "One where no one knows what happened. You're in real estate, right?"

I nodded. "I am."

"Good. I'll give you a call when I'm ready to sell. Thank you for listening."

My hands were still gripping the steering wheel. Reaching through my driver's side window, he put a sweaty hand atop one of them. Immediately, I pulled it away. He winced at the rejection, but he'd earned it. "I did love Marylou, you know."

It was obvious from the way he hovered that he wasn't finished purging his soul. I was trying to figure out a way to graciously exit when his phone rang, saving me. Paul took one look at the call screen and grimaced.

"Marylou's Aunt Ruth," he said. "Didn't think I'd hear from her anymore, considering. Hello, Ruth. How are you?" He waved and stepped away from the car. "No, the only pictures I took were the ones I brought. I didn't touch the high school ones..."

I had pulled away and was watching him in the rearview mirror walk back to his house when I saw a white envelope on the floor of my car next to my brake pedal. Paul must have dropped it when he reached through the window. Sighing, I stopped the car and got out. "You dropped this," I said.

"Probably another bill. Thanks."

As he reached for the envelope, however, I realized it wasn't a bill, but an invitation of some kind. The return address was a picture of an Indian, like the one that had been on Marylou's sweatshirt.

"Marylou's class reunion invitation," Paul said when he glanced at it. "The Pennington Chiefs."

Pennington Chiefs. Why did that name sound familiar?

A sad smile came over his face. "She wouldn't have gone, what with all the bad memories."

I'd say more like a love-hate relationship seeing how she'd held on to the sweatshirt.

Paul was lost in his reverie. "Strange how Marylou seems forever tied to that place. Every time I turn around. Ruth just said Marylou's choir photo was missing from the funeral home."

"It was probably misplaced," I said. "It happens."

He nodded, his attention drawn to the logo on the white envelope. "The police found that sweatshirt by the way. The one you said Marylou was wearing."

"They did?"

"In the trash behind my office. The police found Marylou's blood on it. They think Andrea wiped the murder weapon clean with it."

Then tossed it in the Dumpster near Paul's office where anyone would find it? That didn't seem very well thought out. Andrea had to have realized the police would be searching around Paul's office as a matter of course.

Unless she wanted the police to find the garment and suspect Paul even more.

Wow, hell did hath no fury.

The only thing I could think of to say was "I'm sorry." Again.

"Me too." He tucked the invitation in the stack of bills. "I'll have to let the reunion committee know what happened. Thanks for stopping by."

Talk about karmic revenge. I sat in my car and watched Paul schlump inside. His ex-lover kills his wife, tries to frame him, then kills herself when the guilt gets too much. And Andrea had been so publically adamant about his innocence, too. She didn't show a hint of nerves. Pretty cool and calculating. And yet in the end, she cracked from guilt and committed suicide anyway. Guess she figured as soon as Paul talked about the affair, she'd be found out.

Something didn't feel right. I couldn't put my finger on exactly what, but my stomach told me there was something off kilter about the whole scenario.

29

"CAN you pick up extra water? Jenn and Erin are being pissy about running errands." Lindsay's voice was all business when she called later that afternoon. "I was at the middle school and I heard them talking about organizing a kids' walk as a kind of vigil. If that's the case, we're going to need at least double the amount we have."

I was busy staring at the sheet of paper on my counter, and nodded my reply before realizing she couldn't see me. "Sure. Anything else?"

As she rattled off a few more items, my attention drifted back to the paper. Marylou's list, which I'd recreated shortly after getting home. A thought had been clawing at my brain to get out ever since I spoke to Paul; I simply couldn't find the words to make it make sense.

"...extra propane lighters," Lindsay said. "If they're holding a vigil, they're going to have candles, and I don't want them littering the ground with burned matches. I'll never hear the end of it. I don't want some nature lover giving us a hard time because we littered the street."

I don't feel like dealing with those PC nut bags screaming we're disrespecting the Cherokees or whatever. Bad enough you screwed up the invitations. Use the new logo so we don't get any complaints. That was it. The logo. "Hey, Lindsay," I interrupted her list making. "What was your high school mascot when you were a kid?"

"The Chiefs."

"Were they the Pennington Chiefs?"

"Until someone protested. Then they became the Pennington Mountaineers. Why?"

"No reason, really. I was talking to Paul Paretsky today and he received an invitation to the class reunion. Well, Marylou did."

On the other end of the line, there was a short pause. "He did?"

"Yeah."

Now it was my turn to pause and the thought in my brain became slightly more defined. Still unfocused, but closer than before. "How come you never mentioned you and Marylou went to high school together?"

"I...I didn't know we did. She never said anything to me about it. Are you sure it's for the same reunion? More than one class is having their reunion this year."

"That must be it," I replied. "Although I didn't think you two were that different in age. I didn't think Pennington was all that big a town."

"I'm pretty sure she was older. Regardless, I doubt we ran in the same circles. The kids I hung out with were a pretty select group."

Select. She meant popular. I could see Lindsay being oblivious to someone like Marylou, but I bet Marylou knew who Lindsay was. "Weird that Marylou never mentioned Pennington at all."

"We're talking about Marylou."

"True," I said, though you would think, eager as she was to bond with the committee, Marylou would have mentioned the hometown connection at least once. Especially since Lindsay represented the type of group Marylou and Kim had longed to be a part of. "Did you know Marylou's best friend died in high school? Do you remember hearing about a girl who died of a drug overdose behind the school? Her name was Kim Rivard."

"Now that you mention it, I do remember something about a girl dying. It wasn't anyone I knew, so I don't think I was too affected by it. Did you say drug overdose?"

"Uh-huh."

"Then I definitely didn't know her. My crowd was totally straight edge. Honestly, though, unless it involved cheerleading or musicals, I didn't pay much attention. BJ was always on me about not paying attention to how he played."

"BJ was your boyfriend?" I vaguely remembered her mentioning something about being class couple when we talked the other day.

"All four years." *Except for a little bump during senior year.* I remembered the conversation. There was silence on the other end of the line. "Why are you so interested in what I did in high school?" Lindsay asked.

"I told you, I saw the invite at Marylou's house, and was shocked to learn you two were from the same town is all. You don't think it's a strange coincidence?"

"A little, I guess," she replied, with as much enthusiasm as someone would give a passing bug. "I've got too much on my plate to think about it right now. There's so much to get done before seven o'clock. I haven't even had a chance to shower today. Can you see me standing in front of all those people looking like something the cat dragged in?"

If the cat dragged in a silky angora rabbit, I could. Somehow, I wasn't too worried about Lindsay looking bad.

"Oh! A microphone," she said. "I completely forgot. The one at the rental company wasn't working. Jenn's daughter has one of those kid's karaoke machines. Can you text Jenn and ask if we can borrow it? I would, but I'm driving right now."

"Sure." No guarantee Jenn would reply to me, but I could send the message.

"Thanks. It would suck if I had to sing the anthem without one. When you're outdoors, it's hard to project."

I rolled my eyes. Heaven forbid she have trouble projecting. After ten more minutes of Lindsay's 'delegations,' I hung up and went back to staring at the list. There had been the big slash next to Lindsay's name. Lucky woman. But then, didn't people like her always have good luck? Scoring the best genes, the best homes, and the best team and class placements for their kids. The adult versions of having good skin and dating the high school sports star. Marylou looked for a secret she could hold over Lindsay, of that much I was certain. The more I stared at the slash, the more I remembered how forcefully she'd drawn the line on the page. So hard it dented through on the other side. Like she'd been furious not to find something. She probably was. Lindsay, the ultimate queen bee, and from her hometown high school to boot? I was surprised she wasn't the first person Marylou went after, seeing she'd been looking to buy herself popularity. Equally surprising, she hadn't found anything. No one's past was squeaky clean. Not naturally.

"Don't you think it's odd that Lindsay had no idea she and Marylou were both from Pennington?" I asked Rob when I called him a few moments later.

"You're joking right?" he replied. "No, it's not odd. Lindsay doesn't notice anything unless it involves Lindsay, you know that. Marylou could have been right under her nose for four years, and she'd never realize. Did she really ask for a karaoke machine? What for?"

"So the massive crowds could hear her sing the anthem, of course."

"But of course. Does she want Auto-Tune as well?"

"I don't think Kiddy Karaoke comes with it. Hey…" I grinned into the receiver. "Maybe after, you and she could sing a duet."

"Very funny. You do know we lip-synced those concerts, don't you? Besides," he added, a grin evident in his tone, "something' tells me you won't be able to pry the microphone out of Lindsay's hands. This is her night. She'd kill us if we ruined it."

I winced at the word kill. "No pun intended," I murmured.

"No. No indeed," he agreed. "Did you talk to Lindsay about a memorial?"

"I did. We decided to create a separate memorial circle on the opposite side of the track." At first, Lindsay balked at the idea, not wanting to show sympathy for a killer, but she eventually softened for the sake of Andrea's kids. Along with the fact that I said I was putting up a memorial regardless. Having spoken to Paul, I felt a little more sympathy for her, in a there-but-for-the-grace-of-God way.

"Her obituary is up online, by the way," Rob told me. "I just read it."

"That was quick."

"Sad is more like it."

I pulled up the listing and saw what he meant. Andrea's obituary was even shorter than Marylou, and focused largely on her husband's various positions. Matt didn't even remember to list her work on the Night Walk Committee. Why she got so attached to Paul made more and more sense.

"I wonder if Tim will rush to bury me when the time comes," I mused aloud, mostly to break the mood. I was concerned about how short my own obit would be.

"I don't know about Tim, but I will, if it conflicts with the playoffs."

"Which playoffs?"

"All of them."

"Nice to know my bestie has his priorities straight. Hey, this is odd."

"What?"

I'd moved from Andrea's obituary to Marylou's. "According to her obituary, Marylou graduated high school twenty years ago."

"So?"

"So, that's when Lindsay graduated. She, Marylou, and Kim Rivard were all in the same class. How could she not have remembered a classmate who died?"

"There were a couple thousand kids in my secondary school. I was lucky if I remember a third of 'em, and I knew everybody."

"Lindsay's chairing the freaking reunion committee! Even if she weren't, Pennington isn't Manchester, England. The whole town isn't more than..." I checked the online encyclopedia. "Four thousand people."

"Well, then that does seem odd."

More than odd. It was downright disturbing. Curious, I went to the website I'd bookmarked a couple nights earlier and skimmed the article on Kim's death. Two lines leaped out at me.

Marylou Commeau insisted one of the popular kids did something to her.

The party's host, Brian Jorgusen.

Popular kids.

Brian Jorgusen.

BJ.

No. Too many deaths had my brain jumping to conclusions. Andrea killed Marylou. She'd confessed in her suicide note. She was the one who tried to run me off the road when she thought Paul was interested in me. I remembered that night clear as could be. The SUV veering into me. The taillights as the car pulled ahead of me and drove away. "There wasn't a sticker," I said.

"What? Sadie, are you still there?"

"The car that drove me off the road. I didn't see a Woodbridge Soccer sticker."

"What are you talking about? Of course, there was a sticker. It was Andrea's car. You didn't see it because of the rain."

Maybe. I had been distracted by other things, like not crashing, at the time.

Still...

I looked at the article. The words "popular kids" leaped off the screen. Marylou had had a long memory when it came to high school and popularity.

And Marylou's list had had a dark slash next to Lindsay's name. A dark, almost angry looking slash.

What if Lindsay did have a secret? One that Marylou didn't have to write down because she already knew it by heart?

Do you ever wish you could go back in time and fix what went wrong?

"I've got to go, Rob. I'll talk to you tonight."

Hanging up before he could reply, I called Dan Bartlett.

Maybe my brain was making up things, but there were way too many coincidences for my taste.

30

BARTLETT WASN'T AVAILABLE. Neither was Tim. I left messages and went to get ready for the walk. By the time I'd located my turtleneck and flannel-lined jeans, I was relieved I didn't get through. What would I have said?

Marylou's best friend overdosed senior year of high school, and Lindsay didn't remember either of them, even though she graduated with Marylou, and her boyfriend at the time had the same initials as a boy who hosted that party. Oh, and it was totally possible Marylou was blackmailing her over something to do with the overdose, though I haven't a clue what that might be, but don't ask me how I know that because then I'd have to mention a piece of evidence I destroyed days ago. By the way, try not to hate me, Tim, when I explain what Mercedes means.

Yeah, I could see that going over well.

Maybe it was just a bunch of weird coincidences. Like the comments on the story said, murder over a singing solo was pretty farfetched.

But murder over a boy? Didn't Ruth say something about Kim having a crush on one of the popular kids?

"Will you listen to yourself?" I said to my reflection. I wasn't talking, but I knew what I meant. I'd gone from weird coincidences to

Lindsay killing Kim over Brian Jergins or Jorgenson or whoever and being blackmailed for it in the span of five minutes, and Kim hadn't even been murdered! She'd died of an overdose.

Just like Andrea.

And Lindsay, being wealthy, would be the perfect blackmail target. Didn't Paul say Marylou told him she had a solution for their money problems?

All right, now I was just crazy talking to myself. Andrea killed Marylou and herself. Dan Bartlett told me so. Why was I buying trouble with unfounded suspicions? Hadn't I already lost enough friendships this week? If I kept this up, the only person who'd want to deal with me would be Mr. Buffles, and his affection was 50-50, based on how close it was to dinner.

So, it was a good thing I hadn't reached Tim or Detective Bartlett. When they called back, I'd make up something about the Night Walk.

My doorbell rang.

Figuring it was probably Rob, checking on why I'd hung up on him, I pulled last year's T-shirt over my head and headed to the door.

The doorbell rang a second time.

"Give it a rest; I'm fine!" I hollered. "All the mystery and mayhem this week got to me for a minute, is all."

I opened the door.

"Hey." Lindsay stood on my threshold, a cup of Cuppa's coffee in her hand. "Did you know you've got pumpkin on your siding?"

"I...uh..." My voice lagged behind my mouth.

Did she ever look bad? That was my first thought. Her ponytail was the perfect combination of messy and coiffed and her yoga pants were perfectly uncoordinated with her top.

My second thought, I managed to vocalize. "What are you doing here?"

"The middle school's only a couple miles from here. I figured I'd stop and see if you wanted a ride."

"You did?"

"Sure? Save us trying to wrangle two parking spaces. Unless you'd rather drive that clunker of a loaner."

My fingertips dug into the molding. "How did you know I had a loaner?" I'd never told her about my accident.

"That is a loaner, right? Unless you traded in your car for an older, more banged-up model?" She pointed toward my driveway where the car sat.

My hand muscles relaxed. "No, no, that's a loaner," I said. If she considered that car banged up, it might be time to look at a new car. I looked over at her large, black SUV. From where it was parked, I couldn't tell if there was a sticker on the rear window or not. It was a little too large. The one that ran me off the road was smaller. Maybe. I couldn't be sure though. All of a sudden, I wasn't sure of anything.

"Are you coming?" Lindsay asked.

It was official. Didn't matter how much logic I fed myself, my gut didn't trust her. I also didn't have a good excuse to say no. "All the supplies are loaded in my car," I said, trying.

As expected, she waved my attempt off. "There weren't that many, so I already moved them."

"You did?" I must have been distracted and failed to double check the locks.

"Uh-huh. This way they'll be in one place making set up easier, and we can save a parking space."

"Wow," I said, "You've thought of everything."

"That's why they asked me to be the chairperson. I'm very good at logistics." She smiled, and I swear the sparkle in her eyes looked triumphant. "So, are you ready to go?"

"Um..." I hovered at the threshold.

"Hurry up," she said, ignoring my reluctance. Turning around, she practically skipped toward her SUV. "We don't want to be late. Tonight's going to be huge."

"I HAVE A CONFESSION," she said, once we were on our way toward the middle school. "The reason I wanted to drive together is so we could spend time together."

"Really?" She'd never been overly keen to spend time with me before. Funny how her desire had coincided with my asking about Pennington High.

Busy fishing her ponytail through the hole in her baseball cap, while waiting for the light to turn green, Lindsay didn't answer right away. "Ever since I heard the news about Andrea. I keep thinking if I hadn't been so involved with this event, I might have noticed how distraught she was. I feel horrible."

"Me too. For both her and Marylou," I replied.

"Right. To think we might have stopped her. Anyway, it made me realize I need to be a better friend. Oh, speaking of which..." She pointed to a tray of four drinks from Cuppa's nestled in the console. "I stopped by and picked up coffee for the gang. Jose helped me figure out what you all drink. Who drinks peppermint tea?"

"That would be me."

"Since when? I thought you were a coffee person."

The aroma drifted to my nostrils through the opening in the plastic lid reminding me of Dan Bartlett. "This week. I thought I'd try something different."

"I should do that. All that caffeine is not good for me."

"But you hardly ever drink caffeine," I said. "Whenever I see you, you're being healthy and drinking water."

She laughed. "Does this look like water to you?" she asked, holding up the cup. "Trust me; I'm not as healthy as I appear to be."

"I'll bear that in mind." I sniffed the tea again, thinking of all those movies where crazy people drugged people's drinks, and told myself I was being paranoid. After all, Jose was the one who'd made the drinks; Lindsay didn't even know which one was mine. Unless she drugged all four cups, I was safe. "And thanks, for the tea."

"Oh, it's no problem. Like I said, I want to be a better friend. I mean, it's been a hell of a week or so, hasn't it?"

"You don't know the half of it."

"Tell me about it," she said, not realizing I'd meant the comment literally. "Here I was all stressed out that Marylou's husband was a killer, and it turns out I'd hosted the murderer under my own roof. I'm still in shock. Honestly, the things you don't know about people."

"Like finding out Marylou was from your home town?"

"Exactly. Is that a wild coincidence or what?"

Or what indeed. I picked at the plastic lip on my lid, finding comfort in the rhythm tick, tick, tick my fingernail made. "You want to hear something wilder? I looked up her obituary. Turns out she was in your graduating class."

Lindsay turned her head, and I met her gaze. "Her and Kim Rivard," I said.

"Is that so? We must have hung out in completely different crowds, because I had no idea."

"Not even when you were doing the reunion invitations?"

"I'm the reunion chairperson, Sadie. I don't do invitations," she said, tucking a stray hair under her cap.

"I thought this committee was inept and you had to do everything."

"Don't tell me you're going all literal like Jenn. And regardless, the invitation list had people's maiden names. I don't know Marylou's maiden name."

"Commeau," I replied. "We were introduced to her aunt, as well."

She blinked, but not much more. "Still doesn't ring a bell. The other one does, a little. What did you say it was, Prevey?"

"Rivard. Kim Rivard. They found her propped up against a tree behind a high school."

"Oh her! One of the girls on the committee mentioned something about a dead classmate, but I didn't connect the two. She totally wasn't part of my circle."

Interesting, how her memory improved since our phone call. "Well, you did say you hung out with a select group," I said.

"To be honest, I mostly spent time with my boyfriend. Between him and all my extracurriculars, I didn't have a ton of time for hanging out. You certainly are interested in my high school."

"I told you, I think it's really funny how you and Marylou were both from Pennington, and didn't realize."

"Hmmm."

We were stopped at the red light a couple of blocks away from the school. Across the street, some kids and their parents could be seen walking in the same direction. Night Walk participants, no doubt.

Turning away from the window, I found myself meeting Lindsay's gaze. "What about you? What were you like in high school?" she asked, reaching for her coffee. "Let me guess. Debate team or marching band."

"I'm not much of a musician," I replied.

"Then debate team."

I let her keep her guess.

"I bet you were one of those kids who got along with everyone too. Floated through all the cliques."

"I had plenty of friends, if that's what you mean."

"Yeah, that's what I figured." She leaned sideways, bringing her head close enough to mine that I could smell the orange blossoms in her hairspray. "Can I tell you a secret?" she asked.

I gripped my cup a little tighter. "What kind of secret?"

"I don't think the others like me."

Not what I expected. "Which others?" I asked. "The rest of the committee?"

"Them. Other people in town. None of them like me very much."

"What makes you say that? Where I sit, you're very popular."

She looked at me like I had two heads. "Sadie, popularity isn't about being liked. Jenn and Erin spend time with me because it makes them look good. Same with Andrea, God rest her soul."

That had to be the most narcissistic thing I'd ever heard, yet at the same time, it made a kind of sense. Queens needed a hive; hives needed a queen. Where did that put me?

"I don't hang out with you because it makes me look good," I said, taking a drink. The tea tasted bitter and strong from having steeped too long.

"I know. That's why I know you were one of those nice people. You like everyone."

"Not necessarily." I could think of a person in the car I didn't like —or trust—at the moment.

"I admire that about you," Lindsay continued, as though I'd never spoken. "You don't let gossip or opinion decide who you'll be friends with. Like Marylou. You were friends with her even though the rest of us thought she was a raving bitch."

"Marylou came with a lot of baggage," I said. "I'm only now beginning to see how complicated a person she was."

She waved off my comment with a manicured hand. "You give her too much credit. Complicated implies interesting, and we know that wasn't true. Why else would her husband need to have an affair?"

"Did you know she was blackmailing people?"

Was it my imagination or did she grip the steering wheel a little tighter? "That list she wrote. Turns out she was digging up dirt on her friends."

"No. Way. How the hell did you find that out?"

"I did a little digging myself."

"Wow. So, all those crazy words actually meant something? Unbelievable. Good thing I wasn't on that list, wasn't it?"

31

I GOT a knot in my stomach, one not even the peppermint tea could untie. "Yeah, lucky break there," I said. "What with you being the wealthiest of all of us.

Unless she died before she had a chance to dig anything up on you," I added.

Lindsay set her coffee back in the holder. "Thanks for the vote of confidence. What makes you think she'd find anything worthwhile?"

"Oh, I'm sure she'd have found something. No one is completely innocent."

"Listen to you being all cynical."

"Hard not to be," I said. "Seeing as how two of our friends died in a little over a week."

"So true," she agreed, giving a sigh. "I still can't believe we missed the signs regarding Andrea. Poor thing was messed up, and we had no idea.

"But, enough of this sad talk." Reaching across, she patted my knee. "Have I mentioned how glad I am that you're on the committee? You and I really ought to spend more time together. I get the feeling we could be really good friends, don't you?"

I smiled and took a long drink.

Thankfully, before we could continue the conversation, we turned into the high school parking lot. I spotted Rob by the tailgate of his hybrid, opening luminaria bags. He was chatting with a handsome silver-haired man while he worked and was more interested in the man than the bags.

So much for him being my human St. Bernard. Lindsay pulled into a parking space under a shedding maple tree, yards away from the other cars. "I don't want my doors dinged," she said.

I got out and walked around to the rear of her car. Why I thought looking at her taillights would jar my memory, I had no idea. The rear window looked like dozens of other SUVs in Woodbridge, many of which were in the parking lot.

This was silly. Lindsay answered my questions. The police had a confession. What was the point in trying to connect dots between Lindsay and a twenty-year-old drug overdose?

My brain was tired of thinking about it. Like Lindsay said, it had been a long week and a half. I just wanted to get this fundraiser done, go to bed, and sleep for twenty-four hours straight.

"Hey, look alive there, McIntyre! We've got work to do." Lindsay was all energy as she joined me. Like a woman without a care in the world. It was jarring, especially after hearing her talk about being disliked.

"We're running a little behind schedule. That's what I get for grabbing coffee." She paused to finish off the one in her hand. "Fortunately, it looks like Rob and the others have most of the luminarias built. I'll have Jenn and Erin start placing them along the route while you and he do the track circle. I'll grab some volunteers from the snack table to unload the car."

"Sounds good," I said, setting down my tea and reaching for a case of water.

Lindsay grabbed my arm. "Hey, I said I'd get volunteers to do the supplies. You go help Rob."

She did say that, didn't she? "Sorry," I replied, shaking my head clear. "I must have flaked out."

"Try not to do it again until after we're set up. Are you feeling okay?" Beneath the lid of her cap, her eyes narrowed. "You look a little pale."

"I'm fine. Tired is all."

"Aren't we all? A few more hours and we can all collapse. Sound good?"

"More than good," I told her. I went to drag Rob away from his handsome friend so we could place lit bags every five feet like a glowing yellow brick road. He was not going to be happy with me.

"Don't forget your tea! I think you'd better switch back to coffee," she said, trotting over with my cup in her hand. "Your system clearly needs the caffeine."

What I needed was for my brain to stop thinking about Lindsay and Marylou.

Having illuminated the track for a couple of years now, Rob and I had the system down. First, we loaded as many luminaria bags as we could in the red wagon. Then, dragging the wagon behind us, we'd work in tandem. I would place the bag, and he would follow with his trusty propane lighter. Usually, our chatter kept the task from being overly monotonous. Tonight, however, a somber cloud blanketed the field, and neither of us felt like talking.

"Sorry I had to break up your conversation," I said, as we walked back for our second load of bags.

He shrugged, his normally luminous looks as sober as the atmosphere. "No worries," he said. "It was just fantasy league talk. We'll catch up this weekend."

"Fantasy league, huh?"

"We're just friends," he replied. As he said it though, I caught his cheekbones turning pink from the corner of my eye. Friends, huh? He and I were going to have to talk.

We had just stuffed the last luminaria in our wagon when Jenn's car drove up. Erin's stare could freeze boiling water as she got out and began loading luminarias into the back.

"In case you're wondering, I never told Bartlett about the list," I said.

"What are you going to do with the information?"

The question came from Jenn, whose blonde head leaned out the driver's window. She was waiting expectantly, and I realized both of them were afraid I'd pull a Marylou.

I never thought about the power that gave me.

"Nothing," I replied. "I burned it." When push came to shove, I didn't have any Marylou in me. "You both said you were going to stop, so I don't see a reason for any of it to go farther than Erin's kitchen."

Rob added, "I also agreed to give Jenn a loan to get a new lawyer. They'll be better able to get Nick to stick to his child support payments."

"That doesn't change the fact you thought we had something to do with killing that witch. People shouldn't suspect their friends of murder."

"Seems like a pretty rational suspicion, considerin'," Rob replied.

"Are all the luminarias on the course?" Lindsay's voice rang out as she approached us from the bleacher area. "The walkers are starting to arrive. Here, everyone should have a walkie talkie radio in case of an emergency." She held out three handsets. Jenn and Erin each took one. Rob reached for the last one, then looked at me.

"Since we're down two volunteers, I'm going to need Rob to help out on the course. You'll be okay setting up the luminarias on your own, won't you, Sadie? If you need anything, you can always call for me."

"If I need anything, I'll shout it across the parking lot."

"Or you can find me," Lindsay replied, her tight smile saying she wasn't amused. "I'll talk for you. Now, as soon as you're finished with the luminarias, meet me by the flagpole. I want to make sure everyone has this year's T-shirt. I've got a fun surprise, too."

"Better be pizza," Rob grumbled as she headed back with our cart.

"Unless she sent someone, don't count on it." If the chairperson didn't stuff envelopes, she certainly didn't get pizza.

"I'll have to call Arturo and have him send some food over." Arturo, of course, being the pizza shop owner.

Rob waited until I set down the next luminaria, then clicked his propane lighter. "You think they'll keep their word, Jenn and Erin? 'Bout closing up shop?"

"I think Jenn already has. She's wearing an old jacket. Erin, I don't know. I'm going to say hopefully, if for no other reason than the fear that I might say something."

"And if she doesn't?"

"Then we'll have to cross that bridge when we come to it, won't we?"

I set down two more bags, and he lit the candles. "Did you really burn Marylou's list?" he asked after the second one caught.

"Yep." I planned to burn my notes too. What purpose did they serve? Marylou and her killer were both dead. Jenn and Erin would destroy any evidence before the police got there. In the end, the only thing left would be broken friendships, rumors, and a bunch of other damage that couldn't be undone. Woodbridge had had enough of that this week.

The fact that we were lighting Marylou's and Andrea's memorials might have helped me come to that conclusion.

"Pick up the pace, people!" From her place by the flagpole, Lindsay clapped her hands. "Five minutes to start."

"Lovely, someone gave her a microphone."

"Kiddie Karaoke," I corrected. The sparkly pink and purple box sat on the ground by Lindsay's feet. "She had Jenn bring it since it's difficult to project in this kind of weather."

Rob rolled his eyes. "All the things Jenn sold off, and she couldn't sell that? She and I are gonna have to talk. I don't care if she pays back the loan, but she's dumping that piece of rubbish before next October."

"Convince her to sell it, and I'll build *you* a luminaria tribute."

I placed the last luminaria in the circle, and stepped away. The entire track glowed with soft white light. Dozens of tiny white lights merged to create one unified beacon of hope. That was, after all, the message behind Night Walk. With all the craziness, it was easy to forget.

Marylou's and Andrea's circles burned side by side. We decided not to label them, for fear of repercussions. Marylou might not have had many friends, but murder tended to make people loyal to your memory. Especially if the other circle belonged to your murderer.

That nauseating knot in my stomach twisted again. It'd been tossing and turning since my conversation with Lindsay. My gut was making me wonder if something wasn't right with the picture.

"I told Lindsay about Marylou being in her class," I said to Rob. "She still didn't remember her."

"I don't know why you thought she'd change her mind."

"I guess because I can't believe the topic never came up. If you met someone from Manchester, wouldn't you compare notes?"

He thought for a moment. "Depends on if I could work it into the conversation. Could be the topic never came up. Do you bring up high school when you talk to people?"

"Never."

"See?"

"Excuse me." Lindsay's newly amplified voice was an impatient bell. "Could I have the committee members up here for one moment?"

"Look, I know it's been a crap week friend-wise, but that doesn't mean everyone you know is hiding a secret."

"No," I replied. "Just five of them."

Laughing, he draped an arm around my shoulder. "Who'd have guessed Lindsay was the purest of us all, eh?" he said, giving me a squeeze.

"Not me."

"Exactly. There's a karmic irony to it, don't you think?"

I guessed so. The pieces still didn't feel aligned in my head, even though they should. A little voice kept saying I was missing something. Something important.

I lay my head on Rob's shoulder. "What I think is that I'm exhausted. Can I curl up in one of your heated seats and take a nap?"

"Wake up, Sadie. I need everyone to stick it out for four more hours." Lindsay appeared in front of me, and thrust a pale blue bundle at me. "This year's T-shirt," she explained. "I'm going to tell everyone to look for people wearing this color, so please put them on."

"I knew there was a reason I wore layers," I joked as I switched out last year's shirt.

"I can't believe you kept last year's shirt," Rob replied. "I toss mine in the rubbish as soon as I get home. Got a reputation to keep, you know."

"Says the man who wore gold lamé for three years."

Lindsay had returned to the front of the group where she stood with her hands clasped behind her back. "And now," she said, "Before we officially begin, there's a tradition I started with the other committees I've chaired, and I'd like to start it here as well."

From behind her back she produced a bottle of vodka and a stack of cups, which were greeted with a ripple of laughter. "I think we could all do with a little something to keep us warm, don't you?" This must have been the "fun surprise" she mentioned in the car. "Everyone step up and get a glass so we can have a toast."

"You're not getting one?" Rob asked, when he returned with his cup.

"Of course she is." Lindsay had one in my hand before I could shake my head. "Everyone on the committee has to have a glass. It's tradition."

"Tonight's the first night," I said.

"I mean, tradition on my other committees. Don't be so literal. Besides, if any committee deserves a toast, it's ours."

"She's got a point there," Rob said. "If you get drunk, you can curl up in the front seat."

Well, if he was going to offer me heated seats...

Lindsay held her glass over the crowd. "Okay, the rules are simple. After the toast, we all have to drink the entire cup. Otherwise, it's bad luck. Got it?"

I looked at my cup, which was half full. "Ready?" She raised her cup higher. "Here's to a fantastic group of volunteers and to the best Night Walk ever! Now, drink!"

A small cheer went up around the crowd as people raised their glasses in response.

I had no choice but to drink the contents in one big swallow. Thanks to some bad college experiences, straight vodka wasn't my favorite drink in the world. The acidic tasting liquor did what the peppermint tea didn't do, and that was warm me from the inside out. For the first time all night, I felt myself relaxing. Of course, relaxing made me want to sleep more... Four more hours, I told myself.

"Want to take bets on how long before you get an emergency call from the route?" I asked with a smile. "You haven't had one yet. Do you want over or under five minutes?"

"Over," he replied. "Lindsay still has to sing the national anthem. Besides, Jenn's over me, remember?"

"Oh, sweetie," I said, patting his cheek. "No one can ever be over you."

I was right. Jenn called on the radio two minutes later needing a replacement table.

Lindsay did a great job with the anthem. Like amazingly great. Goosebumps rippled across my skin as I listened to her belt out "rockets' red glare" in a crystal clear voice. They weren't the good kind of goose bumps. They were caused by the knot in my stomach.

"That was amazing!" Penny Galvin, president of the Youth Soccer League, gushed once the walk was underway. I was in charge of winding up the electrical cord, and thus got a front row seat for the shower of compliments.

"You have to help us with the holiday sing-along at the school this year. The music teacher, Ms. Mathews, is good, but when it comes to singing, her voice isn't...well, you know."

I yawned. Ms. Mathews' singing always sounded fine to me. The mothers always took the sing-along way too seriously, anyway. They were kids singing about snowmen in the auditorium. It wasn't the Christmas Show at Radio City Music Hall.

"I don't want to step on anyone's toes," I heard Lindsay say.

"You won't. I'll talk to the principal myself. I just can't get over how amazing you were. Did you take lessons? You must have taken lessons."

"No, although I did think about studying voice in college. The choir director suggested it after she heard my senior solo."

The choir director? In Pennington? That meant Lindsay had been a member of The Pennington Warblers.

With Marylou.

32

I DROPPED THE ELECTRICAL CORD. The plug slapped the karaoke's pink top with a bang.

"Everything okay, Sadie?" The two of them stopped what they were doing and looked in my direction.

"N-no," I replied. "I mean, yes. Everything's fine. I dropped the cord is all."

"Sounds like someone should have had a smaller glass of vodka," Penny said with a snort.

"Maybe," I replied.

"I should have warned people. Never toast on an empty stomach." Lindsay was smiling, but her eyes had that same cold look I thought I saw on the porch. They stayed locked with mine. "Are you going to be all right, Sadie? You don't look good. Maybe participating in that toast wasn't a good idea."

"Will you excuse me? I'm going to go...." I didn't finish the sentence, instead gesturing toward the bleachers like I was going to sit down.

Lindsay lied!

There was this little bump senior year, but we got that straightened out.

My head ached.

If Lindsay sang the solo, then she had to be part of the choral group. She must have been the one to take the chorus picture from the wake, because it showed her in the group, and she didn't want anyone to know.

But why? High school was decades ago. And why keep lying now, when Marylou was dead? Even if Marylou had been holding a secret overhead, no one would find out now.

On the other hand, maybe it wasn't the secret she was trying to hide.

The sweatshirt. The one Andrea supposedly left half burned in the Dumpster near Paul's office. The one that hadn't fit Marylou.

The one Marylou kept, despite hating high school. Why keep a souvenir of some place she hated?

Unless it was a reminder of someone she cared about.

Like Kim.

That was it! The sweatshirt didn't belong to Marylou. It belonged to Kim!

Kim, who died wearing a T-shirt in November.

Traces of cotton fibers and vomit were found on the body. Her friend insists one of the popular kids did something.

I got a very bad feeling.

My head was trying to wrap itself around the rest of the details but was like trying to cut through cotton with a butter knife. I needed to share my thoughts with someone who could help string them together in the right order.

Stumbling on the uneven ground, I reached into my pocket for my phone. My fingers were thick and clumsy forcing me to press the button twice. God, I was tired. Maybe when I got to the bleachers, I could put my head down. A five-minute catnap was all I needed.

On the other end of the line, I heard someone say something.

"I thought I'd never shake Penny. She wouldn't shut up about that Christmas festival."

I stuffed the phone in my pocket just as Lindsay made it to my side. She hooked her arm through mine. "Come up to the top of the bleachers with me. I need your help with something."

There were fourteen steps. I tripped over every one as she dragged me to the top, babbling about views and it being a terrific night for the walk.

"I'd hate if something happened to ruin all our hard work," she said. "Wouldn't you?"

"I-I guess." Why was I having so much trouble keeping my eyes open? "I'd like to sit," I said.

"One more step."

She grabbed my shoulders and spun me around so hard the bleachers shifted beneath my feet. "Isn't it beautiful?" she said. "Look."

Below us lay the lit up track with its spiraling circles. Above them were two smaller circles. Marylou's and Andrea's memorials.

"I wanted to make sure we got a picture from high up for the Facebook page," Lindsay said. "Since you're taller than me, maybe you could stand on the top bleacher and take the picture for me."

Below, the lighted luminarias swayed to and fro. My eyes wanted to roll into the back of my head and I had to struggle to keep them focused. "I don't think that's a good idea." My voice sounded very far away. "I'm not feeling well."

"Oh my," Lindsay clucked. "Are you sure?"

I made my head move. "If I could lie down for a minute."

She clucked again. "Oh Sadie, I'm afraid that's not going to help. You mixed alcohol with a whole mess of Xanax which, well, is very, very bad."

Xanax? I didn't take... "The tea..."

"I'm sorry," she said. "If I'd known you had so much medication in your system, I never would have insisted on you drinking that vodka, or climbing all the way up these bleachers. Between the height and the drugs? It's no wonder you're going to die."

33

FOR SOMEONE who'd been told she was being murdered, I handled the news very well. That's what comes from being poisoned with an anti-anxiety medicine. I could feel my body crying to go to sleep. A deep, peaceful sleep.

There was only one problem. I didn't want to sleep anymore. I didn't want to die.

Yanking away from her arm, I stumbled on the step only to lose my balance and grab hold of the bench.

"Whoa," Lindsay said, grabbing my arm again. "Be careful. You need to sit right here, and wait until I get back to the ground. Then you can take the picture with my phone, okay? I'll call up to you when it's time to snap."

What was she talking about? My eyes started to close again when I felt her arm hooking through mine again, and moving me toward the middle section of the bleachers. "It's good we did this early," she said as we walked. "That way there isn't a lot of people milling around cluttering the shot. And the ones who are here, aren't paying attention. There. This is a good seat."

My back was against the clubhouse. Supporting me. Though I

didn't want to, I let my head loll against the wood. It was getting harder and harder to keep my eyes open.

I thought of the phone in my pocket. "Why?" I managed to ask.

"I had no choice. You were starting to figure things out."

"You mean about Marylou."

She let out a long sigh. "That loser. She just couldn't let go of the past. I mean, it was twenty years ago for crying out loud. Get over it."

"You're talking about Kim's death." Marylou had blamed the popular kids, and no one was more popular than Lindsay.

"It was an accident, for Christ's sake. She was supposed to get stupid, not freaking overdose. Stupid cow."

So it was Kim's fault she died. Made sense. I guess. "But she was in the woods."

"Well we couldn't leave her passed out at BJs house, could we?"

They could have called her parents, I wanted to say, but Lindsay would probably have an excuse for that as well. She seemed to have a real problem with responsibility.

The muscles in my shoulders were dissolving away. I closed my eyes and felt myself sinking into the sensation.

No! I snapped my eyes open. Talk, a voice in my head said. Talk. "Marylou blackmailed you," I said.

Lindsay tilted her head sideways. "Can you believe it?" she asked. "Twenty years later and she shows up on my doorstep demanding I pay her. Fifty thousand dollars! Like I could get my hands on that kind of money. I told her to screw off."

"But she didn't back down."

"No. She doubled down. Said she had Kim's sweatshirt from the night she died. That it had Kim's DNA on it or some crap like that. As if that would prove we slipped Ecstasy in her drink. What a joke. I told her to screw herself, but she wouldn't give up. 'Doesn't matter what they can prove,' she said. 'I just have to show the sweatshirt to your husband.'"

I have to show her, Marylou had said. She'd been talking about the sweatshirt. She must have heard about the posse's party and decided to wear the sweatshirt to Jenn's house. To prove she was serious.

"The bitch actually would have ruined my marriage because of a stupid accident. Can you believe it? I didn't work my ass off getting Carlos to marry me so she could come to town and ruin my life."

"How dare she want justice for her best friend?"

"Oh please. Marylou didn't want justice. She wanted money."

In the cotton that was my brain, tiny pieces of the picture began to show themselves. Lindsay must have gone to Marylou's house Sunday night. They argued; Lindsay hit her with one of the dragons, stole the sweatshirt and..."

"You erased Marylou's computer."

"Of course I did. She had the damn file open. Fortunately, you pick up a few things being married to a software guy."

"But why Andrea?" Why kill her?

"Oh, Andrea," she said with a sigh. "Poor, deluded Andrea. She had to go and have a breakdown over Paul Paretsky. She really was stalking him, you know. Parked outside his office in her car? Talk about pathetic."

She must have seen Lindsay putting the sweatshirt in the trash, and said something. Lindsay got nervous and...

"How?" I asked.

"How do you think? People in this town love their coffee. They don't even ask what's in it; they just take the cup from whoever offers."

I thought about the tea she'd so generously brought me and winced.

It's a terrible habit," Lindsay was saying. "You never know what's in a drink."

I made a note to be careful, if there was a next time.

Was this how Andrea felt before she died? The world spinning and darkness pulling you under?

At least it was peaceful. My eyelids started to close only to flutter when Lindsay squeezed my knee. "I better get to the field before one of the volunteers come up looking for me. Now remember, listen for me to holler for you to take the picture. I doubt you'll be able to do much, but you should still listen." I felt the air around us shift as she got to her feet. "It was interesting working with you, Sadie. Shame you wouldn't let the whole Marylou business go. I think we might have become friends."

"Not on your life. You're a bitch," I slurred.

She glanced over her shoulder at me. "Whatever."

No way could I let her get away with this. She'd killed two people —three if help didn't get here soon. If I was going to die, I was going to go out with a flourish. Took effort, but I raised my arms.

And shoved her.

Lindsay's arms flailed. Stumbling, she lost her balance and pitched forward. Only her shin catching the bleacher bench saved her from the same fate as Marylou. Instead, she landed face first on the cold aluminum.

"You bitch!" she screeched. Lifting her head, she revealed a river of blood running from her nose over her lips. "Look what you did."

She lunged for me. The back of my knees hit the bench and I was shoved into a sitting position against the clubhouse wall. Right against the *Sponsored by Renee Drake Realty* sign I knew hung there. "I do not have time for this," I heard Lindsay hiss. "Just sit there and die, for crying out loud."

I tried to raise my arms to push her again, but the last effort killed whatever strength I'd had. There was darkness on all sides trying to swallow me. Head falling against the clubhouse, I gave in. *At least I broke her nose*, I thought as my eyes closed. *That had to count for something.*

The walkers were arriving. I could hear shouts. And footsteps. Someone was running up the bleachers. "Over here!" I heard someone shout.

I let the blackness wash over me. A hand touched my shoulder. Just as the darkness ascended, I heard a familiar voice calling "Mom."

———

I woke up in the hospital to find, of all people, Dan Bartlett in the chair next to my bed. When he saw I was awake, he jumped to his feet. "Rob took Tim to the cafeteria to get something to eat, so I said I would sit watch until they got back. How do you feel?"

"Tired." My mouth was dry. I tried swallowing for moisture, but it didn't work. Bartlett noticed, and poured me a glass of water.

"You gave your kid quite a scare," he said. "Here, let me help."

He cradled my head and held the glass while I took a few sips. "Better?"

I nodded. "Tim wasn't the only one who was scared." I'd been pretty sure "You're a bitch," were going to be my last words. "You got there fast."

"Fortunately, I was on my way to the school anyway. That was a pretty smart idea, by the way. Leaving your phone on. We didn't hear the entire conversation, but we caught enough." Sitting on the edge of the bed, he gave me one of his sexy eyebrow arches. "Was that your plan?"

I hadn't a clue. Most of the night was a blur. "Does saying yes make me sound smart?" I asked.

He grinned. "Brilliant."

"Then yes, that was my plan."

The two of us smiled at each other until the reality of where I was and why completely sank in. "She killed two people." Three, if you counted Kim Rivard, and none of us had a single clue. "I am a lousy judge of people," I muttered.

"She fooled a lot of people for a long time. The first death was likely an accident. The way she tells it, she dropped some Ecstasy into Kim's drink so she would make a fool out of herself, but it backfired and the girl stopped breathing."

"So they dragged the body to the woods."

"Exactly," he said. "The idea was to make it look like Kim wandered off to get high. It worked too, largely because the boyfriend –"

"BJ."

"His father knew a lot of the guys on the force."

Meaning Marylou's charges fell on deaf ears. "Did she say why? Lindsay, that is?"

"Social ostracization?" he offered. "Ruining her chance at a solo? Revenge for singing better than Lindsay? I don't think there was a clear-cut motive beyond embarrassing her."

She got away with it for almost twenty years, too. Until Marylou came to town, recognized her and decided she could get justice for Kim as well as save Paul's business.

Another memory pushed its way to the surface. "Marylou told Lindsay she had proof. DNA evidence from Kim's sweatshirt. The sweatshirt Marylou had taken off Kim's body the night she died."

Bartlett shook his head. "A bluff. She had nothing."

Sad. Twenty years of holding onto a memory, in case the opportunity for revenge arose, and in the end, it'd been useless. "Didn't matter though," I said. "Just talking about what happened would cause enough damage. Who wants to hear his wife might have drugged someone to death?"

"Try hearing your wife offed two people and covered up a third death and see how that sounds. Carlos Herrara walked out of the station this morning and hasn't returned. Your pal Lindsay is on her own."

"She's not my pal," I said, tugging on the blanket.

He reached over and tucked the cloth around my shoulders. "I know."

"Did she say why she killed Andrea?"

"After she failed to burn the sweatshirt, she decided to dump it by Paul's office, thinking it would incriminate him. Only she didn't realize Andrea was sitting in the parking lot."

Thinking about Lindsay's and Andrea's intense conversation the night of the storm, a theory formed in my head. Andrea saw Lindsay putting the sweatshirt in the trash, and asked her about it at the meeting. Realizing that Andrea might tell the police, Lindsay must have laced her coffee with Xanax, the same way she drugged my tea. Poor Andrea, pumped up on cold medicine, didn't stand a chance.

"But Andrea left a suicide note," I said. "How?"

"She typed it. We suspected from the start it might be a forgery.

Andrea's body was found with a pad and pen nearby. Plus, the note didn't mention her children. How many mothers forget them?"

Certainly not Andrea. They were her life. Hopefully, her husband treated her memory with more respect than he did her.

"Anyway, once you started asking questions, Lindsay started to panic, and decided you needed to be eliminated immediately."

Clearly, as evidenced by my lying in the hospital bed. "I knew the tea tasted funny, and shrugged it off to over steeping." I was such an idiot.

"Don't beat yourself up too much," Bartlett said. "I kind of like that your first thought isn't about murder or potential murder. It's refreshing."

It was naïve, is what it was. But I returned his smile anyway. "I don't suppose Lindsay said how she planned to get away with killing me in front of the entire town."

"Her acting skills." Rob and Tim appeared in my doorway, Rob looking as relaxed and charming as he always did, my son looking a bit paler. Never had I been so glad to see them. "Sorry I worried you," I said to Tim.

He leaned over the bed and kissed my cheek. "Let me guess; this is payback for the time I got a concussion playing baseball."

"Close enough," I told him.

Bartlett cleared his throat. "By the way, our computer guys finally got into Marylou's computer."

"Oh?" My fingers twisted in the sheets. I knew this day would come.

"Turns out Lindsay wasn't the only one she was blackmailing. She had files on your friends too. We're going to be paying Jennifer and Erin both a visit later today."

I let his words wash over me. Confused. "Just my friends?"

"Were you expecting a file on you, Mom?" Tim asked. "I'm not sure asking Dad to fix a speeding ticket is really blackmail worthy."

I'll never betray our friendship. That's what Marylou said the night she died. She must have buried whatever she found about Mercedes.

Or never recorded it on the computer to begin with. Whatever she did, I closed my eyes and sent her a silent thank you.

Bartlett cleared his throat. "Now that your family's back, I'll get out of your way and let the three of you talk."

"You don't have to," I said, reaching for his wrist and missing.

"Actually, I do. I've got a ton of paperwork to fill out. That's one of the unknown problems with crime."

As he walked by he let his fingers brush along the top of my shin, making my whole leg feel alive. Our eyes locked. And the thrill moved to the rest of my body. No doubt about it, Dan Bartlett did something to me that I hadn't felt in a long, long time.

"See you around, Sadie," he said.

"You too, Detective Bartlett." Soon, I hoped.

After he left, Tim plopped himself on the bed and gave me a long, gentle hug. "Don't ever do that again," he whispered in my ear.

"Yes sir, Officer McIntyre," I whispered back. For the first time in a long time, I felt like all was right in the world.

34

TWENTY YEARS AGO, Lindsay Herrara, then Lindsay James, nearly got away with manslaughter. She almost got away with it a second time. It wasn't until she turned to full core murder that she tripped herself up.

Marylou, meanwhile, tried to use the secret only to end up as dead as her high school friend. And Andrea, poor, unhinged Andrea, succeeded in finding a love match with Paul Paretsky, and lost her life because she couldn't say good-bye.

All of which could be read as "Don't push your luck."

After hearing Jenn's story, Detective Bartlett intervened and cut a deal with Nick. I have no idea what was said, but Nick agreed not to press charges, while Jenn agreed never to step inside Nick's home again.

Erin wasn't so lucky. Fortunately, her lawyer negotiated time served and community service.

Two days after I woke up, Rob brought me home where I found three fresh pumpkins on the step. A note under the top one read "Feel better, Jenn."

I smiled and tucked the note into my pocket. Erin was still—

would probably always be—angry, but perhaps things with Jenn had a chance, after all.

That night, sitting on the couch with a toasty warm blanket, I turned on my laptop, and did the same thing I'd been doing since computers and the Internet became a thing. I typed in the name Joey Albano, just to make sure he was still in prison. That's right, Joey Albano, the crime leader.

My father.

Tim's grandfather.

My real name is Mercedes Albano. That's what Marylou had discovered. One night I stood in the shadows and watched my father and my boyfriend Dougie beat a man death for owing them money. I testified against them. I didn't move to Woodbridge. I was relocated to the east coast so I could give my unborn child a good life.

A chance meeting in a restaurant with a cop named Jack McIntyre made that good life even better. He adopted Tim before he was born, and gave him his name.

Tim doesn't know his father and grandfather are murdering sons-of-bitches. Nor do they know Tim exists.

Not a day goes by that I don't pray that all of them stay in the dark forever. Thanks to Marylou's silence, I get to pray another day.

What can I say? Everyone's got a secret.

THE END

What did you think? Your feedback is most welcome.

COMING SOON

Woodbridge's Favorite Detective Returns In

BACKYARDS HAVE BODIES

When local businessman, Alex Johnson, is found murdered, her best friend, Rob is suspect number one. To clear his name, Sadie—with help from Dan Bartlett— will have to unravel a whole new tangle of neighborhood secrets.

ACKNOWLEDGMENTS

If it takes a village to raise a child, then it takes an entire universe to write a book. This was my first independently published novel, a project that would never have gotten off the ground if not for a host of fabulous people. People like...

My husband, Peter, who endures the mood swings of a stressed-out writer whenever I'm on deadline – which is pretty much all the time. You're my hero and my best friend. I wouldn't be a working writer without you pushing me to follow my dreams all these years.

My son, Andrew, the original Tim, who has grown up thinking it perfectly normal for a mother to lock herself in the car so she can write. Thanks for the blood spatter lesson, Lt.!

The amazingly awesome and talented Donna Alward, who talked me off the virtual ledge every time I freaked out about making the leap from romance to mystery.

My mastermind mates, Susan Meier and Selena Blake, and my critique partners, Deb Monk, D.L. Eagan, and Nina Singh, all of whom endured multiple drafts of Marylou's murder.

My wonderful Beta readers Penny, Lesley, and Janet.

My agent, Amanda Leuck, of the Spencerhill Agency, who agreed with me that this story should see the light of day.

My editor, Maria Theresa Hussey, who helped take a rough draft and turn it in to something more polished.

My writing and non-writing friends, too numerous to list, who have supported me throughout my career and who always believe in me.

And lastly, all the readers who have seen me through twenty-something novels. You all make what I do worthwhile.

ABOUT THE AUTHOR

Barbara Wallace can't remember a time when she wasn't writing stories. The award-winning author began her career with Harlequin Romance in 2010. Since then, she has written over twenty novels and seen her work sold around the world, including in the UK, Australia, Spain, Russia, India, Indonesia, France, Greece and South Africa. The Suburbs Have Secrets marks her mystery novel debut.

When not writing, Barbara can be often be found watching the wildlife behind her house with her husband, Peter, or catering to one of her three rescue pets. Fans can find her on social media at where she talks about her writing, her pets, the Boston Red Sox, evil butlers of Downton Abbey, and/or her son — not necessarily in that order.

Stay in Touch At

www.barbarawallace.com

Barbara@Barbarawallace.com

KEEP THE CONVERSATION GOING

Cuppa Joe's is the exclusive online home for fans of the Sadie McIntyre Mysteries.
Visit Cuppa Joe's Today